NO RESISTANCE

NO RESISTANCE

Evelyn Anthony

Severn House Large Print
London & New York

This first large print edition published in Great Britain 2007 by
SEVERN HOUSE LARGE PRINT BOOKS LTD of
9-15 High Street, Sutton, Surrey, SM1 1DF.
This title first published 2004 by
Severn House Publishers, London and New York.
This first large print edition published in the USA 2007 by
SEVERN HOUSE PUBLISHERS INC., of
595 Madison Avenue, New York, NY 10022.

British Library Cataloguing in Publication Data

Anthony,   Evelyn
  No resistance. - Large print ed.
  1. Romantic suspense novels 2. Large type books
  I. Title II. Anthony, Evelyn. Rendezvous
  823.9'14[F]

  ISBN-13: 9780727875716

Printed and bound in Great Britain by
MPG Books Ltd, Bodmin, Cornwall.

To Betty and Desmond, with love

AUTHOR'S NOTE

So much, both fictional and otherwise, has been written about the methods employed by the Gestapo in interrogation that it hardly seems necessary to say that the details in this book are authentic, but I must explain that the fourth floor referred to as the interrogation centre in the Avenue Foch was in fact located in the Rue des Saussaies. I have taken the liberty of amalgamating the two places. The practice of therapeutic amnesia is comparatively new to Western psychiatric medicine, but has long been used in the Soviet Union for political purposes.

Israeli Intelligence operates in the United States, and is reputed to have its nerve centre in New York itself. In 1966 two former members of the German S.S. were reported to have been executed by the Israelis in Madrid and Buenos Aires respectively for crimes committed against the Jewish people during the last war.

EVELYN ANTHONY
London 1966

Foreword

I had written fifteen historical novels. I was earning good money, being well reviewed. I was also bored and dissatisfied with what I was doing. So I went to Paris, hoping for inspiration. And I found it. We had gone with two friends. The husband had been an active British Intelligence Agent in Europe during the war. We were having a drink at the Ritz bar, which had been taken over by the Germans during the occupation. We started talking about French women who had been in the resistance, and captured by the Gestapo. Some, he said, had been seduced by their interrogators and went to work for them. But they were very few. Most held out, suffered and died rather than betray their comrades. Suddenly, my friend said, 'But some Germans fell for their victims. They weren't all swine you know. Some tried to help the girls, at great risk to themselves.' And on that lovely spring evening in Paris, where these things had happened, the idea for *No Resistance* came to me. It was the start of a new career; it was also a risk, but it worked. And in the horror and terror of occupation, enemies still defied their roles and fell in love.

Evelyn Anthony © 2004

1

'Darling. Darling, wake up.' She leant over him, thought of kissing him to wake him and then decided not to; he was always irritable when he woke up, however successfully they had made love. He didn't like to be caressed or teased. He opened his eyes slowly and they focused on her face. 'Hi,' she said, smiling at him. 'It's nearly five.' He looked at his watch and sat up, throwing off the sheet. He had a lean and splendid body and he kept it in top condition. He was a very disciplined man, and Julia liked this; it was part of what made him different from her two husbands, both flabby, rich and easy to despise. You couldn't despise Karl Amstat even if you did have a million dollars. Foreigners had this strength, this masculinity; you were a woman and treated like a woman. You just didn't take liberties or they weren't around any more. Julia had come to like this aspect of her lover too. He had the upper hand, and she knew it and accepted it.

Otherwise she wouldn't keep him; it was as simple as that.

'I'm going to take a shower,' he said. He smiled at her over his shoulder. 'I know what you're like when you get to the bathroom first. You'll be in there for hours.'

'You're so selfish,' she said. 'I just don't know why I put up with you. I'm going to mix myself a drink.' She got up and draped herself in a long chiffon négligée; it was just like a piece of rag when it wasn't being worn, and it had cost two hundred dollars. She covered herself in it, and brushed her hair, watching herself in the mirror. She looked good, very good indeed. She was thirty-one and beautiful, as well as rich and well connected. She had everything, including a lover who never said he loved her, and went into the bathroom first. She laughed out loud at herself in the glass and went into the lounge to find a drink. She was very happy.

He locked the bathroom door and went under the shower. He was irritated that his mistress wanted a drink before six o'clock. Five, and just out of bed, and straight to the liquor cupboard. He disapproved and she knew it, but he wasn't going to say anything to her. They were very comfortable together; he was proud of her because she was beautiful and she had brought him a lot of clients, rich people like herself, who wanted him to design a new summer place down on the coast, or build them houses where they could spend holidays, till they got bored and took off for somewhere else. He was very successful as an architect. His serious work was designing new office blocks and in fact this was where the money was. Julia's friends were useful for another reason. They provided him with a background – additional cover was a better way of describing it. He had a niche in New York now. After only six years he was part of the scene; people knew him or of him. Karl Amstat, the architect. He went to the mirror and looked at himself; he combed his blond hair flat, and studied himself very carefully. He hadn't changed much; he had dropped all the old tricks like growing a moustache or wearing glasses. In a way his good looks had been an asset. It was much easier to blend into the scene when you had regular features that could be altered by changing your hair colour, almost impossible if you had a big nose or were short-sighted. Now he just looked like himself, only twenty years older, and at last he felt able to relax. They would never find him now.

Julia wanted to marry him. He smiled when he thought of that. It had been awkward refusing her to start with; she was very persistent, like all American women who were used to having their own way. She couldn't understand why he wouldn't marry her. She said she loved him and he couldn't quarrel with that; he wasn't sure what she meant by love, because it was a word she and her friends were always using, indiscriminately. They just loved a show they'd seen, or a new apartment decorated by some smart pansy, or a new man they'd met, or a bloody dog, come to that. She loved him, she said. She wanted to marry him, and she brought it up every few months, casually, as if she didn't really care one way or the other. Once or twice he had felt tempted to say 'Yes'. Yes of course I'll marry you, but first there's a little something you should know...

Amstat had been very lonely for the first year. He had got a job in an architect's office, but nobody bothered to make friends with him. Without money or contacts New York was a cold place to live. It had been a slow process and he had been miserable. When the luck changed, it changed with typical New York speed. He got a commission to do a design for an out-of-town factory. That building made him. He left the firm and set up on his own, and the commissions came with a rush. He had money and he found he had friends too. The two went together, and he had been long enough in New York to accept that without undue cynicism. He had met Julia Adams at a party. She was very smart, wearing something that looked like nothing and was still different to the clothes the other women wore. She had lovely jewellery and a beautiful face, expertly made up, and he had found himself taking her out to dinner. The second time they met he went back to her apartment and they went to bed together. He had had women over the years, but they were mostly tarts and once or twice a girl he had picked up who wasn't a prostitute, though he always treated them as if they were. For nearly twenty years he had avoided any kind of intimacy with anyone.

Julia had been the beginning of his new life. He had begun to enjoy himself; she gave him confidence and he relaxed. He would have liked to marry her. She had even said, very unwillingly, that if he wanted it, she'd have a child. He liked her, and he could keep the upper hand with her; she was marvellous in bed and he couldn't think what more they needed to be happy. But he couldn't do it. He couldn't ever get that close to anyone – she had started asking why he didn't take out American citizenship, and that had clinched it. Papers, investigations, questions. He would have to be alone for as long as he lived. And he was lucky even so.

She was only half an hour in the bathroom; he was already dressed and reading the evening papers. 'Karl?' She was calling from the bedroom.

'Yes? What is it?'

'Bring me a Scotch-and-soda, darling.'

'No. You've had one already. Drinking gives you lines.'

'Oh God, you are hell. You know it worries me if you say that. I haven't got lines, have I?'

'You will have, if you drink this early in the evening.'

She came out of the bedroom and he put the paper down. 'What do I look like?'

She wore a yellow silk dress and a big diamond brooch on one shoulder. The colour suited her; she had very dark hair and brown eyes. 'You look beautiful,' Amstat said. 'Where are we going?'

She came and sat beside him and lit a cigarette. 'If I tell you, you'll say no.'

'Probably. But try me, anyway.'

'Do you really think I'm beautiful?'

'Yes.' He smiled at her. She was very nice, and he liked her. He took hold of her hand and held it. 'Tell me where we're going that I won't want to go.'

'It's a cocktail party.'

'Oh God, no! I can't stand those awful parties – Julia, you know how I hate them. Crowds of people, nowhere to sit – who's giving it?'

'Ruth Bradford Hilton. She's just got back

from a trip to India, and she's got a divine new husband. This party's to introduce him round. Darling, you'll love her, she's divine, and he sounds divine too. I haven't seen her for ages – she went round the world after her divorce and then she met this guy in Italy and then they went to India. I'm going anyway, but I do want you to come with me. Besides, darling, the Bradfords are very important people in New York. You ought to meet them. She says her brother and his wife will be there. They've taken an apartment in New York, usually they live in Boston; he's Robert Bradford the Third. They've got a house in the Bahamas, a place in Florida – honey, they're loaded! Haven't you heard of them?'

'No,' he said. 'I haven't. But I'm only a poor humble foreigner. I'm not an authority on your American dollar dynasties.'

'Then you should be,' Julia said. 'It's where you get your living. It's six-forty – I want to get there early and talk to Ruth. Come on, darling. Just for me. I need a handsome man to take me around.'

'All right,' he said. 'But we're not staying too long.'

'Just an hour,' Julia said. Once they were there it wouldn't matter. She wanted to show Ruth what she'd picked up for herself right in the middle of New York. He really was divine, and she was never going to let him go.

The Bradford Hiltons' apartment was on Park Avenue, eighteen floors up. They could hear the noise of the party coming up in the elevator, and Amstat looked at Julia and winced.

They went into the crush, Julia pushing ahead, stopping for a moment to shout at someone she knew and then pushing on. He followed her because he didn't see anyone he knew and there was nothing else to do.

'Ruth – darling! How are you? How wonderful to see you – you look divine!'

Mrs Ruth Bradford Hilton had a handsome weather-beaten face and a loud laugh; she was a small woman who looked much older than American women usually did; she couldn't have been more than forty-five. He could imagine her going on a tiger-shoot in India or crossing the Sahara with whichever husband she happened to be married to, and enjoying every moment of it. She was very typical of a certain type of very rich American woman. Tough as hell, and born out of her time. She was the direct descendant of the old pioneers who founded America, and the fact that she was worth fifty million and dressed at Balenciaga didn't make her any different. The man she introduced as her husband was a pleasant, well-bred Englishman with a stupid face, who hardly said a word.

She turned to Amstat, taking in everything about him. He could see her doing it, making a thorough judgment of Julia's new boy friend – he hated that expression with its patronising implications. He smiled at her and asked her how she enjoyed India.

'It was fabulous, fantastic. Have you ever been there, Mr Amstat?'

'No,' he said. 'Please call me Karl.'

'Karl then, how nice of you! Well, you really must go. We stayed with the Jam Singhs, you know – Aysha's an old friend of mine, we spent a summer in Europe together as girls – she's such a beauty – you know how dainty Indian women are – well, George just adored the idea, he's a wonderful shot, you know, so we thought we'd go and pay the Jam Singhs a visit for our honeymoon...' She talked on and on, interrupted by people rushing up to kiss her and scream the same old inanities about how marvellous it was to see her and how divine she looked. She kept coming back to him, going on describing the palace where they stayed, and how her hostess had become a political power in India, and then she was telling him about the tiger-shoot. He had lost Julia, and he couldn't see her anywhere. Suddenly Ruth said, 'That's enough about us, Karl; tell me about you. What do you do, and where do you come from? You're German, aren't you?'

'No,' he said. 'I'm Swiss. I'm an architect, Mrs Hilton.'

The sun-tanned face opened out in a dazzling smile. She had a compelling charm. 'You must call me Ruth, if I'm going to call you Karl. I hate formality, so does George – don't you, sweet?'

Her husband looked down at her. 'Yes, I do. Can't stand it.'

From the way he looked at her Amstat thought he hadn't married her just for her money. He might end up by staying with her for it, though.

'And you're an architect – how fascinating. How long have you known Julia?'

'Two years,' Amstat said. He wondered if she were going to ask him if they lived together. She was the kind of woman who might, if she wanted to know.

'I'm so glad,' she said. 'She's looking marvellous. That last husband of hers was a drag – thank God she had the sense to get divorced. Are you married? Oh, George, get that waiter, darling, he's taking the champagne away and I'm just dying for a glass...'

'No, I'm not married. I'm a bachelor. Confirmed, I'm afraid.'

The smile came at him again. 'Don't count on it. I know little Julia. Oh, there's my brother, and his wife. Damn, where's George – no, don't go, Karl, I want you to meet them. Robert, sweetie; Terese – Robert, this is Karl Amstat.' He shook hands with a tall, good-looking American man, and then he heard Ruth Hilton say, 'And this is my sister-in-law, Terese Bradford. Mr Amstat.'

The woman had been half turned away from him, speaking to someone. Now she came round and held out her hand. Her blonde hair was cut short, her eyes looked straight at him. 'How do you do,' she said. After twenty years he found himself face to face with Terese Masson.

'What's your name?'

'You know it. You have my papers.'

He saw Willi Freischer make a move beside him.

'No,' he said. 'Leave her alone.'

Freischer always began an interrogation by hitting the prisoner. If it was a man he punched him and kicked him in the kidneys or the groin. He slapped the women backwards and forwards till they had bloody noses and split lips. If they answered back he thumped them in the breasts. It was a good idea to let the girl see Freischer so she would know what to expect if she didn't co-operate. He looked up at her quite calmly; it was his function to be calm, to maintain a balance between the big, beefy Gestapo butcher standing behind him at the desk and his own polite line of questioning.

She was very young, the girl they had arrested when she got off the train from Lyons. Her papers said she was eighteen. If she hadn't been so frightened she would have been very pretty. Fear made the human face ugly, it stretched the skin, turned it sallow, hollowed out the eyes.

She was terrified; he could tell by the way she held her hands tightly together on her knees. They were shaking and she was tensing up, trying to control them. Two years in the S.D. section had taught Alfred Brunnerman a lot about human reactions to things like pain and fear. It was his job to assess the individual, to judge how strong or weak they were, how long he needed to break them. If he hadn't the time to waste on them he passed them on to Willi Friescher who took them up to the fourth floor. This girl, Terese Masson, was an important prisoner. Not important in herself; she was little more than a courier, taking messages from place to place, but it was her bad luck to know something which really was important. That was why General Knochen had sent her up to him first and not left her to Freischer to interview. Freischer was apt to overdo it; many of his prisoners died.

Knochen believed in Brunnerman's intellectual approach to his job; he held a long list of successes behind him since he joined the Gestapo in 1940.

'Your name is Terese Masson, you are eighteen years old, you were born at Nancy on June 18th, 1925, your father is dead, and you live with a Mademoiselle Jerome at 22 Rue Bonnard. This is all in front of me. Major Freischer, that's all for the moment.'

Freischer saluted and went out. As he walked past the chair where the girl was sitting he looked at her. He hoped she stuck it out; he hoped he got his hands on her. He'd make the little bitch squeal. He hated the French more even than the Poles or the Jews or any of the inferior races. He couldn't have explained why, but it was something to do with their culture and their good cooking, and the way everyone talked about Paris as if it were something special, better than other cities. He was not, unlike two of his assistants, one of them a Frenchman, a homosexual, but he enjoyed roughing up French women. They were supposed to be so smart, so pretty, so hot in bed. He felt really savage towards them. He went out and shut the door. Brunnerman didn't speak, he wrote something down and waited, as if he were thinking.

He had enjoyed his work with the S.S. for

the first year. He liked counter-espionage and he had been rapidly promoted because of the new, intellectual approach he brought to it. Politically he and his family were dedicated National Socialists; his father held the post of Professor of Philosophy at Frankfurt University which had been vacated by a Jew who fled from Germany. The Brunnermans were members of the élite, and the sons of the élite went into the S.S. If they showed real ability they went on to the Gestapo. Brunnerman was a colonel at twenty-four because he was one of the best administrators and interrogators in this particular section. Unlike Freischer and the old beer hall Nazis, he despised brutality and insisted that it was unnecessary and often ineffective. As a young man he had studied psychology and philosophy, and become fascinated by the Russian scientist Pavlov's theory of conditioned reflex. From the thesis that the human being was governed by a series of automatic impulses, and his behaviour could be totally conditioned by interfering with the brain mechanism controlling the reflexes. Brunnerman had gone further still into the structure of the human personality. He believed, and he had proved his point over and over again in dealing with prisoners like the one sitting in front of him, that it was possible to break down resistance without physical pain, and often to transform an enemy into a useful and obedient tool.

He hated brutality and despised his colleagues who resorted to it because they lacked the skill and patience to try other methods. Cruelty was degrading for both sides; he had seen a great deal of it since he was posted to Paris and he was increasingly disturbed by what he saw. This interrogation was going to be more difficult than most because Terese Masson had been brought straight to Gestapo Headquarters on the Avenue Foch without the usual ten days' softening up in Fresnes prison. Fresnes was a filthy, over-crowded relic, full of women suspected of every kind of crime from prostitution to Resistance work. After ten days the suspect came to the Avenue Foch in a condition which made it much easier for Brunnerman to work on them. They were starving, and the first thing they were offered was a meal, and it was a meal of pre-war quality. If they ate it, and many did, they were one step nearer giving way. And one of the most important factors in dealing with women in his kind of work was that they had had time to get dirty and bedraggled, often lousy. Mentally they always saw themselves facing interrogation decently dressed and clean, even attractive; it was easier to be heroic when you looked normal. Rags and stink and vermin did something more fundamentally damaging to a woman than to a man, who didn't care so much how his enemies saw him.

Terese Masson had spent the night in a cell in the basement, with an S.S. man on duty to see she didn't try to lie down or sleep. For the last three hours he had made her stand upright against the wall. Brunnerman glanced up at her; she was looking over his head with an expression of frightened obstinacy on her face. She was a very pretty girl; he could think, quite dispassionately, what a pity it was that she should end up in the Avenue Foch. She was the sort of girl he might have met at a party and taken out to dinner.

'Now, mademoiselle, I've sent Major Freischer away so that we can talk. Would you like a cigarette?'

'No,' Terese Masson said. 'And you're wasting your time. You'll get nothing out of me.'

He smiled at her and lit his own cigarette. 'You don't have to be aggressive with me; I'm not going to hurt you. And it's foolish not to have a cigarette if you want one – you'll be here a long time. You must be hungry by now. Of course, you probably had something on the train coming back from Lyons, a sandwich perhaps – who sent you to Lyons, mademoiselle?'

'Nobody,' the girl said.

She didn't even pretend to tell the truth. She had large brown eyes, which were a surprise because she was so blonde, and they stared at him fiercely, like a cornered animal. A lot of people cursed and swore at him within the first hour; some of the women stood up and shrieked obscenities at him just to destroy the atmosphere of normality he was creating. This girl was going to fight him as hard as she could because he wasn't behaving as she expected. Nobody had threatened her or hit her. He was relaxed, almost friendly. 'How old are you?' he said suddenly.

'You know,' she said. 'You've got my papers.'

'Eighteen,' Brunnerman said. 'You're very young to be mixed up in this. You should be out with your young man this evening, enjoying yourself.'

'I haven't got a young man,' she said. 'You've taken them all for your filthy labour camps.'

He ignored the remark. 'You went to Lyons,' he said, 'to give a message to a man at the Café Madeleine on the Rue Castigilione. You sat at a table and he sat down and tried to pick you up. You moved to another table, but you left a piece of paper for him under your plate. Then you had your meal, walked round the town for a while and then took the train back to Paris. This is what you did. When you got to the barrier at the Gare du Lyons you were arrested and brought here. Do you want to know how I know all this?'

'No,' she said. 'No, I don't want to know anything.'

Her hands had moved from her lap and were holding the sides of the chair seat.

'I'll tell you anyway,' he said. 'Because I think you ought to know. You were betrayed, mademoiselle. One of our agents was waiting at the Café Madeleine – he saw you meet the contact, leave the message for him. Your contact was arrested the moment he left the place. Everything you did was known; we wanted you for interrogation here in Paris, that's why you were allowed to catch the train back. The man you met at Lyons is being interrogated at Lyons now. I shall ring up in front of you and find out what he's told them.'

'He won't have told you anything,' Terese Masson said. 'You needn't lie to me. I'm not afraid of you.' She leant back against the chair; her whole body ached with tiredness.

He picked up the telephone and spoke into it in German.

'You don't have to be afraid of me,' he said.

28

'I told you, I'm not going to hurt you. But you ought to be afraid of Major Freischer.'

There was some delay in getting through; he held on, smoking his cigarette. This was the first part of the technique. The girl had been told what would happen to her if she were caught. She was emotionally prepared for violence, for suffering; she was ready to resist and some of the frailest physically hung on for days, often till they died. There was a spirit in this girl that would take a lot of crushing. But already she was a little shaken, a little disarmed by his approach. And she knew now that she had been betrayed; someone she had trusted had landed her in the mess she was in – a friend, not an enemy, had let her down. And the man she had met in Lyons was being questioned too. How much had he told them – how brave was he being? Her own ordeal hadn't even started. He had confused her already, and he had slipped in the threat without making it seem obvious. 'You ought to be afraid of Major Freischer.' It took time, this new technique of his, but once it worked it worked for ever. It was very simple in theory and immensely complex in practice. Take one frightened human being with something to hide. Isolate them, weaken them physically by keeping them awake and without food, destroy their self-respect by making them evacuate where they stood, surround them with hostility and the threat of agonies to come. Then give them to an interrogator who was kind and even sympathetic; they would feel hate for him, resentment at their own degradation, but finally a pathetic dependence would creep up on them, focusing on the one human contact they had which was showing them understanding. At all costs they must become involved with the interrogator, that's why one man, and not a team, was so essential to this particular method. It was a great strain on the man, but there wasn't a substitute. At the crucial moment, when they were still resisting, the interrogator's patience would come to an end; his friendliness would change to anger, he would reproach his victim and threaten to withdraw altogether. And his replacement was someone like Freischer, the symbol of hate and torture. With only two exceptions in two years Brunnerman's prisoners had all collapsed at this point; a high proportion of them had gone to work for the Gestapo afterwards.

The operator put him through to the Gestapo H.Q. at Lyons. No news, they said. The suspect was undergoing the most rigorous interrogation. They expected to break him before the evening. Brunnerman hung up. 'Your man has told them everything he knows,' he said. 'But he doesn't know the name of your Paris contact. He says you know that.'

'He's lying,' she said. 'I know nothing.'

'Look, mademoiselle, it's no good pretending to me. We both know you know this man's identity; I know that he's your chief in the Paris group and that you know who he is. That's what I want you to tell me, and, believe me, it'll save you a lot of trouble.'

He said it so convincingly that she looked at him for the first time as if she were seeing him as a man. They were nearly of an age; in other circumstances, in another place, they needn't have been enemies.

Suddenly she made a weary gesture, pushing the hair back from her face; she had been under arrest for eighteen hours, most of them spent sitting on a bench or on her feet to keep her awake. She'd had nothing to eat since she left the café in Lyons; he knew perfectly well there was no food on the train. There was little enough allowed on the ordinary rations for the French population. It was nine in the morning, and her whole day stretched in front of her like eternity.

'You might as well know now that I'm not going to give you any information. It'll save us both a lot of trouble if you get on with whatever you're going to do to me and stop playing cat-and-mouse.'

31

'Tell me,' he leant back in his chair and undid the buttons of his uniform jacket, 'what do you mean by do to you? What are you expecting? Torture?'

She shrugged; she wore a coat and skirt and a white blouse; she was very slim, with pretty legs. 'That's what usually happens, isn't it?'

'Not as often as you think,' Brunnerman said. 'In fact it never happens if I can help it; especially to women. You may not believe this, mademoiselle, but not all Germans are brutes. Most of us are ordinary men with wives and sisters of our own, trying to do a difficult job in the middle of a war. It doesn't give me any pleasure to keep you sitting here when you must be exhausted. I'm going to have some coffee.'

He ordered some over the telephone and when an S.S. man brought the tray she saw there were two cups. He poured out coffee for himself and then brought a full cup over and held it out to her.

'You might as well have it,' he said. 'It'll help to keep you awake.'

She took the cup from him; there was a strong, rich steam rising up from it; it was real coffee. She didn't look at him or say anything, but she turned the cup over and poured the coffee on the floor. He went back to his desk and sat down again. 'That was very silly. Why did you do it?' His tone suggested that she was behaving like a spoilt, bad-mannered little girl.

'I would have drunk it otherwise. You must see that I can't afford to take anything from you. I know what you're trying to do, and it won't work.'

'Very well then. Let's examine it. I'm trying to get a piece of information from you which you will give to us anyway – in the end. I'm hoping to get it without putting you through any unpleasantness, and also it will make it easier for you afterwards if you co-operate. I can understand how confused you must be – this isn't the cruelty, the wickedness, you expected of the Gestapo, is it? I told you, we're not all brutes. I hate violence, especially when it comes to women.'

He hadn't quite meant to say that. It had slipped out. He did hate Freischer and what he represented. He had been present at interrogations when men whose courage he respected, though they were enemies, were beaten and mutilated to make them speak, and he had been disgusted. There had been very few women, but these were worst of all. Their pain had been horrifying to watch, but the ferocity of his own men in dealing with them had shaken him more than anything in his life. He had prided himself on his professionalism, his detachment. He did a job and he did it extremely efficiently. He was able to say to himself that it was clean, scientific, this destruction of the will of another human being by a series of psychological tricks.

He had found it necessary to make these excuses more and more since he had come to Paris, because the nightmares of the fourth floor were so difficult to justify. He had conquered part of it; he could shut his eyes to the men, but the women haunted him. He didn't hate like Freischer and so many of his colleagues; he couldn't think of someone like Terese Masson in terms of filthy language and anatomical parts just because she was a Frenchwoman and working against them. He said it again, and it was as much for his own benefit as hers.

'I'm going to make you tell me who sent you, and I'm not going to put a finger on you. Or let anyone else either. It's nine-thirty now. We will begin from the beginning. Tell me your name, your age and where you were born.'

The clock on his desk showed 2 a.m. In the last two hours she had begun concentrating on the clock to stop herself from drifting. It was a fine ormolu and boulle-work pedestal clock, probably about 1801; it reminded her of the table in her mother's old drawing room at Nancy, because that was boulle too, and she had always loved the richness of the red colour. He had been questioning her for such a long time; he had gone out twice during the day, while an S.S. man watched her, but she had stayed rooted on the hard upright chair, without anything but a glass of water. She had studied every feature of the place and kept her mind alert, fighting the demands of her exhausted body and brain to drop down on the floor and sleep.

His office was a fine room with a high moulded ceiling and a red fitted carpet; the coffee would make a permanent stain. Terese Masson made that stain – she's dead now, they beat her up and she died. She threw her coffee on the floor and the Gestapo colonel got fed up with her and gave her to the major who had put his head round the door towards midnight and been sent away again. She had never believed it was possible to shake like that just because a man opened a door and put his head into the room and looked at you. He was waiting for her. The thought of it made her want to cry, but she wouldn't give way to it. She wouldn't tell the colonel who had sent her because she was not a traitor. She held on to that thought and kept her exhausted brain from sliding into confusion.

Raoul was an old family friend. Raoul was a very brave man and he had warned her that taking messages for him was dangerous. He had known her father before he went off to fight in 1940 and was killed. She was not going to tell anyone about Raoul, whatever this German said. The German looked tired too. He had taken off his coat and tie and it made him look younger, not in the least frightening. He had gone on, patiently asking her the same question, asking her other questions about herself which had nothing to do with the war, and she had found herself answering. This was wrong. Never get involved with them, say nothing, or you'll end up by saying too much. This she had always understood, it was part of the basic instruction given to all Resistance members. But somehow during the hours they had been shut up together in that room she had forgotten it and begun talking to the German and letting him talk to her. He had told her about his home and his family; she had begun to talk about her mother and their home in Nancy. He was beside her suddenly, and she jumped; she must have closed her eyes for a moment. He put his hand on her shoulder; it was the first time he had touched her.

'Have a cigarette.'

'No, I don't smoke.'

'Yes you do, Terese, there were cigarettes in your bag. Why don't you stop fighting me?

36

I'm only trying to help you.'

Suddenly she began to cry; she hid her face in her hands and wept, her body shaking. 'You're not trying to help me! You're trying to make me give away my friend – you're worse than that horrible major who keeps coming in. He's just a brute, but you're a hypocrite, trying to trick me!'

She had no handkerchief, she wiped her streaming face with the palms of her hands. 'Here, use this.' It was his handkerchief and she had taken it before she knew what she was doing. She went on crying into it, unable to stop. Brunnerman brought a chair and sat beside her, waiting.

It was the beginning of the end and he was surprised at his own relief. He was very tired; his head ached from smoking and he had drunk so much coffee that his mouth felt coated with the taste. She was tough, the girl, and courageous; she had done her damnedest and he was really happy to see her crying for her own sake. 'Come now,' he said quietly. 'That's enough now. Take this.'

She put the cigarette between her lips and drew on it Even with red eyes she was still pretty. He put his hand out and touched her arm She looked at him and she saw something in his face that disappeared immediately.

'Is that it? Is that what you want, Colonel?'

It was, and he had known this too, and tried to hide it from himself. He had been thinking of going to bed with her for hours. He looked at her without answering and he saw something in her eyes, some kind of fear.

'If you give me this man's name, I'll let you go,' he said. 'I'll drive you home myself. You don't have to sleep with me if you don't want to; that's up to you. I also promise you that I'll go easy on the man. I'll treat him as I've treated you. Tell me his name, Terese.'

'Oh God,' she said. She got up and moved away from him, then she stopped in the middle of the room because there was nowhere she could go.

'How many women make this kind of deal with you?'

'More than you'd think. They're not all as brave as you. But it's not a question of bravery now, is it? It's common sense. I'm not your enemy; I'd like to be your lover.' He got up and came face to face with her. He knew what she was afraid of now. She was afraid of herself with him. He had a sense of excitement that was near exultation.

He caught hold of her and pressed his hands into her back, flattening her body against his.

'I'm the only friend you've got, and you know it. You don't even hate me. You'd like to go home now, and forget all this nightmare.

And it hasn't even started. You've seen Frei-scher; do you know what he does to women? Well, I'll tell you – I've got to tell you, so you really understand the alternative to me.'

He told her very quickly, and for a moment her hands clutched at him in terror.

'I can't keep you here much longer,' he said. 'My superiors will want an answer; we haven't much time, we want this man of yours and the whole business cleared up. You'll tell Freischer; I've seen men scream-ing information out at the tops of their voices. You'll tell him; for the love of God tell me first and let me protect you.'

'I can't, I can't...' She could hear her own voice repeating it, while the warmth and strength of the man soaked into her. She didn't hate him; it was difficult now to realise what he was and what he represented. He was a man and he could get her out of this. He could take her home. She had fought him as long as she could, and closed her mind to the fact that she couldn't stay shut up in this room with him for ever. The next time that butcher with the beefy hands and the murderous eyes came into the room he'd take her with him. 'I can't tell you, don't make me ... please don't make me.'

'Don't make me send you upstairs,' he said. 'I'm asking you something for myself now. Don't make me do that.'

'Why should you care what happens to me?'

'I've told you, I like you.'

He was completely in control of the situation; he could hold the girl's body, press her against him so that she was aware of his sexuality for her, and feel that he had won. She was going to break down, and it would be more than just a piece of first-class work. It would be a personal triumph, a personal vindication. He looked down into the pale, frightened face, the dark eyes staring up at him in a mixture of misery and pleading. She was lost and she knew it; she was going to tell him because he had attacked her as a woman and made her see that she was fallible. She could respond to the enemy in spite of herself. She would go to bed with him too, and not from fear but because she wanted to. He could feel that she wanted to by the way her body fitted up against him and the pitiful fight against it in her eyes. She'd survive her betrayal; she'd come to like him and be grateful. They'd have a good time together. He would keep his promise and get her out of the Avenue Foch; he could explain it away to his general by saying she was going to work for them. In a week or two, after she'd been with him, she would probably do that too. And he could live with himself and what he had done to others because of what he hadn't done to her.

He could blot out the middle-aged woman he had seen strapped down on the table in Freischer's interrogation room, screaming like an animal as they passed electric currents through her body. He could forget the great courage of an Englishman who had taken all that they could give him in terms of physical torture until he was confronted with one of his own agents who had defected. He could ignore the evidence that the men he worked with were sadists and perverts, under the command of inhuman bureaucrats only interested in results. He could stand apart from them and still go on with his work – he could go on in the Gestapo and remain a human being; if only he could have Terese Masson.

'Who sent you to Lyons?' He held her face with one hand, forcing it upwards; her eyes were closed and the tears were streaming down her cheeks. 'Tell me now. Tell me the name.'

At that moment the internal telephone on his desk began to ring. He knew what that interruption meant when she began to struggle, and he let her go and picked up the telephone.

It was General Knochen himself.

'Have you still got the Masson girl?'

'Yes, General, I'm just...'

'Has she given you this man's name?'

The voice barked at him over the line; he could imagine Knochen sitting at his desk, making notes in his crabby handwriting. He very seldom lost his temper but when he did he was without mercy.

'No, not yet, General, but any moment now.' It was dangerous but Brunnerman's own nerves were stretched like piano wires, and he couldn't help saying, 'I'd have had it now, if your call hadn't interrupted me.'

'You've had fourteen hours to break her,' Knochen snapped. 'That's long enough. Send her upstairs and let Freischer see what he can do.'

The sweat came out on Brunnerman's face. 'Give me another hour, half an hour. It's just coming – I'll guarantee it!'

'Not another minute!' There was a moment's pause. 'What the hell are you doing, anyway? What's all this fuss about the girl? She's to go upstairs, Brunnerman. Immediately!' The line clicked, and Brunnerman hung up. Terese Masson had gone back to her chair; she was sitting with her hands clenched on her knees and her eyes weren't looking at him. He went over and stood in front of her.

'Get up!'

She did as she was told, and he could see that she was calm. His own hands were shaking. 'That was my chief. He wanted to know if you'd co-operated and I had to tell him you hadn't. I even asked for more time, but he wouldn't give it. They're coming for you, Terese. For Christ's sake tell me, before they get here!'

She shook her head. 'No,' she said, 'I can't.'

'You stupid little fool!' He shouted at her, overcome by anger. He did something he had never done since he joined the S.S. He hit her across the face.

'Tell me the name!'

She had collapsed on the chair, covering her head with her hands, trying to protect herself. He stopped and turned away from her. He went back to his desk and lit a cigarette; it took some seconds before he got the lighter flame steady enough to light the end of it. 'I'm sorry I did that,' he said. 'It's never happened before.'

'It's all right.' They were facing each other across a distance now, and she managed to smile at him. She looked very small and even younger than she was. The carpet was like an ocean between them.

'It showed you meant what you said, in a funny way. That's why you hit me – as a last resort.'

'I meant it all.' His anger had gone now; he felt a sense of total emptiness. 'All I can do is advise you. Don't try and hold out. Don't

43

get Freischer in a bad mood. Tell them quickly.'

There was a loud knock on the door; it opened and the two S.S. men in uniform came in and saluted. He saw the girl raise both hands to her mouth in a gesture of fear, and then get up without being told.

'Major Freischer requests the prisoner Masson, Colonel.'

Brunnerman refused to look at her. 'Take her.'

She moved to meet them, and at the door she turned. 'Don't worry,' she said. 'If I wouldn't tell you, I'll never tell them.' Then the door shut, and a moment later he heard the whine of the internal passenger lift as it went up.

There was a single low-voltage bulb in the ceiling; it hung on a length of flex and when she opened her eyes it was moving gently, backwards and forwards. She recognised the light as a sign that she was conscious for short periods; she tried to keep her eyes open so as not to lose it and slide away again. The descent into the dark was worse than the pain which was associated with the swinging bulb; it was like being drowned in that bath all over again. There were big oval blisters on her breasts where Freischer had burnt her with his cigar; they hurt, but the sensation ran into all the other feelings of injury in her body. They had broken the fingers of her right hand one by one and there was an intolerable ache somewhere at the end of her arm. It was over, that's why she was looking at the light bulb and slowly coming back to full awareness. She was in a cell, lying on a plank bed, naked except for a dirty blanket that was as thin as paper. She shivered continuously with cold and shock; she had vomited up all the water she had swallowed while they held her head under the water and she hadn't even the strength left to cry because of the pain.

'Terese.'

It was impossible to turn her head; she could see him bending over her, but his face was blurred. It wasn't one of the others. It wasn't the man with the little eyes that had the cigar, or the thin one who turned out to be a Frenchman when she heard him speak. This was the other one, the one who had tried to help her. The kind one. Tears rushed up into her eyes and overflowed, running down her bruised and sunken face.

'Don't cry,' he said. 'It's all over.'

'It hurts; my hand – everything...' She tried to speak, but it was only a whisper; he had to bend close to hear her.

'I know, I'm going to send you to hospital.' He knew what they had done to her, because he had received a full report. He had put in a report of his own, written in desperate haste after she was taken away, saying that in his opinion she didn't have the information they wanted. But it hadn't saved her. He had stayed on in the office till she came down from the fourth floor, and then come down to the basement to see her. He hadn't been able to work all day, and he refused to go back to his hotel room and sleep. After a day and a night without going to bed he had reached a pitch of nervous exhaustion where it was impossible to sleep at all. His mind kept returning to Terese Masson, nagging him with questions about himself and his reactions. Why had he lied to try to save her from the ultimate interrogation – he wasn't in love with her, wanting to sleep with her wasn't love. He had never been in love with any woman and he had gone to bed with a great many and enjoyed them. It wasn't courage either, because a lot of the people who came to the Avenue Foch were brave; at least in the beginning. He didn't know what it was, but the effect upon him was obsessional. She had come into his life at a crisis point of which he was unaware; what happened to her was an extension of what was really happening to him. Even before he went down to see her he had decided to resign and ask to be transferred to a Wermacht combat unit. Now he couldn't bear to look at her; when he left the cell he was going to be physically sick. If he had come on Freischer at that moment he would have shot him.

There was another whisper, forced out with great effort.

'Did I tell them?'

She hadn't been able to remember; she had a confused memory of someone screaming and screaming, but there were no words. She might have told them. She probably had told them, otherwise why had they stopped?

'No.' He said it very firmly and clearly so that she would remember. 'You were very brave. You didn't tell them anything.'

It was true. Her contact at Lyons had given enough away to put a lead on the man in Paris. Even Freischer had to admit that if they gave the girl any more that day she'd be dead by the evening. She closed her eyes. 'Thank God,' she said.

'Major Bradford, could you come a moment, sir?'

Robert Bradford was sitting behind the desk in the S.S. Commandant's office; he had a huge pile of cards in front of him and he had been trying to go through them, checking them from a special list. So far he had ticked off four names and drawn a line through nearly a hundred others. These had been shot, hanged, or gone to the gas chambers, the other four had been discovered among the starving thousands in the camp. There were many more names still unchecked. They were supplied by the French resistance. Other officers were dealing with the Dutch, Belgian and Scandinavian survivors. He looked up at the young sergeant; his name was Broome but his grandparents had come to the States from Poland. He was only twenty-three and what he had seen in the twenty-four hours since his company liberated Buchenwald had put ten years on him. He was permanently green; nobody wanted to eat much, few of Bradford's men were even talking while they went through the camp, rounding up the prisoners, opening one Bluebeard's chamber after another in the building and finding walls of the dead and living piled in rows one upon another. The stench of the place alone was indescribable. They had found the guards too, and the camp commandant, and when he was confronted by them Bradford found himself too benumbed by horror to feel anything so human as anger or hatred. He had put them under guard, and then ordered them to begin burying the heaps of dead which lay round the compounds.

'What's the matter, Sergeant?'

'We were going through the block marked J. sir, and we found some women still in there. There's one we can't get out; she's crazy. If you try and get near her she goes berserk. The men don't want to manhandle her, sir, and I don't blame them. I guess we'd like you to come down.'

'Okay,' Robert Bradford said. 'I'm coming.'

'She's over here, sir,' Broome said. 'By those bunks in the corner.'

There was little light in the building; it was full of tiers of wooden bunks, and the atmosphere was thick and foul with human scents. He saw some women huddled together in a corner, all staring at him with eyes that protruded from their waxen faces. One of his men was trying to persuade them to have some of his chocolate ration.

'In there,' Broome said. 'In the bottom bunk.'

Bradford bent down and in the poor light he saw a girl crouching on hands and knees. The hair hung down to her shoulders and her eyes were fixed open in a glare of terror. She wore a filthy camp uniform dress and her body was thin as a child's under the rags.

'I think she's French,' Broome said. 'When you get too close she starts to yell at you.'

'Right,' Bradford said. He moved in deliberately and held out a hand. 'Mademoiselle?'

The girl sprang back, cringing. 'No! Go away! Go away from me! I'm not going to tell you!'

He answered her in French. 'I'm a friend,' he said. 'I'm an American officer. You're free now.'

She used a filthy expression in reply. She shook her head at him and the ragged hair flew round her face. 'I'm not telling you! Never!'

Bradford turned to the other women. 'Anyone know anything about her?'

One of the older women took a pace forward. 'She's been like this on and off since she came here,' she said. 'Her name's Masson. I think the Gestapo had her first.'

'Masson...' he repeated. 'Masson – I think that name's on my list. Okay, Sergeant, it's not nice but we've got to do it. Get her out, and we'll send her back to the base hospital with the other sick.'

He went back to the office and crossed the fifth name off his list. Terese Masson, Resistance agent. Captured the 20th November 1943. Age eighteen years, hair blonde, eyes brown, height five foot four, no distinguishing marks or scars. Eighteen years old. 'Jesus God!' he said out loud. She had been in that hell-hole for ten months. She must have been around nineteen and she looked an old woman. The improvised hospital just outside the camp was bursting with prisoners suffering from every variety of disease. Captain Joe Kaplan was the army psychiatrist in charge of the mental patients and Terese Masson would be under him when she got there. Bradford had tried to comfort her when they got her into the ambulance, but she only moaned and cried, repeating again and again that she would never tell them, never, never ... he seemed to hear the cry following him as he went back to the office and the ambulance drove away, its red crosses looming like plague marks on its sides. He hadn't allowed himself the luxury of personal feelings since he had first driven into Buchenwald; he had done his job with his mind tight closed against sentiment or hate, but the pitiful cry of defiance and the miserable rag-doll body struggling against her rescuers haunted him, like the few statistics on his list. Two days later he drove out to the base hospital and asked to see her.

2

'You know, Bob, this is a very interesting case.' Joe Kaplan took off his glasses, polished them on his handkerchief and then put them back on. Bradford knew the mannerism well; he had known Joe since they were students at Harvard together: he had always polished his glasses when he got excited about something. They had become friends and stayed friends, which was unusual, because the Bradfords were moneyed aristocracy and the Kaplans were Jews. The two sections of society seldom mixed socially even in New York, which was pretty liberal by Boston standards.

'Most neurotic conditions are caused by guilt feelings, you know – but the point about this girl is, she didn't tell the Germans anything!'

'I don't see why you have to wrap it up,' Bradford said. 'It seems fairly simple to me; she's broken down because of what they did to her. For Christ's sake, what's so neurotic about that? Wouldn't you?'

Kaplan laughed. 'No, I'd have opened my big mouth the first time one of them said Boo! Don't get mad at me, Bob. I know you're very close to this. I've tried a simple analysis, drugs and the usual stuff. You must admit I've made some progress; you can get the kid into a room with a bath without she has hysterics. But I have established that she's had some kind of sexual trauma with one of the bastards – no, it wasn't rape. I checked. She's a virgin. But something that makes her feel guilty. I said to her once, "You didn't give them any information, you must remember that. You didn't tell them anything!" She'd had a shot of pethedine and she was pretty woozy. Without the stuff she wouldn't talk at all. And she said, "I would have told *him*. They took me away from him … I wanted to tell him. I wanted to go home with him!" Then she got very upset, so I left it.'

'All right,' Bradford said. 'What's the outlook? What chance has she got of leading a normal life?'

Kaplan shrugged. 'That's hard to say. It might take a year, two years, to get her orientated properly, and even then she'll probably have permanent nervous disabilities. You can't break a leg in six places and then expect to run a mile. If I had the time, and she was back home in a proper clinic with good psychiatric nursing and facilities, I'd say she might be able to live outside in about a year. But here – there's not a chance, Bob. I've got to tell you straight, the girl hasn't a hope in hell of anything but a life spent under care in some institution.'

'If I got her to the States,' Bradford said, 'she can have the best...' He looked up at Kaplan. 'Joe, I've got to help her. I'll do anything!'

Kaplan didn't answer immediately. 'How involved are you with this girl? You're not kidding yourself you're in love with her, are you?'

'No, I'm not kidding myself,' Bradford said. 'Because I know damn well I am. All right, I know you're going to start talking about pity, and me feeling guilty because I was born rich and all the rest of the crap, but whatever the reason, I'm in love with Terese. I've got another couple of months before I get a posting and I'm not leaving her here for the Red Cross to pick up and send to some lunatic asylum. If I can get her to the States...'

'Not a chance,' Kaplan said. 'The only way you'd get her in would be to marry her, and I won't let you do it. I'll go to your colonel if necessary and that'll be the end of that. Besides, she's too sick to take outside the hospital. You think she's a lot better than she

54

is, but that's because she's inside; she associates the hospital with being safe. You wouldn't get her past the door.'

'Then you won't help,' Bradford said angrily. 'Is that it?'

'No, no, I didn't say that,' Kaplan held up his hand. 'Sit down and don't lose your temper. I didn't say I wouldn't help. I was just trying to explain the problem to you. I know what's been happening between you and that girl. You've gone and got yourself all snarled up over her, and she's come to depend on you so much I don't know what effect it'll have on her when you leave the area. I'm thinking of both of you. I've had an idea – it's pretty experimental, Bob, but I think it might just work. Even if it didn't, she won't be any worse off.'

'What is it? You wouldn't have any Scotch around here, would you?'

'In the desk – right-hand drawer. Help yourself. Do you know what the human mind does when it finds a fact too much to bear? It forgets it. That's pretty normal, we all do it. If there's something unpleasant – something we're ashamed of, some awful grief – we forget it as soon as we can: or we try to. Amnesia is an extension of that, only it's an extreme measure taken by the mind, and it wipes out everything as well as the subject causing the problem. Often if that didn't happen the person would go crazy. There's a new theory, it hasn't been practised much, one or two cases have come up – it's called therapeutic amnesia. In other words the memory is erased scientifically, deliberately. This frees the patient of their immediate psychotic pressures and lets the doctor start from scratch. I think this might work with Terese Masson. If I can wipe out the last year or two – she might get well.'

Bradford poured out a second Scotch into the glass and drank it. 'Is this really possible? You mean you could make her lose her memory?'

'I don't see why not. She'd like to lose it; this is a big help. Her mind would like to forget what's happened to her. But I can't do it unless she agrees. And there's another point. She has no family, just one old aunt of seventy who lives some place in Brittany – she's going to come out of this without a past; I said two years, it might be her whole background, her identity! Who's going to be responsible for her then?'

'I am,' Robert Bradford said. 'You know that.'

'I have to be sure,' Joe Kaplan said. 'Think about it, Bob. Think what this really means when you say "I am". It might be for ever.'

'That's what I want,' Bradford said. 'Will you let me talk to her about it?'

56

'I was going to suggest that you did,' Kaplan said. 'She likes you, Bob. You're prettier than me.'

'You look better today. Did you sleep well?'

She looked at him and smiled. 'They gave me something; I always sleep well now. Thank you for the dress, Robert.'

'It suits you,' he said. 'I'd like to see you in some really nice clothes.'

She smoothed the skirt of the blue linen dress bringing the edges of the pleats together very carefully. 'It's beautiful,' she said. 'I haven't worn a dress like this for years.'

'Not years, Terese,' he corrected. 'Not as long as that.' The large brown eyes turned to meet his and there were tears in them. She cried very easily, sometimes for no reason at all.

'It seems like years to me. You're very kind to me. Robert. You've given me this dress, and all those nightclothes and my hairbrushes. Most of the people here haven't got anything but what the Red Cross can find for them. I feel quite rich.'

'I'd give you more, if I could get it,' he said. 'I'd give you anything. Think of something – think of something you'd like.'

'It's a beautiful day,' she said suddenly. 'I've been thinking how nice it would be if we could go out for a walk when you came today.'

'Why don't we? That's a wonderful idea!'

Her blonde hair had been cut short, one of the nurses had curled it with a pair of tongs; rest and food had put flesh on her. She had begun to look young again. Sometimes she even smiled. Even then she was so pretty that it hurt Bradford to look at her; it made him ache inside when she smiled at him.

She shook her head. 'I can't go out,' she said. 'I'm afraid. I'm afraid of everything, really.'

'You're not afraid of me,' he said. 'Or Dr Kaplan.'

'No, not you. Most of all not you, Robert. And the doctor is kind. Everyone is kind here. It makes me feel so safe. He says I must try and take a bath soon. I can go into the bathroom and it's not too bad. But I won't let them turn on the water ... I can't bear the sound of it.'

'Of course you can't,' Bradford said. He moved his chair close to hers: a few weeks before she had shrunk away when he tried to get near her. Now she let him sit with her and even hold her hand. He understood about the bathwater. It made him feel ill with anger. He took hold of her hand and held it tightly. 'Terese, I've got something to say to you. I want you to listen to me very carefully.'

'What is it? Is it something bad...? Oh, Robert, are you going away?'

She had turned white and her mouth was trembling. 'Are you leaving here?'

'No, no, I'm not going anywhere! This is something good – good news, that's what I want to talk to you about. Listen, Terese – you said just now you wanted to go out? You want to get better don't you? You want to put all this behind you and live your life like other people?'

'Of course I do,' she said. 'But it's not possible. I know what I was like when I came here – I know what you and Dr Kaplan have done for me. But I'm not a fool, Robert. I'm sick; I'll never be normal. If it hadn't been for you I think I would have killed myself. Life has nothing left for me.'

'Supposing I told you it had,' he said. 'Supposing I told you Kaplan could cure you, make you just like you were before anything happened. What would you say to that?'

'How?' she said. 'How could he do it?'

Bradford took her other hand and held both in his.

'He can take the memory away. But it may mean that you won't remember other things as well. You won't remember who you are or where you lived or anything about yourself. You'll have to be – re-born, Terese. But you'll be well – cured. Will you let him do it?'

'It sounds impossible. And frightening. What will happen to me afterwards?'

He bent his head and kissed her hands. 'I love you.' He said it very gently so as not to frighten her. 'I'll take care of you afterwards. Please, darling, let Joe do this.'

'All right.' She said it simply and without hesitating. 'If you'll promise to be with me.'

'I promise,' Bradford said. 'Right the way through.'

Colonel Baldraux lit a cigarette; he smoked continuously, lighting one Gauloise off the butt-end of the last. He sat in the Bradfords' Paris hotel suite wreathed in blue smoke. He was a tall, thin man with sparse fair hair and blue eyes and an Alsatian accent.

He was irritated by the American sitting opposite him; rich Americans annoyed him on principle, and he had found it difficult to track the Bradfords down. 'You realise how difficult this sort of attitude makes our work, Major?' he said. 'All I ask is ten minutes with Madame Bradford to establish a few facts.'

'I've told you,' Bob Bradford said. 'My wife was tortured by the Gestapo and spent ten months in Buchenwald. I wouldn't let anyone question her about it.'

'Very well,' the colonel shrugged. 'I can't force you to let me talk to her. Perhaps you can remember something that might help us.

60

Does the name Brunnerman mean anything to you? Did your wife ever mention him?'

'She's never talked about it, not to me. She was too ill. Who was Brunnerman, anyway?'

'A colonel in the S.S., one of their best men,' Baldraux said. 'It's on the Gestapo files that he questioned your wife. This was before she was tortured. We have arrested most of the Gestapo staff, including a man called Freischer who actually tortured Madame, and members of the Vichy Militia who were working with them, ex-criminals like Rudi de Merode – of course he had his own establishment at the Rue des Saussaies – your wife was lucky not to have been taken there; some of them were worse to their own people than the Germans ... But I am getting away from the point...' He lit another cigarette and swallowed a huge mouthful of smoke. 'We are interested in any lead we might pick up on Brunnerman because he seems to have escaped. All the Allied Security forces are looking for him, but he operated mostly in France, and naturally we want him. He was transferred to a Waffen S.S. division on the Eastern Front and that was the last we can trace of him after the retreat began. His division was responsible for the murder of twenty thousand Jews during the Russian campaign. It would be a pity if he were to slip out to Spain, for instance. We've lost hundreds of the top men in the confusion just after the war ended. I would very much like to find this one.'

'I'd like you to find him too, believe me,' Bradford said. 'But my wife can't help you. I promise you, Colonel, I'm not being obstructive; she has no memory of anything that happened during the war. That whole period is a blank, thank God. To be honest, she didn't even know her own name or anything about herself.'

'She's very fortunate,' the colonel said. 'How does she account for this gap in her life?'

'She believes she was ill. That's all we told her and she hasn't ever tried to question any further. She's well and happy, and that's how she's going to stay.'

'Nothing can bring the past back?' Baldraux said. 'You are sure?'

'As far as we know, nothing in the world.'

'Very well then. Thank you for the interview, I shan't be troubling you again.'

'I hope you catch the bastard,' Bradford said.

'Ah, Major, so do I.' The slate-blue eyes were bright with hate. 'And we will, don't worry. Sooner or later he'll be found.'

Ruth Bradford Hilton smiled at her sister-in-law and then at Karl Amstat. He had taken

Terese's hand and seemed unable to let go of it; he hadn't said anything to her at all.

'Darling, Mr Amstat's an architect, isn't that fascinating?'

'Yes.' Terese Bradford smiled. He had let her hand drop and there was a fixed, artificial smile on his face. He might even be a little drunk; so many people got high at cocktail parties and it was such a bore. 'What sort of building do you design, Mr Amstat?'

'Industrial, mostly,' he heard himself answering, and his voice sounded quite normal. There were people pressing in all round him, it was impossible to get away for the moment. 'And I do some private commissions, if they're interesting.'

'I'm very ignorant about it,' she said. 'I make all my family furious by saying I prefer traditional styles to the modern.'

'It's really a question of extremes,' Amstat said. It was the same person. She was unmistakable: the same eyes, the same face, voice, everything the same, only older, more sophisticated. He must be going mad. She didn't recognise him; she was becoming quite animated talking about architecture, and there wasn't the slightest hint of recognition. He shivered in the hot-house atmosphere, and his hands shook round the empty glass he was holding.

63

'Here, let me give you some champagne.' The English husband was back with a bottle, smiling under his ridiculous little brushy moustache.

'Darling,' Ruth said, 'you are sweet; where's that waiter got to, this is his job!'

Amstat's glass was filled, and he found himself drinking it straight down. 'It's so hot in here,' he said to Terese Bradford. 'It makes one so thirsty.'

'It does,' she agreed. 'I've been fifteen years in America and I still can't get used to the heating everywhere. There's a balcony over there – why don't we go out and get some air? I'm stifled.'

'Why, yes of course, but I must watch the time.' He made a futile gesture of looking at his watch, but she had taken his arm and they were moving into a larger room. He opened the balcony doors and they stepped out. It was little more than a narrow ledge with a parapet; below them stretched a magnificent view of the glittering skyscrapers, and the incandescent, changing glow of neon signs like an electronic rainbow.

'It's a wonderful sight, isn't it?' Terese said. He was standing beside her in the dark; the roar of the party went on behind them, and the roll of traffic in the streets far below came up very faintly like an echo. 'Better than all the Swiss mountains – are you

Swiss, Mr Amstat?'

'Yes,' he said. 'My home was in Berne.' It was crazy to go on talking to her, but he had to be sure. 'You're not American, are you?'

'No, I'm French. I met my husband after the war and married him in France.'

'I thought I detected an accent,' he said, 'but being a foreigner myself I wasn't sure.' He took out his handkerchief and wiped the sweat off his face.

'I love America,' she said. 'Are you married, Mr Amstat?'

'No, I'm afraid not. So far, I've escaped.' He always said this when women asked him that question. He had said it to Julia the first time they met. He wondered where she was. She was probably looking for him. 'Have a cigarette?' She held out a case to him, it gleamed in the dim light, and he took one. When she shut it he saw diamonds sparkling on the front. He lit her cigarette and watched her face in the moment while the flame lasted. She had changed very little. It was astonishing how clearly he remembered everything about her. She must be thirty-four, thirty-five, but she hadn't grown hard, or aggressive like the American women of the same age. She had a gentleness about her still – she had always had it.

'Have you been here long?'

'Only six years. I was in the Argentine,

studying, before that. I like it too. Your sister-in-law was telling me all about India; she was very enthusiastic.'

'She's a great enthusiast.' Terese looked up at him and smiled. He smiled back; he had seemed very tense and odd when they first met. Now she liked him better. He was more relaxed.

'She goes mad about people and about things. The trouble is, they don't always live up to her, and she can't understand that. She's such a strong person herself, and she's never married a man who could match her. I hope this one is different to the others. He seems very nice.'

'Yes, if you like the type. What were her other husbands?'

'Two Americans and one Bolivian. They were all disastrous, especially the Bolivian.' She gave a little laugh, and in spite of himself he had to laugh too. 'He was terribly rich and very temperamental. He threw fantastic scenes when he didn't get his own way about everything, and one night poor Ruth called up to say he was running amok in the apartment smashing everything he could get hold of, just because he wanted to go to Salzburg for the festival and she wanted to visit friends in Kenya! It was too ridiculous, really, but they got divorced and she swore it was the last time. The trouble is, she's miserable living alone. She needs a man in her life, and, being a good Presbyterian, she has to marry them, one after the other.'

'She sounds even more formidable than she looks,' he said. 'And she looks very formidable. How does she like you? Were you a disappointment too?'

He didn't know what made him ask that. It was all so strange, like a nightmare mixed up with a pleasant dream. The pleasant part was standing talking on the balcony; when they leaned over the parapet their elbows touched. He was very much aware of her. How did she fit into this milieu of an ultra-sophisticated society? It didn't serve any purpose but he wanted to know. It was like playing the children's game, grandmother's steps. He had seen children playing it in the streets in France. It was one of the oldest suspense games in the world, where you crept inch by inch towards the one whose back was turned. If you were seen moving, you were caught. The thrill was in the fear of being caught. That was what he was doing now, asking her questions, instead of getting out of the place as fast as he could.

'Was I a disappointment?' She repeated the question and then hesitated. 'I don't know. Not to Robert, my husband, anyway. But probably to Ruth and the others. I've never had any children.'

'I'm sorry,' he said.

'It doesn't matter. I've stopped minding now,' she said. 'One can't have everything. I've got the best husband in the world.'

'It's very rare to hear a woman say that here,' he said. 'I should think your husband's pretty lucky too. Can I take you back inside now? I have a friend with me – I'm supposed to take her out to dinner.'

'Oh, I'm so sorry, of course. I'm afraid I've kept you out here talking...' Inside the room, in the bright lights, she turned to him again. She definitely liked him; he was very charming and there was something warm about him. 'Don't think me rude, Mr Amstat, but I would like your address, so you can come to dinner with us. It's so seldom one meets another European. Will you come?'

'I'd be delighted; it's very kind of you. Here is my card.' He shouldn't have given it to her and he knew it. But it was too late. Not that he would ever go, if she remembered to invite him. He didn't even look for Julia – he wanted to get out.

'Goodbye, Mr Amstat. I'm so glad we met.' She held her hand out again and he took it.

'Goodbye, Mrs Bradford. Until we meet again.' He didn't shake hands with her; he lifted her hand and kissed it, and he saw what he expected to see. Freischer had broken Terese Masson's fingers. There were

68

small scars on the back of it, where her broken bones had been re-set at some later date. He hadn't even needed to prove it, but now he couldn't try to fool himself. He left the party and went straight back to his apartment. He mixed himself a large whiskey and then rang down to the basement for his suitcases. After four years he would have to start running again.

Terese opened her eyes and listened to her husband breathing in the dark beside her. She hadn't slept; she was waiting for him to fall asleep before she moved away from him. She got free very gently, sliding out from under his arm. He always wanted to sleep lying close to her, their bodies still engaged after they had made love, and she had always had to crawl away from him before she could relax. He had been a little drunk that night, that's what had started it, and when they came home after dinner with Ruth he came up behind her when she was undressing and kissed her neck. When he began feeling her breasts she tried to break away from him, but he either didn't or wouldn't notice. He had undressed her and begun the patient, tender assault on her body which had brought her closer to him over the years without ever carrying her through the barrier into a proper sexual fusion. She hadn't wanted any of it, but she couldn't bear to see him turn away, rejected and hurt, pretending not to mind. She loved him too much and owed him too much not to bear with his need for her; she even pretended to share his enjoyment, imitating his passion.

Now that he was asleep she wanted to lie on her own, to put on a nightdress, because nakedness worried her. It made her feel uneasy, as if she had some reason to be afraid when she was stripped. It wasn't because she didn't love Robert; he didn't repulse her, he had never been a brute or slept with another woman or done anything which could lay the blame for her frigidity on him. She had never tried to blame him; she blamed herself instead. She could be tender with him, respond to affection, enjoy his caresses and return them freely, but the convulsion of intercourse, with its sense of helpless subjugation, was something it had taken her years to endure without horror.

She knew her way round the bedroom without turning on the light. She didn't want Bob to wake up, she needed to be alone before she could hope to relax and sleep. She went into the living room and sat down, lighting a cigarette. It was a beautiful, restful room, and Terese had chosen the décor and furniture herself. Ruth had tried to persuade her to follow the fashion of five years ago and have everything modern from the paintings on the walls to the angular, black leather chairs and cubist tables which were the rage of smart New York interior decorators. Her own house at the time was a riot of violent colours, Swedish sofas and Reginald Bacon paintings. Terese had refused to be influenced. The colour scheme was muted; soft green silk walls were matched by a fine Aubusson carpet and several rare pieces of French furniture, including a Roetger commode which had once been in Versailles. The sofas and chairs were deep and comfortable, the pictures English eighteenth-century landscapes with an exquisite Gainsborough conversation piece Robert bought for her when it came on to the public market in England. Everything in the room was a reflection of the best of French and English taste, and this was only their New York apartment, which was empty three-quarters of the year. The Bradford home in Boston was like a museum. Terese had never felt at liberty to change anything or add anything of her own, and she had never regarded it as her home, though they spent most of their time there. She leant back, drawing in the smoke and thinking about Boston and the house and Ruth. Fifteen years ago she had come there to meet his family, so dependent upon her husband that she was uneasy if he was out of the room. Her mind was a blank. It had reminded her of a piece of paper which had to be filled up with pictures of a past drawn by someone else. She could remember the hospital and waking up, seeing Robert sitting by her bed. She hadn't known who he was or where she was or her own name. Strangely she had felt no panic, and afterwards when they pieced a little together for her she understood that Joe Kaplan had prepared her for this moment by hypnosis, so that she wouldn't be overcome by fear. 'I am Robert,' the man in American uniform had said. 'Don't be frightened, darling. I'm Robert.'

Why in God's name hadn't she ever been able to love him properly? And why hadn't he ever reproached her? She got up, threw her cigarette into the grate and called herself an ungrateful bitch out loud.

She lit another cigarette and went into the kitchen. When she switched on the light it was like walking into a room in Provence on a day of the brightest sunshine. Everything was polished wood and brass, with yellow walls and tiles and a pine floor. She and Bob would have liked to eat there, only they never dared because of the servants. She made herself a cup of coffee and sat down at the table. She stretched her right hand out in front of her; it was white and smooth-skinned, with long pale nails; she looked at the little scars along the back of it. She didn't know how she had got them; Joe Kaplan had told her not to worry about it and she had accepted that. He had treated her for weeks before she married Bob, after she left the hospital and Bob had put her into a hotel with a nurse. Every time she saw Joe Kaplan he drew in a little more past on the blank paper, so that she had a name and a birthplace and she knew how old she was. And her mind accepted the facts, but without any great curiosity. It was odd how little she cared about what she didn't know, and she couldn't make herself care. She had had an accident and lost her memory, and it didn't matter. Even trying to speculate made her feel lost and miserable. Bob had been very good to her that first year; he had made her see that a present and a future were all she needed, and he hadn't tried to sleep with her until Joe Kaplan said he could. She only knew that because of something Joe's wife Vera had said years afterwards. Vera didn't like her; Terese had the feeling that the older woman was holding herself back whenever they were together, like someone trying not to pull a knife out of their pocket and stab to the heart. Perhaps she was jealous of Joe. He had a famous practice and he was on the staff of Belleview as a leading consultant psychiatrist. There were so many neurotics beating on his door that he couldn't possibly treat them all. And he wouldn't treat the bogus rich sick, as he called them. 'There's nothing the matter with these damned women that a day's washing and six kids wouldn't cure!' He was ruthless with them; Terese had known one or two women and the odd man who had come out of Joe's rooms quicker than they went in. But he was wonderful with people who were really ill. He had been so wonderful with her. He wasn't just her doctor, he had always been Bob's friend and he was her friend too; perhaps the only one she had. It hadn't been easy, meeting Bob's family when they came back to America from France. His mother had been alive then, and she was an older, more terrifying, version of Ruth. The old Mrs Bradford had been kind, but it was like being received by royalty, however graciously, and Terese had been at a permanent disadvantage. They all knew she had been hurt in the war – it was generally accepted that it was during an air raid, so nobody could ask her questions about herself, and she had sensed how inhibiting this was to her mother-in-law. Mrs James Bradford II was a terrible snob because she could trace her own ancestry back to an early English settler in the late 1700s, and she was dying to ask her son's little French wife all about herself. If she ever attempted a reference to Terese's family, her son turned the subject on to something else. She had dominated his father and even Ruth, though with some difficulty. But where Terese was concerned she found that she had no authority over her son at all.

Ruth had been kind too; they were all kind when she first arrived, all Bob's relatives and his friends, but she could see them looking at her awkwardly; she sensed that she made them uncomfortable, and in return she clung to him more and more. She had said to herself that Joe was her friend and this was true. Her only friend was truer still. She had a lot of acquaintances, married couples she and Bob mixed with socially, women she lunched with and worked on an odd charity committee with because it was expected of her, but no intimates. No real friends. Only her husband, and Joe Kaplan. It was time to ask the Kaplans to dinner; it didn't matter about Vera. She was a bitch to everyone, and everyone disliked her. She could ask that Swiss she met at Ruth's party. He was nice. Perhaps it was because he was a European that she had found him so easy to talk to; he was a very good-looking man. Ruth said he was Julia Adams' lover; Ruth had thought him attractive too. Terese had met Julia once or twice but she couldn't remember much about her except that she was beautiful and very smartly dressed. She would have to ask Julia with the Swiss. It might make a pleasant combination, especially with Joe, who knew a lot about modern architecture. She had finished her coffee and the mood of restlessness had passed. When she got into bed Terese knew that he was awake. He stretched out his hand, feeling for hers.

'Where have you been?'

'Drinking coffee, darling. I couldn't sleep. Would you like me to make you some?'

'No, thanks. Come here, darling, close to me.'

She went into his arms and kissed him. 'I love you, Robert. Sometimes I forget to tell you how much. Did I make you happy tonight?'

'Very happy,' he said. 'You always do, my sweetheart. I'm such a lucky guy I can't believe it. You know, I looked round those people tonight at Ruth's party, and I thought, There's only one woman in the place, and she's mine. Only one really feminine, beautiful woman among the lot of them.'

'I wish we'd had a child,' she said suddenly. 'I'd give anything to have one. I feel it so terribly that you've missed that because of me.'

'You're not to feel anything like that,' Robert said. 'I don't give a damn about children. You're all I want. You know that.'

'I'm the lucky one,' Terese said gently. 'Not you, darling, me. Did you see Julia Adams tonight?'

'Yes, pretty briefly. She was looking for that architect you took out on the balcony. He's the current boy friend. Why?'

'I thought I might ask them to dinner with Joe and Vera. He gave me his card – the architect. I mean. Amstat, Karl Amstat, that was his name. He was rather nice, Robert. I think you'd like him.'

'If you like him, I guess I will too.'

'All right, I'll call Julia this week.'

Amstat didn't answer the door immediately; the bell rang twice while he was in the bedroom, emptying clothes out of the closet, two suitcases gaping open on the bed. He wasn't expecting any caller and he let them ring. It wasn't the first time he had packed in a hurry, but he had begun to think it wouldn't be necessary again. He had been safe for six years with the expectation of being safe for ever. But not now, not after meeting Terese Masson. It was the kind of damnable coincidence that couldn't be foreseen, it was incredible that she hadn't remembered him, but this was only temporary luck. The next time they ran into each other she might see something about him which she had missed in the middle of a crowd of people or standing on a balcony in the dark.

He was going to have to run again. The doorbell went on ringing. He swore and went out to see who it was.

'Well,' Julia said, 'so nice of you to walk out on me at the party. Would you mind telling me why?'

She didn't wait for him to answer, she walked past him into the living room and sat down.

'I'm sorry,' he said. 'You know I hate cocktail parties. I couldn't see you, and I couldn't stand it any more, so I left. Now I'm tired, and I want to go to bed.'

'Not with me, presumably,' she said. She made no attempt to get up; she took off her gloves and lit one of his Turkish cigarettes; she was so angry at the way he had humiliated her in front of the Bradfords that she was going to have a row with him whatever the outcome.

Amstat didn't move from the middle of the room. 'No, not with you,' he said. 'Or anyone else tonight. I'm sorry I didn't wait for you, but I've told you before, Julia, I'm not an American lap-dog. Now I'll take you home, if you like, but I'm not going to waste time quarrelling.'

'I'm not going home,' she said. 'I want to know what's the matter with you, Karl, and you're not going to brush me off. You've never walked out on me before, you didn't even call me afterwards and now you're trying to throw me out. I want to know why, that's all.'

'I've given you the reason and I've said I'm sorry. Twice. That's all there is to it. Now please go home.'

Julia hesitated; she had never seen him like this. He had become a stranger. 'Karl,' she said, 'don't let's fight. The last I saw of you was when you went out on the balcony with that crazy wife of Bobbie Bradford's – then you vanished. I thought maybe you'd picked her up, and I was furious.'

'What do you mean, Bradford's crazy wife?'

He felt anger rising in him as he looked at her, sitting smoking and swinging one foot backwards and forwards, using the word in that contemptuous way. He really disliked Julia at that moment.

'What I said! Crazy – well, sort of, anyway. She lost her memory during the war. Why are you looking at me like that? What the hell do you care if I call her crazy?'

'What do you mean, she's lost her memory? She seemed perfectly normal to me.'

He turned away from her, getting a bottle

of whiskey and two glasses out of the cabinet; he couldn't let her see his face.

'Well of course she's normal,' Julia said irritably. 'She just can't remember anything that happened before she married Bobbie. I heard she'd been in some kind of air raid – anyway I don't know, it's just what Ruth told me. Who cares?'

'Have a Scotch,' he said. He had poured himself a drink and gave her one.

She patted the sofa beside her; he looked tense and angry still, and she was frightened. More frightened of losing him than she had ever been about anything in her life before. 'Come and sit down and make up with me,' she said. He didn't come, he went on standing there, looking at her without seeing her, sipping his drink.

That was the explanation. That was why Terese hadn't known who he was, and it meant, incredibly, that she would never know.

'Darling,' his mistress said again, 'come here. I hate fighting with you. I know I was bloody and I'm sorry.' She managed to laugh as if it were all very unimportant. 'I'm just a jealous female. Come and kiss and make up.'

He sat beside her and immediately she put her arms around him. She was never diffident about initiating love; she gave him a long deep sexual kiss which left him com-

pletely undisturbed, while his mind registered that he must keep her out of the bedroom
or she would see the suitcases.

'No, Julia, not tonight,' he said. 'I'm tired
and I've got a lot of work to do. I'll take you
home.'

She looked at him and shook her head. 'I
wish we'd settle this thing, Karl. I wish you'd
marry me.'

'Why spoil it?' he said. 'Why try and tie it
down? It didn't work with you before – it
probably wouldn't this time. I'll come round
tomorrow early, about five. We'll spend the
whole evening together.'

'And the night,' Julia said. 'I'm getting so I
want to wake up in the morning and find
you still there.'

'You will,' he said, 'if that's what you want.'
He kissed her and made an effort. 'I'm sorry
I made you angry, darling. I really meant to
call you later and explain.'

Julia stood up, collecting her bag and
gloves; she was a very graceful woman and
she had recovered her poise. 'Forget it,
sweet. It was just a jealous fit. Amnesia or no
amnesia, she's a very attractive woman, and
that's a very cosy balcony. You needn't drive
me home; my car's out front.'

He went down in the lift with her and put
her in the car, and kissed her open mouth
through the window before she drove off.

Then he went back up to his apartment, into his bedroom and began to unpack. There was no danger from that incredible encounter. She would never be able to identify him. He didn't have to run, after all.

3

'I don't think the Bradfords give good parties,' Vera Kaplan said. She traced her mouth in bright pink lipstick and smiled at herself to make sure that none of the colour had gone on her teeth. Her husband was dressing in the next room and the communicating door was open. 'She's so dull, that's the trouble,' she went on, raising the vocal tone a little to make sure he heard. 'I find going to dinner there as bad as your medical friends.'

Joe was not the type of man who had a dressing room, it wasn't part of his background to dress apart from your wife, but she had made him do it, and now it was useful because they quarrelled so much that he spent many nights there. He heard every word and disciplined himself not to answer, not to be irritated.

'She's so dull.' His wife had hated Terese Bradford from the moment she met her; he had tried hard to analyse the particular compendium of jealousy, suspicion and symbolic resentment that made Vera so implacable, and even his professional understanding baulked at the intensity of her dislike. But then people often chose quite unrelated objects on which to focus their own failures, their own sense of inadequacy and injustice. He was so far out of love with Vera that he could see her situation and feel genuinely sorry for her. He was a Jew, and when Vera Calston Hughes married him she had broken the most important of all the social taboos governing the American upper class. If she had been a drunk or a nymphomaniac, or just stupid, ugly and a bitch to the world, she would have been kept within the magic circle of those who could actually trace their descent to some free thinker of the eighteenth century who had emigrated to the States from England or the Netherlands. But she had married a Jew, and made herself a member of the untouchables and not just the medium-grade untouchables like the Irish or the Italians, but a Jew who was despised and discriminated against even by the last two. At such a level Negroes didn't exist at all, except as servants or a Cause, like spastic children. Poor Vera. He tied his bow tie and made himself go into the bedroom and let her take a few more jabs. She must feel the need to hurt him or she wouldn't try so hard to do it.

'It won't be too bad tonight,' he said. 'Bob says there's a Swiss architect they're inviting; he sounds like an interesting guy. You may like him.'

'I may.'

She didn't turn round; she went on making up her face. She had been a pretty girl when she met Joe and fell in love with him; she had money and a name that got into the social columns and he was the most intelligent man she had ever met, and one of the nicest. More often than he knew Vera recognised how nice he was, and looking into her own embittered character, grieved that she hadn't been strong enough to see the marriage through without losing her self-respect and then her love for him. She hadn't spoken to her family for ten years. She would never forgive them and she took refuge in this attitude because she envisaged someone dying and her being able to refuse forgiveness. And it wasn't only on her side, it wasn't just the stiffnecked Boston aristocrats in their rigid entrenchment in the past; they had thrown her out and refused to meet her husband, but his Jewish parents and their tightly knit community had rejected her in a different way. Vera could go into their homes and be treated with great courtesy, offered everything first, deliberately made part of every conversation, and still be completely alien to all of them, the stranger who didn't understand, didn't belong.

Joe had his work, he had his career to compensate, and anyhow Vera felt he hadn't lost anything by the marriage. Nobody cut him, or asked them to parties where the guests were picked for their tolerant racial attitudes. Joe didn't even notice these things; they were part of a system which he had never penetrated deeply enough to be aware of the subtlety, the cruelty of the snubs his wife was made to suffer by her friends on his account.

But he knew what the trouble was; he knew the real reason why she didn't move when he came near her, or answer when he said he liked the way her hair was done. She just went on fitting a big pearl and diamond earring into her left ear, and letting him see she didn't love him any more, and she could have screamed because he understood the reason.

'They don't usually go in for intellectuals,' Vera said, returning to the attack. 'Tell me, darling, I said she was dull just now, but maybe I'm unfair. Did all that psychiatric stuff you did affect her – slow her down a little?' Now she did turn and she smiled up at him.

'No,' Joe Kaplan said, 'it didn't.' He hadn't meant to rise, but he had had a long day and it came out in spite of the futility and, above all, the repetition of this particular argument.

'Vera, why don't you get off Terese's back? What's she ever done to you?'

'That's just it,' she said. 'I'm not sure. Anyway, I'm not the one who's on her back – or ever has been. How about you?'

It always made him furious, though she'd been accusing him for years, and he became violently angry yet again.

'I have never had an affair with that woman. I have never touched her. She was my patient and she still enjoys that kind of immunity as far as I'm concerned.' He breathed loudly and deeply to control himself and said the next thing very calmly. 'I'm not a violent person, Vera, but the next time you make any kind of a crack about me and Terese I'll slap the bitchery right out of you. Now I suggest we might get a move on or we'll be late. As a doctor I appreciate punctuality, and as a Jew I like to be polite. I'll be outside in the car.'

He walked out of the room, closing the door quietly as if nothing had happened. His wife sprayed herself with Casaque, put a sachet into her bag and checked that she had her lipstick, vanity case and kleenex; she wore a black dress by Jakes and her figure was like a girl's. She was an immaculately groomed woman and it was all part of a routine she had learnt long ago and never relaxed. The result was what she saw as she took a last look at herself, sables over the left arm, dress, bag, shoes, everything in perfect harmony, with the right amount of jewellery. 'As a Jew I like to be polite.'

He knew what was wrong with her, and she was suddenly very sorry that she hadn't been able to deceive him. He ran a Volvo 28, and in spite of her protests that it was vulgar and unsuitable, he had ordered it painted bright red. He loved the car, and he drove it at high speeds. She got in beside him and they began moving downtown through Park Avenue towards the Bradfords' apartment on the corner of 56th Street. At the last traffic lights Vera said, 'Did you really mean that? You've never slapped me in ten years, and God knows you should have done.'

'I guess not,' Joe Kaplan said. 'I spend all day trying to sort out other people's problems and then I come home and threaten to sock my own wife.' He put out a hand and squeezed hers. 'I'm sorry honey. Forget it.'

'I just don't like her,' Vera said. 'He's sweet,

87

poor Bob, and he could have married any-one – I suppose it annoys me to see another woman being fussed over all the time.'

'She's earned it,' her husband said: he slipped the gears with unnecessary force and left the standing traffic twenty yards behind. 'Believe me, Vera, you'd never understand what Terese suffered unless you'd been there to see it for yourself.'

She didn't answer, because she would only say that she was sick of hearing about it, and the only difference between Terese Bradford and thousands of other people was the lucky way her life had turned out. Europe was full of camps where Nazi victims rotted away what was left of their lives, scarred in mind and body, unacceptable anywhere because they were casualties of a war which nobody was interested in any more.

'You don't need to be jealous of her,' Joe Kaplan said. 'I wish you'd see that. I admire her, I like her. To me she's a kind of symbol, one of my biggest successes. There's nothing personal in it for me, darling, and there never has been. If you can't like her, be neutral. For tonight anyway, and see how it works.'

'I'll try,' Vera said. She smiled at him, and for a moment it was like it used to be and there was a warmth between them, a moment's unity. She made a joke of it and this was an old means of communication between them. 'I'd better, hadn't I, if I don't want to get a poke in the eye!'

Karl Amstat had never meant to accept the dinner invitation. He had gone out of town for a few days on an assignment in Chicago for a department-store project, when the night he flew back, the phone rang and he heard her voice at the other end asking if he remembered meeting her and inviting him to dinner. Julia had already accepted and she was so looking forward to meeting him again. He had said yes, that would be delightful, and then reached for the telephone to call back and cancel it. But he hadn't gone further than dialling the first two numbers. He wanted to go, and it was perfectly safe. He had brought the subject up several times to Julia and everything she told him confirmed the fact that he had nothing to fear. Terese hadn't remembered him and never would. It was an ironical situation and he made the excuse to himself that it amused him to exploit it. It would be interesting to go to dinner with them, meet their friends and talk to her husband. He had known by instinct that he wasn't going to like Bradford, and within a few minutes of arriving at the apartment he felt antagonism towards this impossibly rich, nice, good-looking man who had married Terese Masson. He tried not to go near her, but she sought him out immediately, taking him by the hand to show him the Gainsborough portrait her husband had bought her as a present.

'Isn't it beautiful.' She didn't ask the question, she stated it, looking up at the picture.

Personally he thought it very English, very stylised and didn't care for it at all. It gave him the chance to look at her, while she was looking at it. The lack of change was remarkable; time had improved her without altering the air of frailty which he found so sexually disturbing. 'It's magnificent,' he said. 'But I'll be honest with you, Mrs Bradford, I prefer landscapes.'

'Most men do,' she said, and smiled. 'Please call me Terese. You know, I'm so glad you could come tonight. We had such an odd conversation that first evening, all about my sister-in-law's husbands, do you remember?'

'I found it fascinating,' Amstat said. 'You haven't invited them tonight?'

'No, you'll have to meet them again another time. It's just you and Julia and Joe and Vera Kaplan. They're old friends of ours. He's the sweetest man – you'll like him.' She wanted everyone to like each other; she wanted this particular small dinner party to be a real success, and she had taken a great deal of trouble over the food and wine, and spent the afternoon arranging flowers, which was an extra she usually left to the parlour-maid. Terese turned away from the portrait and Amstat followed her back into the small study where they gathered for informal parties. Immediately Bob came towards them.

'Darling, come and have a drink. Karl, you need a second helping of Martini – I know Terese when she starts a conducted tour!'

'And this is only a little pied-à-terre – you should see maison Bradford in Boston!'

Vera Kaplan said it with a laugh that only emphasised the sting in the remark, and held out her glass to Bob. 'It's like a museum. Every piece of furniture came out of somebody's palace, and as for pictures – my God, that latest acquisition you gave Terese would find itself hanging in the john!'

It was so rude that for a moment nobody said anything. It was Terese who took the empty glass out of Vera's hand and filled it.

'I have always heard your family were very rich and very distinguished. I'm sure *they* wouldn't hang a Gainsborough in the lavatory. See if you need more ice in this.'

'I think there's enough ice around already,' Julia remarked to Amstat. She had taken a place beside him as soon as he sat down, and she let one hand rest on his shoulder, casually, with the long painted fingernails showing up like drops of blood against his dark suit. She was smiling, leaning back and looking up at him. 'This is going to be a hell of an evening, my sweet,' she said. 'Our Vera just can't help being an eighteen-carat bitch. Give me a cigarette, will you?'

'Mrs Bradford said they were old friends,' Amstat said.

'*He* is.' Julia drew on his lighter and inhaled. The others were talking and the incident had passed over now, but the atmosphere was acrid. 'She apparently hates Terese, God knows why, there's nothing to hate about her.'

'No,' Amstat said, 'there isn't. Except perhaps that she's very beautiful. Maybe that's what annoys the other woman.'

'It'll annoy me too, if you say it like that,' Julia said. 'I think she likes you. Every time I look up she's looking at you.'

'Darling,' he said quietly, 'don't be ridiculous.'

'Oh I don't mind,' Julia said. 'I enjoy other women giving you a nod. Just so long as you don't give it back.'

'Come on, you two,' Bob Bradford came over to them. 'Stop acting like you were married and talk to the rest of us.'

'We're not doing anything of the kind,' Julia corrected him. 'We're just acting like very good friends, as that bastard Winchel calls it.'

She said it for Terese's benefit, in case she didn't know that Karl and she were lovers. It was all very pleasant and sophisticated and it said 'Hands off'. The next moment Amstat had moved away and was talking to Joe Kaplan. The hand Julia had left resting on his shoulder suddenly dropped as its support was taken away. He hated her making their relationship public and he would be angry and they might even have a row, but she had done it just the same. She didn't like the way Terese Bradford took hold of him as soon as they came in. And she was looking at him, most of the time. Julia was not seriously afraid of losing him. She had enough experience of marriage and lovers behind her to compete with someone like this French-woman, who apparently had never looked at anyone but her own husband. She had just made it awkward for her to monopolise Karl, that was all. The last fifteen minutes before dinner passed without incident. At the table, Amstat found himself on Terese's right, and he was aware immediately that at last he was going to enjoy himself, that being left with that unpleasant wife of the Jew, or even with Julia, would have meant the party was a total failure. He could look at Terese and talk to her and it would seem quite natural. He admired the way she had reduced Mrs Kaplan; it was so dignified, so un-American.

It showed the same deliberate courage that he had seen in an exhausted girl twenty years earlier when she turned his cup of coffee upside down to show she wouldn't take his bribe. He could think back on that with pride; he could sit beside her, smelling her expensive scent, making social talk to her and to Kaplan the Jew, on her left, and remember how she had spilt the coffee during that interrogation. The difficulty was to keep the memory from going on, from gathering momentum into the re-living of that early physical experience. That was foolish and dangerous; it could have been enjoyed if it hadn't been so much a potential on his part. He hadn't gone to bed with her then; he hadn't done any more than hold her to him, but the desires were moving in him, waking and beginning to trouble, like the details of an old dream.

He could sense Julia watching him across the table; she was very clever, making Bob Bradford laugh, keeping Vera Kaplan a little at bay too, and still watching him without making it obvious. He had made love to Julia so many times in the course of the last two years; since the evening a few weeks ago when he had been packed, ready to run because of meeting Terese Bradford, he often spent all night with her and they had breakfast together before he went to his office. But only because she asked him to, and made everything easy and attractive for him. He knew her so intimately that there were no surprises left. He thought how unwise she was to reveal herself completely to a man and then remembered that this was because she was in love with him. And lovers, as she so often said lately, had no secrets from each other; they were one. The biblical expression coming out of Julia's mouth, usually in the post-coital phase of extreme sentimentality, made him smile. He had secrets; she might explore her childhood, bore him at times with revelations of her life with other men, but he said nothing, because there was nothing he could say except the lies he had learnt off by heart. His birth and childhood in Berne, the school he went to, his parents' professions, their deaths, his decision to start a career in the Argentine and study there – it was all part of the façade, and he could recite it with slight variations while thinking intently of something else. Julia knew his body as intimately as he knew hers, but she was completely ignorant about him, and her own passion for self-revelation did not attract him. Contrary to her motive, it created an additional barrier between them. He found himself hoping he wouldn't be asked to go back with her that night.

'It's so lovely to have you here, Joe,' Terese

was saying. Kaplan looked so strained in his efforts to be amusing after the clash between her and Vera that she went out of her way to be nice to him, to show that none of it mattered. He had very dark brown eyes, and when she looked into them they always held a sad look.

He was very unhappy with his wife; they had no children either, and someone had once hinted that this was Vera's fault. A deliberate choice, because she wouldn't be embroiled in family life, by which was meant Joe's family and the additional problem of half-Jewish children.

'It's always nice to be with you and Bob,' he said. 'And you get prettier every day.'

'I heard that,' Bob said from the other end of the table, 'and I can tell you what does it. Me!' There was a laugh, and he added, 'Not to mention Terese's dressmaker! That's new tonight, isn't it, darling?'

His wife blushed, as if she had done something guilty. 'Why yes, it is. But it came from Bergdorf's. I bought it this morning.'

'Very nice,' Joe Kaplan said. 'It suits you.'

'In fact,' Bob went on, 'she's taken a lot of trouble with herself this evening, haven't you, my sweet – and you look like a million.'

He looked down the table length at his wife and smiled; for some reason there was an added lustre to the effect she usually created.

She was still young, with the kind of pointed, unlined face that didn't age for years, but that night she seemed unusually animated, less of a foreigner with a pronounced accent which she couldn't understand was an attractive thing to have. He was particularly relieved to see that Vera Kaplan's bitchery hadn't affected her. She seemed very relaxed, as if she were enjoying herself. She was talking to the Swiss, and they were laughing about something. He decided to make an effort with Vera for Joe's sake and started a conversation with her. It was only because of the close ties they both had with Joe that Vera was allowed in the door. It was such a pity Joe had married her; he could never visualise her as Kaplan had once described when they talked over this problem, a year or two earlier. Bob couldn't see the gay, attractive Vera Calston Hughes who had thrown up everything to marry him, and Joe had emphasised that everything was the right word. Bob couldn't see the courage or the charm, or any of the things which his friend insisted were still in his wife and only stifled by outside factors. He just saw a woman who was socially ashamed of her own husband and took her feelings out on the world. Just to watch his own wife made him feel good. He didn't give a damn about not having children any more; he didn't think of her in connection with the war, or that hellspot at Buchenwald. For Bob it was all over and forgotten. Terese was there, created instantly like Pygmalion's Galatea, by Joe Kaplan. He adored his wife and he had one of the nicest guys in the world as his best friend. His self-satisfaction was so intense that he spilled some of the warmth of it on to Vera without knowing, and she responded like a shut flower being prised open by the sunshine.

In the study after dinner they sat round drinking coffee, and Amstat took the place next to Terese; he didn't wait to be invited, he just sat down beside her.

'Cigarette?'

'Thanks, Karl – oh, wait, have one of ours, there in that green box on the table. Anyone want more coffee?'

'I'd love some,' Julia said. 'Don't get up, Karl can bring it to me.'

But the manoeuvre was defeated by Bob, who took the cup and brought it back. Julia sipped it slowly, and lit one cigarette off the last, while she watched her lover with Bradford's wife. No wonder Vera didn't like her. Maybe there was something in her suspicion that Joe and she had been more than just doctor and patient. She'd never really seen her giving a man a workout before and it was quite something to watch. Karl was right, she was beautiful. Not in a flamboyant

98

movie-star way – so many of those camera-perfect types were as sexless as cheese when you came close to them. This woman had something different, not just looks, because New York was full of beauties, but a kind of fragile femininity, a sort of wanton helplessness that invited outrage. No, Julia decided, she didn't like her either.

'How long are you staying in New York?' Amstat asked.

'I don't know,' Terese said. 'Bob and I only came back to spend a little time with Ruth and her husband; Bob prefers Boston.'

'And you,' he said. 'Which do you prefer?'

'New York, I think. It's more my home in a funny way. Vera was quite right, you know, when she said that the Boston house is like a museum. I've lived there for fifteen years and I've never liked to move even a chair from its place. It's that kind of house, you see...'

'I see,' he said. 'But that doesn't excuse her being rude to you. Nothing would excuse that.' She looked at him with surprise; he had been so vehement, as if he minded personally about the stupid woman's insults. She had cared for Bob, because it was Bob's present to her which was being denigrated. 'Don't take any notice of Vera,' she said. 'She's nasty to everyone; half the time she doesn't mean it. We're all so fond of Joe we

99

just put up with her. Perhaps she senses that.'

'If I were your husband,' he said, 'I wouldn't have her in the house. Your friend Dr Kaplan may be a great psychiatrist, but he obviously can't choose a wife for himself.'

'She wasn't always so unpleasant,' Terese said. 'I expect all this is very odd to you, because I'm sure there's no race prejudice in Switzerland, but over here, you see, someone with a family like Vera's couldn't accept a Jew as a son-in-law. All sorts of people dropped them flat after they married. It must have been very hurtful.'

He didn't answer that because he couldn't. He had stood in the middle of a wood in Lodz, with the snow thick on the ground and the tree branches bending under its weight, obeying an order to have an entire Jewish community dig their own graves before his men machine-gunned them into the open pits. There was nothing he could say about prejudice against the Jews.

'I hope you decide to stay on a while,' he said. 'It would be so nice for me; you must remember I'm even more of a foreigner than you are.'

'Oh, you're different.' Terese played with the coffee-cups, pouring out some for herself which he realised was too cold to drink because she put it down after one sip. 'You've got a great career – lots of our friends have mentioned you – you're a bachelor in the most social city in the world. It's not the same at all with me.'

'Why not?' he said it quietly. 'You've given a list of all my advantages. What about yours? You're a woman, and beautiful; you have a multi-million-dollar husband and a museum in Boston all your own. You can't still feel a foreigner after all that. Besides, I've only been here six years. A lot of things are strange to me still.'

'Yes,' she said, and now she looked straight at him and left the refuge of the coffee-tray. 'But it's different, as I said. I'm the one who's strange, not the other way about.'

'In what way?' Amstat asked her. They were very close on one of the comfortable upholstered sofas, and he had let his arm lie along the back of it. When she bent backwards her head rested against the arm. It was one of the few physical contacts between them, beyond shaking hands or her guiding him to show him the picture; they had brushed against each other leaving the dining room, and he had put his hand on her arm when he apologised. It was like touching a live switch. He had no idea whether she noticed anything, whether the current flowing so strongly out of every sexual nerve-ending in his body was strong enough to communicate itself to her. But there was something a little too relaxed about her; she leant backwards and let her hair brush his wrist, and stayed like that for some time, half turned and looking up at him.

He had never kissed her. He could remember holding her face between his fingers so hard that when he let go there were red thumb and finger marks on the line of her jaw. She had been crying then because she was so ashamed of her own body, and the betrayal it must lead her into, when his telephone rang, and the course of both their lives had split into completely different channels. Now by some extraordinary coincidence the two lines of existence had converged again in New York, twenty years later. He had never kissed her, and he wanted to do it, to find out what it was like. He repeated his question. 'In what way are you the stranger? I don't see it.'

'Oh, it's not important really. You know you're a very unusual person, Karl? I mean that quite sincerely. One day I shall probably tell you what I mean by "strange". And I don't think I've ever talked about it to anyone before.'

'I'd be flattered,' he said. 'I think perhaps we might lunch one day – unless, of course, you go back quickly to Boston, or your husband objects to me taking you out?'

'No to both,' Terese said. 'We're in no hurry to leave, and Bob would be delighted. I can tell he likes you.'

'So soon?' He looked across at her husband; he was laughing at something the psychiatrist had said. She was wrong, of course. The husband didn't like him, just as he didn't like the husband. Being an American he probably wouldn't dare forbid his wife something so innocent as a date to have lunch. It was a very curious society, all these rich people with their personal loves and hates, transforming everything into a problem with a capital P. You had a problem in your business, or a problem if you were too rich to need to work, because this was a breaking of taboo and you had to take up space and waste time going to some broker's office for part of the day. The women had problems when they grew older, because youth and sexual desirability were idols worshipped in every American woman's heart. As a place of refuge for so many millions over the last few centuries, America was the worst place in the world in which to fail, fall sick, get old or die, because then your problems had crystallised into the unforgivable sin. Failure. That was why he was safe and enjoying Bradford's superb brandy, with money behind him and people 'mentioning' him as Terese had said. Because he had succeeded. But it could change. It could change with one big flop in design; within three months he would be as friendless as he was when he first stepped off the train at Grand Central. Within minutes people like these would be holding their noses and screaming for the police if they knew about the other thing. But they would never know. He finished his brandy, aware that he was a little drunk, or high, as these ridiculous people called it, their vocabulary a bastard version of every language spoken under the sun. A word from Italy here, or Germany, or Poland, Jewish words come into common use. English distorted until the same word could mean two completely different things. Yes, he was a little drunk. Not enough for anyone to notice; he had been watching that kind of thing for years and he would never lose the habit, or rather the inhibition, to really be himself in case some slip came out. But Terese knew who he was. Sitting beside him, bombarded like an enemy target with the neutrons of his unconcluded desire – she knew in some recess of her brain that Alfred Brunnerman was sitting there right in the middle of them, smoking a cigar and offering to take her out to lunch. And he would. He'd call and do it, because it was safe, perfectly safe. It was like having a doll to play with, secretly in a locked room.

'Julia, have you seen the time? Forgive me, we've stayed far too late – I have a lot of work to do tomorrow morning before I go to my office.'

Everybody stood up and the party was over; he saw Vera Kaplan go up to Terese and kiss her; the custom nauseated him.

'Darling, it's been such a lovely party. And I adore your picture – I really do!' Amstat saw Kaplan say goodbye; he too kissed Terese, but it was friendly, quite without guilt. There was nothing there; that wife was a fool as well as a bitch if she were jealous for that reason. And he was glad. He would have hated someone like Kaplan to touch her.

'Goodbye, Terese.' She held out her hand to be shaken and he turned it palm down and kissed it.

'Thank you for a wonderful evening. I will call you and perhaps we can have lunch.'

'I'd love to,' she said. 'Don't forget.'

'I won't. Early next week. Good night.'

He and Julia drove back without speaking; she seemed in a good mood. Though she didn't talk, she turned and smiled at him, and when he drew up before her apartment she held out her hand.

'Darling, come on up.' Her fingers twisted in between his, and, leaning forward she kissed him on the mouth. 'Leave the car here; the porter can put it in the garage.' He didn't want to make love to her, but it was difficult to refuse. He didn't want a scene with Julia, or to break off with her. They had been lovers for a long time. When they made love it was very successful and she went to sleep beside him almost immediately. He didn't sleep, because he had been thinking of Terese Masson while he made love and the force of passion which had so satisfied his mistress was mentally expended upon someone else.

When all their guests had gone, Bob came up to his wife and kissed her. 'It was a lovely party, darling, I'm only sorry that bloody woman took a crack at you. But you handled it beautifully.'

'I can take care of myself,' Terese said. 'I don't take any notice of her. I just feel so sorry for poor Joe, that's all. I'm tired, Bob, aren't you?'

'We'll go to bed, then. We can have all the post mortems in the morning. By the way, that's a very pretty dress, I like it.'

'Yes, I liked it too. I was just passing Bergdorf's this morning and I went in...'

There were a dozen cocktail suits and dresses in her closet; she normally bought twice a year from the Jacques Heim collections and that was the way she had shopped for clothes for the past ten years. She had never walked into a shop and bought an expensive dress, just casually like that. But that morning she had gone out and bought the dress specially for that dinner party.

Not to attract her husband or Joe, or compete with the other women, but because she wanted something new to wear so that Karl Amstat would think she looked nice. That was the reason for the senseless piece of extravagance, and the realisation shocked her. She sought safety in the one direction where it was always to be found.

'Darling, do you like me in this? Really?'

'Of course I like it, I told you. It's quite a sexy dress. You'd better buy there more often. That Amstat guy couldn't take his eyes off you all evening.'

They were in the bedroom; she was undressed and brushing her hair. She had begun to panic that he would want to make love to her because tonight, for some reason, she mightn't be able to pretend. He might realise that he had never pleased her, that his caresses were agreeable, even stimulating, but in spite of everything, her emotional virginity was still intact. 'I'm exhausted,' she said. 'I don't know why, really.'

It was such a clumsy subterfuge; it made her feel cheap as soon as she said it. And he deserved so much better, so much more than she had ever given him. She turned round and said, 'Do you mind very much, Robert? Just tonight?'

'You know me better than that,' he said. 'Come on, sweet-heart, stop looking so guilty. I'm pretty tired myself.' He put his arm round her in bed and kissed her. 'It's not a crime, you know,' he said.

'Most men would have a mistress,' Terese said suddenly. 'Have you ever had one, Robert?'

'No. You're all I need, or ever will. Just don't ask that sort of question again, will you, please?'

'Don't be angry. I just feel such a failure sometimes. Darling, Karl Amstat asked me out to lunch one day.'

'I'll bet he did,' Bob said. He laughed and they both relaxed. 'Do you want to go?'

'Not particularly, but would you mind if I did?'

'Why should I? Or do you want me to be jealous and say I'll beat the hell out of the guy for asking?'

'You don't need to be jealous of anyone,' Terese said. 'Not of anyone, ever in our life.'

The next morning she took two phone calls, one from Vera which was short and the result of a row with Joe who insisted she rang up to thank the Bradfords, the other from Julia, which was long and unnecessarily fulsome, as if they were old girl friends. By mid-morning two dozen red roses were delivered addressed to Terese, with a card inside.

'Thank you for a delightful evening. Can you lunch with me next Tuesday? Karl Amstat.'

She put the roses in a bowl and arranged them, knowing that she hated doing flowers. It was an American custom to send candy or flowers after a party. There was nothing unusual in that. She looked up her diary and found that Tuesday was free for lunch. She had known it without looking, but she made herself go through the motions, pretend that it was nothing out of the ordinary.

Lunch on Tuesday. It was very quick to follow up. He was Julia Adams' lover and she had noticed how much Julia seemed to be in love with him. They were both sophisticated, and their relationship was so very ordinary these days; people lived together and some-times they married and sometimes they never got around to it. There was no reason why she should mind about it; no moral objection to account for her dislike of the idea. He was a very attractive man. He must be, she had even bought a new dress to please him. And she wanted to go out to lunch with him. She wanted to see him again, because he was amusing and charm-ing – no, that was a lie, he wasn't amusing.

He was attractive; she liked him. And there was no harm in it. There couldn't be any harm in having lunch. They could talk about architecture.

It was a small restaurant, about twenty-five miles out of New York City, in Banksville, the kind of place which was crowded at weekends. They drove there through the maelstrom of midday traffic, and down the narrow straight highway past Brooklyn Bridge. It was the beginning of spring and the countryside was turning green and yellow under a mantle of trees in bud. It was one of the sights of New York state, its beauty immortalised in a once popular love song, and Terese knew the restaurant very well. It was both exclusive and expensive. She had never been there on a weekday before and there were only four other couples there. She watched Amstat go up to the head waiter; he had a curious authority when he wanted something. He was the kind of man who got served first, who could come late and always find his reservation had been kept. He was very foreign, very un-American, when you watched him closely. They chose a table by the big bay window, where they could look out on the slightly undulating wooded view. There was no one near them.

110

'It's very nice of you to come with me,' he said. 'This place is so crowded and stuffy at weekends – I thought it would be pleasant to get right out of the city for a few hours.'

'It's lovely here,' she said. 'And it's not nice of me to come at all. I've been looking forward to it.'

'Would you like something to drink first?'

Julia insisted on at least two drinks at the bar whenever they went out to eat, and he had become accustomed to the habit now, although it bored him. He had taken Terese straight to their table.

'I don't know – perhaps a Cinzano.'

He raised his head and immediately there was a waiter beside him.

'One Cinzano and one bourbon-and-soda. Bring the menu, please, and we'll order.'

'Certainly, sir. At once.'

She asked him about his work and he told her about the Chicago project. It was a department store, and he found this kind of designing the tedious side of his work, but it made the money.

'Ruth said you did a lot of private work,' Terese said. 'Didn't you design a house down at Tobago for some people called Jaravis?'

'Yes, but that's rather like this department store. I make money but I don't really enjoy it. I remember the Jaravis house. It could

111

have been so beautiful, but she was an impossible woman and her husband was such a miserable worm. She wanted all the wrong things, and I had to give them to her; all he did was sign the cheque. I hated it, I remember very well, but I wasn't so established then. I wouldn't do it now.'

'What do you really like to do? What fulfils you as an architect.'

'Art,' he said. 'By which I mean designing as a setting for art. A museum, a theatre. I have a wonderful design, quite revolutionary, for a theatre. One day I'll do it.' He smiled, and she thought how good-looking he was; the eyes were so blue, and she had never seen him smile with them before. 'You must find all this very boring,' he said. 'I'm being selfish and talking all the time about myself and my work.'

'I like it,' she said. 'It's very interesting. Did you always want to be an architect?'

He lit a cigarette and gave one to her. They had ordered coffee. 'No, not always. My family wanted me to be a soldier. When they died I went to the Argentine and studied. I liked the idea of South America – Europe was just recovering from the war, there wasn't much time for new ideas. People were rebuilding on ruins, now they're beginning to design as well as build.'

'Would you ever go back?' she asked.

'No. There's nothing for me there. I have no family alive.'

'I'm sorry,' Terese said. 'Don't you mind being alone?'

'I've got used to it. But I don't like it, in many ways.'

'You've got Julia, though. I mean, I know about it. I hope you're not annoyed with me for saying it.'

'It's common knowledge. We live together. But I'm still alone.'

Terese put out her cigarette. 'Then you can't be in love with her.'

'I have never said I was.' He was watching her so intently, it was disturbing, like the sudden anger when they were discussing Vera Kaplan's rudeness the other night. It was like a door that opened, a shutter that flipped up, and then was quickly closed again.

'Do you realise something,' he said. 'You're the first woman I've been with in six years who didn't talk about herself all the time? You haven't told me about your husband, your sex life, your doctor, or the secrets of your best friend. Will you let me take you out again?'

'Do you want me to talk about those things, then?' she asked him.

'No. But I want you to tell me why you said you were strange the other night. I haven't forgotten, you see.'

She put one hand to her forehead; it was the right one and the tiny scars showed up against the skin.

'I've lost my memory. That's what I meant by being strange. I know who I am and all the necessary details – I can fill out my own passport, but I can't remember any of it. I had some kind of accident in the war – it's no good,' she looked up at him, 'I can't go any further than that, and I'd rather not try, if you don't mind. But people know about it, and it makes me feel odd. A freak. And this is not the kind of society that likes freaks.'

'It ought to,' he said. 'It's full of them. They're the most neurotic, undisciplined people in the world. Give me your hand.'

She held it out to him across the table. The other couples had gone and a bored waiter leant against the farthest wall, watching them and waiting for some sign that they were going to go.

He put both his hands over hers, covering it completely. She felt an impulse of sensuality that went up like a flare inside her. There were blond hairs on the back of his wrists; his hands were strong and not oversensitive, not too artistic. Her own was hidden between them and his fingers touched her wrist.

'It's late,' she said. 'I know it's late. I must

go home.'

They sat side by side in his car and they didn't speak until he had come to the last intersection before her apartment block.

'When will I see you again?'

'I don't know.' She looked up at him, and the look was there again, the fear of herself, the unspoken appeal to him not to press her too hard. He had seen it in the Avenue Foch twenty years ago and it was still there, still inside her as much as it was part of him. Was this love? this indescribable feeling – he didn't know. It wasn't what he felt when he was near to Julia.

'Perhaps we shouldn't meet.'

'Why not?' he asked her. He drew the car into the kerb and switched off the engine. It was nearly five and the lights were springing up like jewels all over the city. She had escaped him once; she had been snatched away from him and he couldn't save her or keep her for himself. This might be a second chance.

'There's no harm in going out with me. Haven't you enjoyed yourself? Did I bore you?'

'No, no! You know I loved it. I loved every minute of it. That's what I mean – that's why perhaps we shouldn't...'

'I will come for you at one o'clock on Thursday,' Amstat said. 'We'll find somewhere different to have lunch.' He got out of the car and opened the door for her. 'You're home, Terese. Thank you for today.'

'Do you really mean to come on Thursday?'

'At one o'clock,' he said.

'Till Thursday, then,' Terese said. She turned without letting him touch her to shake hands, and went into the entrance.

4

'Well,' Joe Kaplan said, 'this is a nice surprise.' He got up from behind his desk and came towards her with both hands outstretched. 'You're looking wonderful, Terese. Sit here.'

She took the chair in front of his desk and began pulling off her gloves. She had never been inside his private consulting room before and it was quite different to what she had imagined. The furniture was English reproduction mahogany; the chairs were leather, the inevitable couch was a day-bed with a tartan rug spread over it. It was completely unclinical, like a study in a private house.

'This is very nice, Joe,' Terese said. 'It's such a comfortable room.'

'It has a homey atmosphere,' he said. 'That's what I wanted. I want people to relax when they come here, feel they're talking to a friend. I guess a lot of white paint and hard angles puts them off; makes them feel they're sick, like being in a hospital.'

'What a wonderful man you are,' she said simply. 'That's just how one would feel. Do you mind me coming to see you like this?'

'Why should I?' He leant back in his chair and took off his glasses; he began polishing the lenses with a handkerchief.

'I suppose it's a professional visit of some kind, so let's be doctor and patient. What's the trouble?'

'Oh, it sounds so ridiculous.' She paused, waiting for him to put his glasses back on. 'The whole thing is absolutely crazy, me making an appointment with you and going through all this rigmarole – but, Joe, I could not come and talk to you just as a friend about this!'

'All right, that's understandable. I'm your doctor *and* your friend. Go ahead.'

'You've been very good to me,' Terese said. She spoke slowly, not looking at him. 'You gave me a chance to live again after whatever it was that happened. You and Bob were the first faces I can ever remember seeing. It was like being born fully grown.'

'I know,' he said gently. 'I know what it was like.'

'You and Bob – Bob and you; I don't know which way round to put it. Am I making any sense?'

'Sure; just get the perspective fixed right in your mind. Bob first, and then me. Bob loved you, I only doctored you. So?'

'I've come to you,' she said, 'because you're as fond of Bob as I think you are of me. And it's Bob I'm thinking of, not myself. Joe, you know the difficulties we've had – about sex, I mean.'

'I know the difficulties you used to have,' Kaplan said. 'But, honey, you haven't been to see me professionally for something like ten years. Maybe more. I've always understood from Bob that everything was fine between you.'

'That's what I've tried to make him think,' she said. 'Joe, I'm frigid. I've never been able to let go with him, love him properly. I've never been able to really respond and lose myself. But I've pretended to, because I couldn't bear to keep on hurting him. I never had a baby for him, that was bad enough. I couldn't go on letting him know that making love to him meant nothing to me. I'd stopped hating it and being afraid, but that was all. Otherwise nothing.'

118

'I'm sorry,' he said gently. He was not surprised by what she told him. It was natural to expect a degree of subconscious revulsion against the sexual act after the horrible parody of it she had suffered during one stage of her interrogation. He could only imagine what forms it might have taken, but the early attempts to probe into her experiences had revealed a definite sexual association in her mind and he had assumed that it was some kind of torture. Whatever it was it was lost, along with all the rest, and it could never be dug up and exorcised.

'I think you've done the right thing,' he said. 'You've made a good adjustment. As for pretending with Bob – well, that's loving him, isn't it, in a different way? Loving a person is making them happy, Terese, and that's what you're trying to do. Is that what you're worried about?'

'No.' She took some moments to light a cigarette, and knowing the value of these kind of pauses, Kaplan let her take her time.

'I've always believed I was incapable of love. I thought I was just one of thousands of women who didn't like sex, and couldn't ever feel anything. I'd accepted that, Joe. But it's not true, and that's why I'm here. I'm falling in love with someone else. Really in love with them.'

She looked up at him. 'I mustn't let it

happen. I won't let it happen because of Bob. I've come to you because you're the only person in the world I'd trust. I want you to tell me what to do.'

'Could you tell me,' he said after a moment, 'what you mean by falling in love? Really in love, you said. What does this mean exactly?'

'It means that I've met a man I want to sleep with,' she answered almost angrily. 'It means the same for me as for anyone else. For the first time in my life I want to do the normal things, I want him to kiss me, touch me. When I'm near him I feel it so much I'm afraid it'll show to Bob, to everyone who sees us. And it's not only that. That's bad enough. But if it was only just wanting to make love with him I could fight it by feeling ashamed of myself. But it's more, Joe, it's worse.'

'How much worse? In what way?' He kept his eyes off her deliberately; he kept his voice level and unsurprised.

'I like him,' Terese said. 'I like being with him; I feel so at ease, there's something so familiar about him – it's as if I've always known him. I mean it, Joe. I'm in love with him.'

'How often have you been together?'

'Oh, about a dozen times – alone I mean. We meet a lot socially now too.'

'Has he tried to make love to you?'

'No,' she said, 'but he wants to; I can feel it. All we've done is have lunch together; or go to an art gallery a couple of times. Once I stood him up – I was afraid of what might happen, I was trying to escape. He just waited outside the apartment for me to come out and then I went and had a drink with him anyway. Nothing's happened between us yet. And for God's sake it mustn't ever happen!'

'It sounds as if this guy's in love with you,' Kaplan said. 'Will you tell me who he is? You don't have to, if you don't want.'

'It's Karl Amstat. Why do you look like that? Who did you think it was?'

'I'd no idea,' he admitted. 'I haven't even been trying to guess. He's a good-looking guy. He's not my type exactly, but then Julia Adams is crazy about him, so obviously he's got something for women. Now he's trying to make you too, eh?'

'If you want to put it like that.'

He saw the hostility in her face and he made a gesture. 'Don't get mad with me, Terese. I don't blame Amstat. I'm just partisan because of you and Bob. This marriage is a precious thing. You've been very happy, haven't you?'

'Yes, very happy,' she said. 'Oh, Joe, I feel so mean – I feel so low just thinking about anyone else after all Bob's given me!'

'You can't help that,' he said. 'If you didn't

love Bob in that way, it's not your fault. It's not your fault now if someone happens along that can make you feel that way. Falling in love isn't a crime, Terese. But busting up a marriage with Bob would be one helluva mistake. I'm glad you've come to see me; very glad. Do you know what I'm going to advise you to do?'

'No. Just give me *some* advice on how to stop this thing.'

'Run away from it. As far as you can get. From what you tell me, you're still in the clear, you haven't been to bed with Amstat – you've got nothing to reproach yourself with but a temptation – right?'

'Yes, absolutely right.'

'Then stop seeing him. Go to Bob and get him to take you away for a trip. Make any excuse you like – say you're tired, think of something. He's never said no to you in his life, has he? O.K. He'll think it's a wonderful idea, and by the time you get back in, say, six months, you'll have gotten over this completely. I'll guarantee that.' The phone rang on his desk. 'Excuse me. Yes?'

'Mrs Kaplan on the line, Doctor. Shall I wait till Mrs Bradford's finished, or shall I put her through?'

'No, tell her I'll call her right back. How do you feel about that idea?'

'I don't know,' she said. 'In a way I don't

want to do it – I want to go on seeing him. But if I do, Joe, I'm lost. And if I let Bob down I'll never forgive myself. And you'll never forgive me either.'

'I wouldn't say that.' He got up and they faced each other. 'But I might be pretty mad with you at that. Do as I say, Terese. This is the time to be really brave and play the coward. Get away from this guy. Ask Bob tonight. And don't see Amstat before you go.'

'All right. I'll do it. Dear Joe. I'm so grateful to you. I'll run away from it, I promise. And then it'll be over – I won't feel the same when I come back?'

'You don't even live in New York,' he reminded her. 'You haven't any problem, my dear, except which place to choose out of the world. Go on a tiger-shoot, like Ruth.' He smiled and took her hand in both of his. 'And don't worry. Everything's going to be fine.'

When she had gone he made notes on a pad. There was nothing medical in them but they would be attached to her original file. He kept all his private patients' files: the one on Terese Bradford was in the basement in the cabinet for old patients, the cured, the vanished and the dead. 'The bastard.' He said it out loud. Waiting outside the apartment for her, determined to get her. Julia

Adams wasn't enough for his ego, he had to pick on a happily married couple like the Bradfords and start working the wife over. Joe had never liked him, and they had met several times since then, once or twice at cocktail parties and at dinner with Julia. He didn't like the type, the Swiss were too near the Germans for Joe to feel at ease with them, and he sensed a hostility in Amstat which was carefully concealed but not carefully enough to escape Kaplan's racial sensitivity. Of all the unlikely people in the world for Terese to fall for – lunch and art galleries and a wall of unspoken sex rising up behind them, waiting to collapse and bury them flat. He must be an odd guy to have taken so long coming to the point. Anyway, it didn't matter. It might even release the wife's tensions in the direction of her husband, now that she found she could experience desire like anyone else. It only showed him, he decided, how little he still knew about the workings of the human mind, that after twenty years a woman he knew so well, that he had almost moulded her personality himself, could escape him and prove his theory wrong. He had never expected her to reach emotional maturity. She had married and adjusted and kept Bob happily in love with her, and by doing this alone she was Joe Kaplan's private miracle. His greatest success, he had called her to Vera, and this was true. He had re-made a human being, getting her and Bob through the early months of marriage, guiding and advising. Terese meant everything to Robert Bradford; she was his purpose in life, the reason why in spite of his millions and all the opportunities for turning into a rich bum, like so many of his generation, he was stable, happy and mature. His wife was the only thing he cared about; she was his lover, his child, his companion, all rolled up in one personality. How lucky Terese had come to him in time. Joe remembered that he had promised to telephone his wife, but when he did so there was no reply. She hadn't waited for the call. It was such a pity about them, but it was far too late. She had probably been unfaithful to him; women often were because they held a grudge, or needed reassurance which their husbands didn't give them. Very few indeed were motivated by the 'fire in the loins' Terese Bradford had described to him, though the quotation would have shocked her. He had had it himself, and so had Vera; he could understand the damned stupid things it made a rational being do. It could lead to a doomed marriage as much as a disastrous affair. The desk phone rang. It was his next appointment. He shut Terese out of his mind completely, and got up to shake hands with his patient. 'Sit down,' he said. 'Have a cigarette – good. Now, how have you been feeling?'

'Darling,' Julia said, 'please come on up. Just for a drink.' They stood on the step of her apartment block on 61st; they had been to the theatre and had dinner at the 21 Club with another couple who were friends of hers, the Staffords from California. Amstat had insisted on leaving early, saying he had work to do. She didn't show her feelings; she just asked him please to come up, and after a moment's hesitation he agreed. She switched on the lights and told him to make himself a drink.

'And a brandy for me. Courvoisier. You'll find some at the back of the cabinet. I won't be a moment.'

She went into her bedroom and took off her theatre coat. It was scarlet silk with a thick brown sable collar and deep cuffs; her dress was a plain sheath of the same colour. She had taken more trouble than usual that evening to go out with Karl. Everyone had looked at her when they went to the theatre and in 21. There had even been a gleam in Donald Stafford's eye and they were old friends, long past noticing each other. It was all for Amstat's benefit. She had done exactly what a clever woman is supposed to do when she feels her lover losing interest. Made herself extra beautiful, bought some new scent, and gone into battle determined to win. Not to quarrel, not to reproach, but to get him back. That had been her original intention when they started out and it had lasted all through the first act of the new English musical, which was a sell-out, with Tony Newley, right up to the moment they ran into the Bradfords taking a walk in the interval. They were with Ruth, and her husband and two other people she didn't know, and Bob had hailed them, calling them over. That was when her plan disintegrated. When she stood back a little and watched Karl with Robert Bradford's wife. There was nothing obvious about it. She had looked ill-at-ease for a moment, and then they began to talk and Julia was able to study Karl, while she pretended to listen to Bob. He was not a man who showed his emotions easily; that had been part of his attraction for her, the sense of discipline over himself and its consequent authority over her. But this was something that he couldn't hide. Never, at any moment in their relationship as lovers, had she seen him look into her face as he was doing to that other woman. They might have been in the middle of the Sahara, they were so absorbed in even their brief moment together. He had reached out and touched her arm, and it was a caress. Julia had gone through the rest of the evening, behaving normally, refusing to let him slide away and leave her at the door. She took a quick look at herself in the mirror. 'You poor deluded bitch,' she said under her breath. Then she went into the living room to have it out.

He stood up when she came into the room; his manners were always meticulous in these small details. 'Here's your brandy, Julia. I didn't make it too large.'

'Thanks; as it happens it's just right. You take such good care of me, Karl darling.'

He sat down, watching her warily; something was wrong but he wasn't sure what. He had never seen Julia in this restrained mood, like a ticking time-bomb in scarlet, smiling and patting the seat beside her. When he came over she put her glass down, twisted her arms round his neck and kissed him.

'You know I really am in love with you,' she said.

'I know you are.' He said it because there wasn't any other answer.

'Will you ever marry me, Karl?'

He put her arms away from him and got up.

'We've been into all this before. I don't want to marry. If I wanted a domestic life it would be different, but I don't. I thought we'd agreed all this!'

'Well, we'd agreed to let it rest,' she said. She leant back with her arms raised, showing the line of both breasts, and crossed one leg so that the line of thigh was continuous under the red silk. It meant nothing to him, any more than the arousing kiss had done. He was cold, dead, as far as she was concerned. 'I suppose I'd resigned myself to living with you and hoping one day we'd make it legal. I was happy with that, so long as you were happy with me. Tell me, darling, how long have you been seeing Terese Bradford behind my back?'

The question was so unexpected that he couldn't believe it – his first reaction, born out of a different kind of guilt, was to try to deny it. 'I don't understand you, Julia. I don't know what you're talking about!'

'Oh yes you do. You've been seen, my sweet, lunching à deux around town. And, of course, a kind friend or two thought I ought to know – people are so nice about these things.'

'I'm sorry. There was nothing in it – I just gave her lunch once or twice. Look, Julia, it's late and I told you, I have work to do – if you want to pick a quarrel for some damn silly reason, like me taking another woman out to lunch, then you'll have to choose another time! I'm going.'

He didn't want to discuss Terese with her;

he didn't want her to say anything derisory or start tearing their relationship to pieces with her jealous verbal claws. They had been seen, Terese and he. It was inevitable, he should have been prepared. He looked at her with a new viewpoint, the slim body in the expensive suggestive dress, the angry eyes accusing him, the woman he had lived with and with whom he found a sort of security instead of love, was now an object of dislike, who had the temerity to open his mouth when she kissed him and imagine that what they had done before gave her some claim on him.

'You're in love with her, aren't you!' She got up and she was between him and the door. 'You bloody liar, I saw the two of you tonight! You were going to bed mentally right there in the middle of the foyer. How long have you been having this affair – you and that cheap little nobody he picked up from some French junk heap in the war – loss of memory! She was probably an army whore!'

He didn't hit her; he stopped himself in time. He had only hit one woman in his life and this one didn't mean enough for him to touch her.

'You spoilt, useless tramp,' he said. 'You wouldn't understand a woman like Terese Bradford. You wouldn't understand why I'd rather go out to lunch with her than go to bed with you. You're the whore.'

'Thank you,' Julia said. She put her hands to her face and began to cry. 'Thank you for what you've said. What are you aiming for, my sweet? What are you going to do when Bob finds out and divorces her? You going to marry the little bitch?'

'I've told you,' he said quietly, 'don't call her names. I'm not her lover. I don't care whether you believe it or not, but it happens to be true. I've never touched her. I told you, she's not like you. She's not a whore!'

As he reached the door she came close to him; her face was wet with tears. He had never imagined that she could cry.

'This is the finish then? You're walking out?'

'I think we've come to the end, don't you? I'm sorry, but my capacity for scenes is limited. Good night.'

'Goodbye,' she said. 'Get that straight. Goodbye.'

He didn't answer. She heard the front door of the apartment close behind him. She went back to the sofa and sat down, shaking. The brandy was untouched in the glass. On an impulse she reached for the phone and dialled the Bradfords' number, without knowing what she was going to say when someone answered. But the ringing went on and on until she put the receiver back. They were still out, probably with Ruth and the others. She finished the brandy and began to cry again.

'Darling, do you want a drink?' Bob Bradford put his arm round his wife and kissed her. It had been a long evening. Ruth had insisted on going on to the Peppermint Lounge to show her husband the dancing, and it was past three when they finally broke up. He was very fond of his sister; unlike so many of the very rich, the Bradfords were a united and affectionate family, but he found her energy a little exhausting. She never seemed to tire, and when it wasn't marriage or travelling that provided her with an interest, it was involving herself in complicated battles with their trustees over the terms of her mother's will.

Much of the evening had been spent in discussing the particular section of the trust it would benefit her and Bob to have broken, and he had felt sorry that Terese had been left out, like the Englishman, who sat gazing down at the mass of gyrating, twisting couples on the floor of the Peppermint Lounge as if he had taken a table at the reptile house in the Bronx Zoo. The Bradfords had millions, but there were so many strings attached that Ruth found it a real brake on her activities.

She was determined, and she had spent a large part of the evening proving it, to her brother, to release more money for their joint benefit.

He thought that Terese looked very tired, and rather silent. She had gone into their bedroom and said nothing since they got back. He stood in the doorway, a whiskey in his own glass, and repeated the question.

'Would you like a drink, sweetheart? I need one, after this evening. My God, Ruth's taken the bit this time! I couldn't do a damned thing with her!'

'I don't want anything, darling. Let's go and sit in the study while you have your drink. I'm not really tired at all.' She had made up her mind to take Joe Kaplan's advice, and to act on it immediately, while her resolution was still strong. And meeting Karl at the theatre had shaken her so badly that she couldn't wait till the morning. If she did, she might never try to go away at all. If he called her, and they met, she couldn't trust herself not to delay, just for a week, just to see him once or twice more.

'I shouldn't worry, Robert; Ruth's always having legal fights. She thrives on them. Surely he'll advise her?'

'He doesn't know anything about our trust laws,' Bob said. 'And I guess he's found out it's not easy to say no to Ruth, especially when it concerns her own money. Anyhow, let's forget it for now. Did you like the play? I was a bit disappointed – I suppose I expected the impossible. He's a fantastic guy, though. One of the biggest theatrical talents for years. Funny running into Karl Amstat and Julia – I wouldn't have thought it was his kind of an evening. She looked really something tonight.'

'Yes,' Terese said, 'she did. She dresses beautifully.'

'By the way,' he said, and he was laughing, 'did he ever take you out to lunch? I just remembered!'

'Yes,' she said, 'once.' It was the first real lie she had ever told him. 'I suppose I forgot to tell you about it. It was quite pleasant.'

'Nothing sensational.' He grinned, and finished his drink. 'He's a bit Wagnerian for you, darling. There's something very tough about him and I don't know quite what it is. Anyway. Julia likes him. Maybe she likes being pushed around. Come on, time for bed. I have an early meeting in the morning.'

'Darling, I was thinking,' she said it very quickly before he could get up, 'couldn't we have a change?'

'Change? What sort of change?'

'Well, I was thinking about what fun Ruth said they'd had in India – couldn't we go,

Robert? Couldn't we just pack up and take a nice holiday? I'd love it!'

'Why, sweetheart, you've really thrown me! You don't mean to say you want to go and shoot *tigers* like that crazy sister of mine? What's got into you? You've never wanted to travel much before – why India, of all places? Why not Europe – we meant to go to Portugal last year and never made it.'

'Portugal would be lovely,' she said. 'I just thought India was different – I thought you'd enjoy it more than going to Estoril. Darling, let's go to Portugal!'

'All right, we'll go to Portugal. May is the best month, or June. We should have cleared this trust business up in a few weeks. That's a swell idea.'

'I don't mean May or June,' she said. She came and sat down on the arm of his chair and put her arm round his neck. 'He's never said no to you for anything,' that was what Joe Kaplan had said to her that morning and it was true. Now what she was asking for was for his sake more than hers. 'I want to go away now, Robert, just on our own. Right away from here, from New York. You're right, I am tired – I need a holiday.'

'Wait a minute, darling, I said May or June, but that doesn't tie you down ... you could go on ahead for a week or two. But I can't walk out on this family business, not at this exact moment. Normally I don't have commitments that we can't change to suit ourselves, but this is serious. There's something like fifteen million dollars involved in this and Ruth needs me here. I'll try and hurry it up, I'll do my damndest, but I can't take off now, just like that. It's impossible.'

He squeezed her and got up, holding her tightly to his side, explaining why he could not leave his sister and avoid his family responsibilities just this once. He was much taller than she was, and he couldn't see her face.

'Please, Robert.' She said it, and drew away from him. 'Please take me away now. I really want to go. I need to get away!'

'But why?' he said. 'Why so suddenly? Look, Terese, if there's anything the matter, anything worrying you – for God's sake come out and tell me. Otherwise this wanting to rush off on a vacation at a minute's notice makes no sense at all. Especially when I've explained why I can't.'

'Yes, you've explained.' The stupidity, the irony, of it made her suddenly angry with him. 'Your sister decides she needs more money – thirty million dollars isn't enough for her, so you have to stay and hold her hand through it. This is the first time I've asked you for something I really wanted, and you can't do it. All right, Robert. Don't let's argue. It was a silly whim, I'm sorry.' She walked past him into the bedroom and shut the door. A moment later he had opened it and was behind her, taking her in his arms.

'I'm sorry, my sweet. Of course I'll take you away. Just give me a week or two. Maybe I can talk her out of it. Say you book for three weeks ahead – that's not too long to wait, is it?'

'No,' she said wearily. She leant against him, and shut her eyes. 'I may go a little before you. Would you mind that?'

'Of course I'd mind,' he said. 'You know I hate being without you. I feel like a man without an arm. But you go if you want to, and I'll follow on, if you can't wait for a couple of weeks to get away.'

'I can wait,' she said. 'Of course I can wait.'

'You're sure there's nothing the matter – nothing wrong?'

She looked into the anxious face, and knew that no matter what the consequences, she couldn't turn to him for help without telling him the truth. And she would never tell him that. Whatever happened, he must never know, never be hurt.

She smiled at him and touched his face. 'There's nothing wrong. I was just being spoilt and stupid. Forget it, darling. We'll go away together when this family business is cleared up.'

'I adore you,' he said seriously. 'I'll even take you to India and we'll shoot a couple of maharajahs, just to be different.'

She found herself laughing and the old feeling of safety came back. 'It would give the tigers a break,' she said. 'Oh, Robert, you are ridiculous! And I adore you too.' At that moment Karl Amstat seemed totally unreal. The idea of running away from him was equally out of proportion, when all she had to do was remember all she owed her husband and refuse to see him again.

For the first time since he had moved there two years ago, Amstat noticed the emptiness of his apartment when he got back that night. It was a luxurious flat, furnished with Julia's help in excellent modern style, and he had bought several good pictures by artists who were considered an investment. It was his home, and he had been proud of it until that moment. Now, as he shut the front door and walked into the living room, it was a cold, echoing place, angular and stark, the impersonal room of a bogus personality. It wasn't him, this place; it had nothing to do with the real man who lived in it; it wasn't his true taste; it was part of the façade he had built round himself, as false as his name and his papers. He looked round at everything, and thought how ugly it was, how alien to what he would have chosen in other circumstances. He did something unusual; it was late and he had meant to go to bed, but he poured out a long whiskey and took it into the bedroom with him. The bedroom was dominated by a big double-bed, covered in brown and white calf-skin; the bedroom walls were white leather, the furniture Swedish designed and very functional. In the closets there were rows of American suits, a rack of handmade shoes, pyjamas with his initials on the left breast pocket, very discreetly embroidered in dark blue. It all belonged to Karl Amstat, who was born in Berne and was a successful architect in New York. And it had really nothing to do with the man who stood in front of the glass and looked at himself, the whiskey in his hand. That woman he had quarrelled with and walked out on, she had nothing to do with him either; she was as much a phantom as the rest of it. The only real thing she had ever done was to tell him he was in love with Terese Bradford; he could admit that calmly now. He was in love with the woman, just as he must have been in love with the girl twenty years ago. Nothing had changed, after all. He was still Alfred Brunnermann.

He hadn't allowed himself to say his own name for years. Terese was in love with him too; he knew it, and he knew that it was

Brunnerman, the hunted outcast, that she wanted, and not Amstat. He had lived a lie for twenty years to save his life. He had tried to think of himself as dead, to obliterate the past; not just for safety but because there was so much pain and shame in it now, that he had wanted to forget. He had run after the war, because everyone round him was deserting, while Germany came down in a thunder of ruin and devastation that shook the world it had so nearly dominated. He was declared a criminal, and he had behaved like one. Unlike so many of those who fled with him, he felt that he *had* committed a crime, and taking on Amstat's personality was a means of escaping that guilt. He had become an architect, dedicated to the construction of buildings where he could marry the functional and the beautiful; he touched nothing that reminded him of the destruction and waste of his past life. And yet the aching need remained, the need to look back with some degree of pride. He had accepted that he must always be alone, but until now he hadn't been free to be alone with himself as he really was. Terese Bradford had made this possible; she had given him back his identity, because she knew it. Somewhere in the blacked-out memory the young Gestapo colonel who had tried to step between her and his own diabolical organisation was alive and in her life again.

That was who she looked at, talked to, gave her hand to hold when they had their meetings. Even though she didn't know it, and never would, her ignorance didn't matter to him. She mattered; she mattered more than anything because she was almost the last thing he could remember of which he wasn't personally ashamed. He had been dismissed from Paris because he had sent her to hospital, and transferred to the Russian front as unreliable. And that was where it happened, during the retreat.

He emptied the glass and sat down on the big bed, on the calf-skin cover which he had never liked, and hid his head in his hands. It had taken a long time to shut the memory out; he used to dream of it, and wake, in some dingy Argentinian lodging house, sweating and choking with horror. He had triumphed in the end, and stopped thinking about it, and dreaming about it. Now, it was back behind his eyes, a cold, white waste of land, dotted with shattered trees, and the smoking ruins of the retreating Panzer tanks which had been caught by the Russian artillery.

And a long uneven crocodile was moving across the snow, moving very slowly, disintegrating in parts and coming together again, as the old people, or the children fell, or lagged behind. There were thousands of them; he had watched from a scout car, through binoculars; men of his Waffen S.S. division were moving the dark human stream along towards a wood. His senior officer, a brigade general called Schaeffer, was sitting in the back of the scout car, drinking cognac out of a flask to keep warm. He didn't want to be bothered to watch; he had told Brunnerman to stand up in the biting wind and tell him what was happening. He had seen it all before; he had carried out so many executions that he was bored, not nauseated. It was routine, like squashing the lice that lived in their filthy, frozen uniforms. It meant nothing to Schaeffer except a duty he could delegate to someone else, while he comforted himself with sips of brandy. They were in Poland, just outside Lodz, and when the order came through from Army Headquarters in Berlin. Brunnerman had carried it out and sent his men to round up all the Jewish population of the town and march them out into the open country. He had known what Schaeffer was going to do with them. But it was an order. And they carried out their orders; this was their glory at that time, when defeat and death were pressing as hard on them as the pursuing Russian armies. Their discipline never broke. Only afterwards, in the hindsight of sanity and civilised values, did Brunnerman see it as his own and his nation's lasting shame. Four thousand Jews had been marched out that day, and taken into the woods where the men dug a series of long shallow trenches and the S.S. set up machine-guns, the crews slapping their sides and stamping on the ground to keep warm while they waited. Schaeffer had stayed on the perimeter of the wood in the car; he had sent his subordinate ahead to see the business was properly carried out. That's what subordinates were for, to stand in the bloody cold and get the men moving with the digging, and see that the mess was covered up properly afterwards.

It had been done very efficiently; within two hours the S.S. were coming out of the wood, climbing into their transports and throttling forward through the snow towards the shelter of Lodz for the night.

To the brigade general's surprise his young colonel had spent some minutes behind the car vomiting. He had shouted at him to get in, and made the squeamish bastard pull himself together by giving a precise report of what had happened, even though the noise of the motor engine made it impossible for Schaeffer to catch more than a few words.

'And you had the trenches filled in?'

He could still hear that voice, after twenty

years, the voice of a man he saw die only two weeks later in a vicious rearguard action with the first Russian troops to catch up with them. He could hear his answer, shouted above the revving engine, fighting its own battle with the soft snow. 'All graves were covered over. Everything was in order.'

Everything was in order. The screams had stopped and so had the steady rattling of the guns, except for a shot here and there, as an officer inspected the heaps in the trenches and fired point blank at anything that moved. He had stood back, on the edge of the clearing, his hands deep in the pockets of his greatcoat, the noises still going on in his head, the figures still reeling backwards into the pits, long after it was over and his men were shovelling the fresh earth and newly fallen snow on top of what they had done.

He could see and hear it all again at the moment, and suddenly his stomach heaved, and he went to the bathroom and retched. He had nearly shot himself once; one night when he was in Buenos Aires, and he had enrolled at the university to study under Diego Bolsa when the chance of the Jewish intelligence agents catching up with him had decreased to a point where he seemed really safe – then he had taken out the little gun he carried for protection, and nearly blown his brains out because of what he had done in the wood outside Lodz. Now he came out of the bathroom and looked round the empty bedroom, and decided that this was not the night to try to sleep. He went into the living room and sat down to work. He owed his life to the German affiliations in America; they had formed an organisation that had its roots in the old outlawed Bundt, and they channelled their own refugees through the South Americas, providing funds and papers, maintaining a counter-intelligence system to the pursuing Israelis who took up the hunt when the Allies declared the war criminals files should be closed, marked dead or disappeared. Germans had helped him, anonymous sympathisers with the men of their own blood who were on the run, and he had been grateful and obedient. The instructions were precise. Keep clear of women, make no intimates, never on any account get drunk, and keep inconspicuous. He had lived this regime for years, existing on odd jobs here and there, until they gave the word that he could safely study seriously. He had accepted the forged identity and the carefully checked background of Karl Amstat and worn the man's personality like a suit of clothes until he felt it had turned into a skin. Nobody had approached him since he first settled in New York. He had forgotten them and they had presumably counted him a non-risk. But then nobody had imagined he would meet Terese Bradford.

He didn't work, he thought about her, and her image eased the sickness of self-disgust and made him calm. She was dangerous; she and what she represented to him were the most dangerous contingency he had faced since his escape through Spain after the war. It was madness to see her, madness to allow this infatuation to develop far enough where Julia could see it and accuse them. His first impulse after they met at the cocktail party had been the right one. To pack and run. He had known it then and he knew it now. There was still time to get away, time to avoid the inevitable ending of that unfinished love affair of long ago.

All he had to do was cut it off, go back to Julia and resume the safe life; the Bradfords would leave New York, go back to Boston after a time. They never stayed for long. He need never see Terese again. That was the right course, the sane decision. But he couldn't make it; it was too late for Julia Adams and the old arrangements that were quite satisfactory for Karl Amstat. They weren't acceptable to him, to Alfred Brunnerman. The past and the present had met and fused in the resurgence of his emotional need, and his need for Terese Bradford was stronger than his caution or his interest in the future. She could be his death, but now life itself was incomplete without her. He wasn't going to run away; he wasn't going to give her up and sink for ever into a vacuum. He was going after her and he was going to get her. His habits of self-discipline reasserted themselves and he settled down to work until the daylight came.

5

'It's a Mr Amstat on the line, madam.'

'Oh.' Terese had made up her mind that she was never going to see him again. That was decided. Now she had only to pick up the bedroom extension and she could talk to him. 'Say I'm out, please, Mary.'

'Oh I'm sorry, madam,' the maid said, 'but I told the gentleman you were here. I can say I was mistaken...'

'No, no,' Terese said, 'it might sound rude. All right, I'll talk to him. I'll take it in the bedroom.' She walked through from her husband's dressing room, closed the door and picked up the phone.

'Good morning,' his voice said. 'Did I disturb you?'

'No.' She tried to sound normal, but the effect was strained. 'No, not at all. How are you, Karl?'

'Very well. It's a lovely day. Are you busy today?'

'Yes,' she said. 'Yes, we're planning a trip; I'm making the arrangements, Bob's very tied up at the moment.'

There was a pause, and when he spoke again his accent sounded stronger; she knew that her own pronunciation faltered when she was upset. Why was it, she thought in the few seconds' interval, why did an emotional pain become something physical, turn itself into a positive ache – heart-ache? It was such a cheap little cliché, but that was where the pain lodged. She had hurt him, and she hated it.

'I didn't know you were going on a trip. When are you leaving?'

'In a week or so, we're not sure. We're going to Portugal.'

'I'm glad it's not immediate.' He gave a little laugh at the other end to show he was relieved. 'For a moment I thought you were going within the next few days.'

'We're not sure of the date,' she said. She had asked Bob to take her away and he wouldn't do it. 'It probably won't be till some time next month.' She had tried to lie, but she was giving in already. Just by hearing him on the telephone.

'Couldn't we meet some time today? I've got something to tell you, I wanted to ask your advice. Let me take you for a drive this afternoon.'

'All right,' she said. 'But if you want to talk to me, perhaps we'd better have lunch first. If you're free.'

'I'd make myself free,' he said. 'I will pick you up at twelve-thirty.'

'No, I'll meet you.' The maid was beginning to notice the phone calls, the porter had seen him drive in the apartment courtyard so often that he called up to the Bradfords' internal number to let her know a gentleman had arrived. It wasn't innocent any more, not now. He had better not be seen too often. 'I'll meet you at the Algonquin, in the restaurant bar.'

It was a prestige restaurant, semi-tourist in reputation, a place where visitors to New York were always taken at least once, because the wits and writers of the city used it, and it had a pleasantly old-fashioned air, like an English club. They sat at a table at the far end of the room, side by side. She wore a simple suit of pale green, and an emerald clip which Bob had given her one Christmas.

Amstat looked at her beside him. 'You look

beautiful,' he said. 'You make me feel very proud to be with you. Everyone stares at you and envies me.'

'You must be used to that,' she said. 'Being with Julia. She's one of the smartest women in New York.'

'That's true,' he said. 'But I won't be with her any more; that's over. That's what I wanted to talk to you about – I'm not quite sure how I'm supposed to behave under the circumstances. In Europe I'd know, but here...' He let the sentence drop unfinished. He wanted her to know that there was no other woman now; he had to tell her about Julia because that commitment had made it impossible to take their relationship any further. And also he had begun to have a conscience. He wanted to do the right thing, so that there was the minimum of ill-will on either side.

'Did you have a row?' Terese asked him. He had broken off with his mistress; he was free. She began to eat the olives on the table, one by one, trying not to show that she was pleased because she hadn't any reason to be jealous now, imagining him in bed with someone else.

'Yes, unfortunately. The details aren't important, but I'm sorry to end it on bad terms. Julia was very kind ot me; I owe her a lot of things apart from the relationship. She introduced me to her friends, she helped me considerably. I'd like to say goodbye as nicely as I can.'

'Then why not say just that. Thank you for everything, with some flowers. I'd like it that way if I were her. It'll make it easier for her too, because you're sure to meet each other.'

'Yes, I'll do that.'

They were through lunch by now, and they had been talking without looking round them once. Neither of them saw Vera Kaplan take a table with two other women on the left-hand side halfway down the dining room.

'Terese – do you remember the first time we had lunch together, at the Cremerie, at Banksville?'

'Yes,' she said, 'I remember. I remember all the places we've been to. Why?'

'I held your hand then,' he said. 'And you got up to go. I want to hold it now. Will you run away again if I do?'

'No.' Their hands came together on the seat and gripped hard. 'Did you love Julia?'

'You told me I didn't that first day, when I said I was lonely. No, I never loved her. I liked her; she was very attractive. And now I want to be nice to her, as I said. I don't want to be cruel.'

'You've lived with her for how long? Two years? And it meant nothing to you, Karl.

How funny, and how sad too. To live with someone and never to be in love with them.'

'How do you know about that?' he asked her. 'Didn't you love your husband when you married him?'

'Why do you say didn't, as if it was all over? I love him now.' She tried to take her hand away, but he was strong and wouldn't let her. Their clasped hands came into view, and he laid his other hand over them both and stroked her wrist as he had done before. 'I wish you wouldn't do that,' she said. 'It's making love to me. Please, Karl, if I ask you, don't make me feel these things.'

'I feel them too,' he said. 'Every time I look at you I wonder what it would be like to kiss you. Just to kiss you as a beginning. I'm going to get the bill, and we're going to drive out somewhere.'

She went out of the restaurant with her head down, not seeing anyone, and Vera Kaplan watched them leave.

He drove up the Saw Mill River Parkway to get out of the city.

'Where are we going, Karl?'

'I don't know, somewhere quiet, where we can stop. I just took the route because it was the first way out. Otherwise I'd have taken you back to my apartment. I know you don't want that yet.'

'I don't want it ever,' she said. 'I don't want

152

it to happen between us. Pull in as soon as you can. I've got to talk to you about it.'

They went on driving and the highway became a quiet road, a place with trees and open country, where it was possible to stop. Outside the village of Chappagua he pulled into the side and switched off. It was a pretty place, with its original Indian name. The city itself seemed many miles away.

'Don't touch me,' she said. 'Don't touch me, let me talk to you.'

'I'll give us both a cigarette,' he said. He lit two in his own mouth and gave one to her. 'I won't do anything you don't want, my darling. I'm listening to you.'

'You talked about owing Julia gratitude,' she said, drawing on the cigarette, her hand trembling as she held it. 'What do you think Robert did for me? He took me out of nowhere, sick, without a memory – ill, penniless, without a relative or a friend in the world. He married me, Karl. I have no beginning before Robert, I'm nothing. I don't exist. I said I loved him and I do, I really do. I don't want to cheat him now, after fifteen years. I don't want to do it and then find that I've cheated you, too.'

'How can you cheat me?' he asked her.

'By not being able to love you either, when it comes to the point. I've never felt anything with him – never. He's been so patient with me, so good to me – but I can't love him, Karl. Oh God, what a thing to have to admit to you! I'm frigid, useless!' She began to cry.

'And that's what you're afraid will happen between us?' He asked the question very gently, and at the same time he took the cigarette out of her fingers and threw it away. Twenty years ago he had given her his hand-kerchief when she was crying. Now he did the same thing, but he wiped the tears away himself.

'You're very tender, aren't you?' she whispered to him. 'You're so gentle with me, always.'

'I love you,' he said. 'I've always loved you.'

'I feel the same.' She let him hold her and she leant against his shoulder with her eyes closed; she felt drained, and yet liberated.

'I feel everything I should feel when I'm with you. But mostly love; can you believe that?'

'Yes. That's what I feel too. Love for you, Terese. Love in my body and in my heart. American is a bad language for expressing these things. It's not our language, is it?'

'No, but it's the best we've got. What are we going to do?'

'Prove that you're not frigid. Not with me. I don't care about your husband. He didn't know how to love you properly. I'm going to prove it to you, darling. Not completely, but enough, so you can decide. Give me your mouth.'

This was where they had been interrupted; his body was at the same physical pitch then and she was open to his conquest. The twenty years fled and no telephone rang, no nightmare intervened. 'Oh don't, don't,' she whispered to him, and it was the primeval contradiction of the female cry of invitation. He put his hand over her eyes, blindfolding her, and lost himself in the exploration of her mouth.

At last they broke apart, and both were trembling. 'I've lost it,' she said, groping, bringing her soaring senses under control with the first inconsequential thing that came into her head.

'What, what have you lost?'

'My cigarette – I've dropped it.'

'I threw it away,' he said, and held her still, making her look at him.

'I'm going down to Chicago the day after tomorrow, on business. My firm has an apartment there; I use it when I have to stay over. Will you come down with me?'

'Will I have an affair with you?' she asked him. 'Yes, I will.'

'Don't use that word,' he told her. 'It's cheap. It's what I've had before, what all our friends keep having with each other, coupling without love. This isn't like that. I love you. I'm going to sleep with you because I love you. And do you know something?' He held her very close to him, as if someone might drag them away from each other. 'We're very lucky, you and I. This is a second chance.'

'It's like that,' Terese said. 'Like going to a place for the first time and recognising something, feeling you've been there before. I knew you before, I think, in some dream of my imagination. Girls dream of a lover, they give him a film star's face, or put him together out of a book. I've made you up and you've come true. I want to come to Chicago with you. And you're right, it's not an affair we're going to have.'

'No,' he said. It was crazy, like driving a car and finding the accelerator jammed and feeling no fear at all. 'It's a rendezvous.'

Vera Kaplan didn't linger over lunch; she was not a woman who really enjoyed the company of other women, and these were two casual acquaintances from Florida, paying a visit to New York to do some shopping and look up the people they knew. They had a good lunch, and she made an excuse to leave immediately after they'd had coffee. She wanted to ditch them and go home; she had a call to make before Joe came back from the hospital. They lived in a large apartment on the corner of 53rd and Park Avenue, and it was all paid for by Joe. One thing her family hadn't been able to say about him was that he had married her for money, and it was about the only calumny they hadn't used. It was funny how fiercely she sided with her husband when she thought of him in connection with her family and any of her friends she suspected of snubbing him or patronising her. It wasn't on his account any longer; much of her loyalty to him had gone as her love diminished and her muddled resentments grew. Now she fought his battles on her own behalf, defending herself, not him. She hated other people trying to hurt him because they inflicted a double wound; nothing could have prevented her hurting him herself, and now she had the best opportunity of their married life. She could hardly wait for him to come through the door. She changed out of her lunch time dress and coat, and put on a long housegown. The preparations heightened her sense of theatre and excitement. Then she sat down and dialled Julia Adams' number.

'Hello, how are you? It's Vera.'

'How nice to hear you,' the cool voice said on the other end. 'I'm just fine. How's Joe?'

'He's fine too,' Vera said. 'Look, dear, I'm calling because I was out having lunch today and I saw a friend of yours. I wasn't sure whether you knew about it, so I thought I'd better tell you. Your lover boy was having a heavy date with Terese Bradford. Maybe I'm mistaken but they looked terribly involved to me.'

'You're not mistaken, Vera. You're too right, as it happens. And you may as well know he's not the lover boy any more. I threw him out. If he wants an affair with her, he's welcome. I'm just so terribly sorry for Bob, that's all.'

'So am I,' Vera said. 'I always said she was a bitch. Darling. I'm so terribly sorry for you too – I hope you're not letting it upset you? He's not worth it, you know – none of them are.'

'I'll get over it,' Julia said; she sounded perfectly cool. The other woman wouldn't be able to guess that she was taking the call on her bed, her head splitting and her eyes so swollen with crying and sleeplessness that she could hardly open them. She needed one full day to collect the pieces up and fit them together before she faced the world without Karl Amstat. It wasn't much, and she was brave in nasty situations. Her two divorces hadn't hurt as much as this disintegrated love affair.

'Two years was quite a long time, anyway; we were both getting a little bored. Don't worry about me, sweetie. I don't give a damn, so next time you see him having a cosy tête-à-tête with somebody, you needn't bother to call.'

The receiver clicked in Vera's ear. Julia had hung up. That was how much she really cared. And she knew about Terese and him; that was why they had broken up. It would help to be able to throw that at Joe too, along with the other fantastic discovery she'd made. The spoiled little wartime heroine, with everyone running round protecting her. She laughed out loud, and went to mix herself a stiff Martini. She knew all about what had happened to Terese Masson because Joe had told her, expecting to enlist her sympathy. All he had done was make her jealous; only real fear of what he would do to her had prevented her from telling anybody else, even hinting at the truth to Terese herself. Once, urged on by an excess of spite, she had cornered the new bride and told her confidentially how glad her husband was that she and Bob were getting along so well. It had been quite a worry to him, advising Bob when it was wise to consummate the marriage. She had been very sympathetic, and said it all in an understanding whisper, one hand on her victim's arm. And she had got away with it, because Joe never did find out. But that was as far as she had dared to go. There had been a row over his seeing Terese in his consulting rooms; Vera had overheard his receptionist mentioning Terese's name when she asked to put through the call; the row became a real issue when he refused to say why she had come there. Vera hadn't learned anything; he had told her that it was private and medical and nothing to do with her. She had been left alone with her curiosity at war with her suspicion that it was just an excuse on the other woman's part, a way of attracting her husband's attention by playing on his professional sympathy. So brave. If you knew how she'd suffered. He'd start off by saying all that again and she was going to lead him into it. And then pull the rug out from under him.

She heard the front door open at seven-fifteen. When he came into the room she was pouring another drink out of the Martini jug.

'Hi,' she said. 'You're late – do you want a drink?'

'I'm sorry, I was held up just at the last minute. I'd love one, darling.' He went over and she let him kiss her cheek in the meaningless ritual that was practised between them. If just once he took hold of her and really kissed her it would have been a help, but she'd rebuffed him too often to leave the impulse alive. When he made love to her now it was because he wanted it, like being hungry and taking something out of the ice-box. It was passionless desire, and it made them both miserable afterwards. She sat down and sipped her drink.

'I'm tired,' he said. 'It's been a hell of a day today. Patients right the way through, and never enough time, never enough time to really help!'

'I don't know why you don't cut down that hospital work,' she said. 'It only drains you and you only touch the fringe of most of these people's problems; you keep saying this, and you still go on. Personally I can't stand neurotics. They give me the creeps.'

'They give most people the creeps,' he said slowly. 'That's their trouble. They're sick and they're in pain, and it doesn't show like a cancer or a broken leg. It doesn't arouse pity, mental sickness, and it should, Vera. It's agony for so many of them, and it's dressed up in the most unsympathetic disguises like aggression, delusions or withdrawal. You can see how normal people just get mad at them, or else decide they don't want to know any more.'

'I guess I'm very normal, then,' she said.

'There's no reason why you shouldn't be,' he said. 'But they're special to me, these people. I love them, because I can sense their suffering. And that's what they need – to be reached, understood, even if it is only for twenty minutes. I'll never give up the hospital. I couldn't.'

'The trouble with you,' his wife said, 'is that you get so emotionally involved. Doctors aren't supposed to get too close to their patients. You talk about loving a crowd of psychotics as if you were Jesus Christ or something. I should be careful, darling, you got involved once before and that didn't do you any good.'

He looked up at her sharply. 'What the hell do you mean – involved. Involved with whom?'

Vera finished her drink and set down the glass. 'Mrs Bradford. Brave, Resistance heroine rescued from the Gestapo's clutches. Or whatever the guff was.' She reached over and took a cigarette and lit it.

His reaction was that of a man who was too tired to react at all. He put his head back, took off his glasses and sighed deeply.

'Oh God,' he said, 'are we going to have that again this evening? Think of a new angle, Vera, for Christ's sake. It's like a record. On and on and on.'

'You know you're right,' she said, 'that's just how I feel about the whole subject. I go on saying she's a spoilt phoney, and you go on saying she's some kind of symbol, like a female General de Gaulle! I still say she's a phoney!'

'Vera, you are the biggest bitch sometimes. I've had a bad day – I told you. But you want to attack me about Terese Bradford. Okay, attack me. Let's have it, and get it over. Maybe we can have dinner and look at television afterwards. Just let me get another drink first.'

'If you weren't so sensitive about her,' she said, 'you wouldn't make me so bloody mad. But you're too busy analysing other people to think about what your own wife feels – that goes without saying. I just brought it up because I happened to see her today, and I didn't like what she was doing. Bob, believe it or not, is someone I really admire. He's a good guy. He's kind, he's straight – and she's cheating him with Karl Amstat.'

'I don't believe you,' Joe said slowly. He put his glasses back on and pulled himself up in the chair.

'Oh, I don't expect you to,' she said. 'It doesn't fit in with the picture, does it? She's not the sort who goes behind her husband's back and sleeps with another man? Well, I saw her having lunch with him today, holding hands and playing footsie in front of the whole damned restaurant. It was coming out of their ears!'

'Did she see you?'

'Did she hell – she wasn't looking anywhere but into his big blue eyes. And suppose we accept that she's gone off the track – suppose we drop the chastity angle about how delicate she was, that poor silly boob had to wait months before the great Dr Kaplan would even let him touch her.' She had got up and was standing in front of him, her hands clenched into fists, years of hate and jealousy pouring out of her mouth. 'Let's accept you were wrong about that! If she suffered so much during the war, if she was tortured and all the rest of it, how can she go to bed with a German, tell me that!'

'I don't understand you,' Joe Kaplan said. 'Amstat's a Swiss.'

'Oh no, he's not.' Vera stood there and laughed at him; it was her triumph, her sudden hindsight of a forgotten conversation that gave her the knife and she was going to drive it in. 'It shocks you, doesn't it?' she said. 'Well, it shocks me, and I'm not Jewish. They didn't murder six million of my people.'

'Why do you say he's German?' her husband said. 'Why, Vera?'

'Because I was educated in Berne; I spent five years there, learning to be a nice young lady and speak good French and all the rest. That's where he said he was born and brought up. We talked about it that first night at the Bradfords', and I kept meaning

164

to tell you. He's never seen Berne in his life. I mentioned the Magnus Hotel, and he went right in, saying how nice it was, and how his family used to lunch there on a Sunday. All very convincing, very cosy. Except they pulled the Magnus down in 1947, and he told me he left home and went to the Argentine in 1952. He said they had their farewell dinner at the Magnus, just before he left. No, darling he's a phoney too. It's like me telling someone all about the Waldorf five years after it was demolished. He's a German, covering up. Maybe she liked what they did to her – if they ever did it. Where are you going? Joe – where are you going?'

He turned at the door; he looked very pale with dark circles under his eyes; his glasses were off and he was polishing them as he stood in the aperture. 'Nowhere, Vera. Just to my dressing room to change my clothes. Call me when dinner's ready, will you?'

'Is that all?' she demanded. 'Is that all you can say...?'

'What more do you want?' He asked the question quietly. 'She's sleeping with a German. You're right about him, Vera. If he made that mistake about the hotel, you're probably right about him. I don't see that it's any of our business any more.' He went out and shut the door, quietly without slamming it. There was a sense of anticlimax that was

165

worse than any scene between them. She went back and sat down and wondered what she'd actually achieved.

'Would you repeat that please?' Kaplan checked as the operator read back the cable he had phoned through. 'Cable Urgent Rate to Hoffmeyer, Meyerexport, Buenos Aires. Please check credentials Karl Amstat, Swiss national, architectural graduate University of B.U. arrived Argentine fifty-two. Age around forty, Aryan appearance, no distinguishing marks. Applying for job and thorough character research essential. Regards, Kaplan.'

'Fine,' Joe said. 'Thank you.' He put the phone back and looked at his appointment book for the morning. He hadn't done anything last night; he had had dinner with Vera and they had watched a programme on medical research in Asia and seen an old Claudette Colbert movie. She had said nothing and neither had he; he had been thinking very carefully what he should do, and the more he considered it the more certain his course of action became. There was no Hotel Magnus standing when Amstat said he had his farewell family dinner there. There could be a dozen explanations for the mistake, but he personally couldn't think of one that satisfied him. Except what Vera had

166

said, without knowing what she was really saying. Amstat was a German, pretending to be Swiss. If Terese had disregarded his advice and was cheating on her husband, that hurt and angered him, but it was not important, compared with the incidental information Vera had uncovered for him. If Amstat were masquerading under a false nationality, then this was very important to Joe Kaplan indeed. He had been working for the Israeli Intelligence ever since it came into being after the establishment of the State of Israel. His family had strong Zionist sympathies and he had contributed and collected money for his people which Vera knew nothing about. She knew nothing about his involvement with the Jewish Intelligence organisation, and she wouldn't have believed it if he had been fool enough to tell her. As a native-born American he could see the incongruity of the situation. In fact the Israelis' intelligence service was probably the most efficient and ruthless in the world, with agents in every country and a trained commando corps whose abilities had first attracted public notice when they kidnapped Adolf Eichmann. They had taken the big fish alive, but scores of the minnows in the murder pool had faced a summary execution in quiet places all over the world. And there was a long list of names still unaccounted for, a series of old, unspeakable crimes to be avenged in the name of millions of dead. Cousins, uncles, parents, brothers and sisters – their ashes mingled with the atmosphere, for ever absorbed into the air from the chimneys of Auschwitz and Buchenwald and a dozen other places of immortal horror. Their bones were buried in Russia, in Poland, in woods and fields and the shattered ruins of ghettoes; their blood cried in the language of the Israelis under the tyranny of Egypt, and Joe Kaplan heard the cry.

'I'm shocked,' his wife had said. 'And I'm not Jewish. They didn't murder six million of my people.' If Amstat was a German, then he might have only one reason to hide out; other reasons, criminal activities of other kinds didn't interest Joe or involve Israel. They weren't exactly part of Interpol. But if he owed the Jewish people justice, he would pay what he owed. Hoffmeyer was the principal contact in Buenos Aires; most of the war criminals who had escaped had taken refuge in the South Americas, many had even got their wives and families over afterwards to join them. They too had organisation behind them, and money, and it had successfully absorbed men who should have stood before the court at Nuremburg. They had taken refuge in Africa too, exchanging the concentration-camp experimental laboratories for the primitive bush hospitals.

Some had been left to expiate in their own way; their victims had not been predominantly Jewish, and Israel didn't undertake the vengeance of other races. A man in Joe's position was an invaluable contact; he met people from all sections of the community in the course of his hospital work, many of them of German extraction; once or twice he had picked up some piece of information and sent it on. Once he had established that a man on their wanted list was dead, through the weeping confessions of his daughter under sodium-pentothal injections. He had died in Chile, before they could get him into the States, and she was being treated for a severe depressive condition as a result of having a former S.S. major as a father. Joe had treated her with sympathy and shaken hands with her on her discharge from hospital. Israeli Intelligence had taken her father's name off their list.

Now they would begin to check that list against the name of Amstat, when his cable arrived, while enquiries began at the University, places where he had lived, people he had known. It might take weeks, or even months. It depended on how well his tracks had been covered over, and whether he was genuine or not. Joe buzzed his secretary and the first patient came into his consulting room. There was nothing more to do but wait.

'Darling, I think I'll go down to the house tomorrow. I want to pick up some clothes, and see that everything's all right. I'll come back on Thursday.' Terese had rehearsed it all before he came home, and it seemed quite natural when she said it. Bob was busy that evening, going through papers connected with their trust. He was expecting his sister Ruth and the family lawyer within the next quarter of an hour and he didn't pay much attention to what his wife was saying.

'Of course, sweetheart, that's fine. I'll call you.' He looked up for a minute to smile at her; he thought she looked strained, almost unhappy.

'Don't rush back for me, darling, if you're tired. Stay a couple of days if you want. I'm up to my eyeballs in all this stuff. Maybe it'll sort itself out quickly and we can take off for Portugal. How about that?'

'Don't worry about it,' she said. 'We can go any time. And don't call me tomorrow, I'll probably ring the Phillipses up and ask myself round to dinner. I'll call you. Here's Ruth now, Robert. I'll leave you all in peace.' She stopped midway in the hall to kiss her sister-in-law and shake hands with the lawyer, and then she went into her bedroom to pack for Chicago.

He met her at the airport; they had travelled separately, and he had spent the day trying to work, which was impossible because he couldn't keep his mind on the department store and office block, or his patience with the demands of his clients. He wasn't in the right mood for designing eighteen storeys with a cubic footage of forty thousand feet in an area of an arc. He had bought flowers for the apartment, red and white and pink roses, and then found there weren't enough vases, so he sent one of the girls in the company office of his client out to get some. She had brought them back and he didn't have time to take them to the apartment before meeting Terese at the airport. They were still in the back of the hire car, wrapped up.

He took her case – it was a light travelling valise, with her initials on it – and threw it into the boot, among the vases, and neither of them said anything. The apartment was small, in a discreet modern block on the outskirts of town, and it was on rent while the department-store deal was going through. It was easier than hotels, which were always booked and where Amstat found the service inadequate, and there was a service restaurant which supplied meals in his room if he preferred to eat and work in peace. He opened the front door and stood aside to let her go in. 'It's not very elegant,' he said, 'but we can be alone. We can have dinner up here too.' She walked into the living room slowly and looked round; she saw his roses, and she turned to him suddenly and held out both hands.

'It's full of flowers, Karl. Far too many flowers, darling. You needn't have done it.'

'I bought some vases too,' he said. He kissed her hands one after the other. 'But I left them in the car, of course. I haven't been able to concentrate at all today. I thought every moment you'd ring and say you'd changed your mind.'

'I nearly did,' Terese said. 'Several times I nearly called you. But I didn't, did I?'

'No.' He drew her close and put his arms around her. They didn't kiss, they just stood and held each other. 'Thank God you didn't. I couldn't have borne it if you changed your mind. I've got some champagne too; let's drink it!'

'You open it while I unpack,' she said. 'Then I must put a call through to the house at Boston and tell the housekeeper I'm staying the night with some friends, the Phillipses, in case Robert calls. I told him I was going there. I told him not to phone me, but he might. I want to get it over before we have our drink together, Karl.'

'You feel guilty?' he asked her. 'I can understand that.'

'If I let myself,' she said it simply, 'but it's wearing off, every minute I'm with you, I feel it less and less. It's only the details that are sordid, like telling lies to the servants. I won't be long. Is there a phone in the bedroom?'

'Yes, it's through there.'

He had put flowers in the bedroom too; a large bunch lay on a chair still in their wrapping, waiting for the vases he hadn't had time to put them in. She tore the paper and saw that they were already dying. Her little case was on the bed; she opened it, and then shut it again; she put the telephone call through first and after a few minutes she was on the line to her housekeeper, making the explanation which would satisfy Bob if he telephoned her. It was sordid, as she had said; lying was sordid, laying deceitful little trails so that her husband wouldn't know she was in bed with someone else, making love to them, instead of going out to dinner with the Phillipses in Boston.

She had tried not to do it; she had gone to Joe Kaplan for help and to Bob himself; she had made up her mind to keep away from Amstat because she couldn't trust herself if they went on meeting. It had all failed, and she was there with him, coming nearer and nearer the inevitable conclusion, and nothing could stop it now. If this was really love, then she had lived all her life without knowing it, not even having the shadow, much less the substance. She was miserable because of Bob, but she was happy too, frightened and expectant, but committed past any chance of turning back. She loved Karl Amstat. It sounded so trite, so simple. It meant lies, dishonesty and adultery, and when she thought of Bob she could only take refuge in making sure he never knew, that no matter what the subterfuge, he would be protected. She could bear the guilt of this association, so long as she never saw the knowledge of it on his face. She began to take her clothes out of the valise; there was a dress to wear for the next day, and a lightweight suit for the flight back, the gold-and-ivory toilet set Ruth had given her as a Christmas present after she had been married five years. It was like a mark of acceptance, as if the Bradford family had decided she was going to last. And there was the nightdress and négligée she had bought the day before, made of pure silk satin and costing a thousand dollars from Lord and Taylor. She had gone there deliberately instead of to Bergdorfs', because she paid by cheque and she didn't want the nightdress on her charge account. She didn't want Robert to pay for it or see her in it. It was probably ridiculous. When you took a lover you didn't go to bed in white like a bride. You came to him naked, experienced.

'Have this.' He came in with the glass of champagne in his hand. 'Darling heart, you look so worried. Don't be afraid of me, please.'

'I'm not, Karl. Look – this is what I bought.'

He picked up the exquisite white silk, and laid it back on the bed. Everything she did was what he hoped she'd do. All his life he had maintained a certain prudery where women were concerned. It was part of his background to associate a respectable relationship with going to bed in some kind of covering. And this was respectable; this woman was as special to him as if he had just married her in the church in Frankfurt where his father had married his mother and he had been christened and confirmed. They might have been on their honeymoon in a hotel on the Rhine, with magnificent views outside the windows and flowers in the bridal suite. That was what he had tried to do, make up for what might have been. That was what the roses meant, filling the impersonal, American apartment bedroom with the scent and colour of the past they had never had. There had been no marriage, no house to buy, no wife and children to come home to; nothing but a day to day existence in semi-shadow, with nothing to live for except life itself and nothing to look back on but destruction. His parents were dead; his home was rubble. He had had nothing for the first ten years out of the twenty since the war, and now he had his career, his alias, his niche in a society which only accepted him because he was a liar. Terese and what was going to happen between them was the only real thing he had known since the war ended. This was not going to be like Julia Adams, who took off her clothes without any shame at all, and demonstrated how clever she was at making the most of their desire as if it were admirable to know the tricks of love.

'It's beautiful,' he said. 'And you will look beautiful in it. Come and have the champagne in the other room.' This too was how it should be; he had never felt so German, so much himself. He even made her a little bow before he took her hand. A man did not hurry these things, or behave with vulgar haste, however much he wanted her. He waited, he courted her properly, and then when the time came his dominion in love would be complete.

'You must think me an awful fool,' she said. They were sitting side by side, drinking with their glasses held between them like a barrier. 'I've been married for fifteen years and I'm so nervous, it's ridiculous! I don't know what to do – how to behave.'

'It's not ridiculous to me,' he said. 'I like it. A woman should be nervous – just a little. I'm going to make you very happy, my darling. You've nothing to fear, you can trust me completely. I shall look after you.'

'It's the first time,' she said, defending herself. 'If I'd done this before it would be different. Oh, Karl, I hope to God I don't disappoint you.' He lifted the bottle; it was empty. He took the glass away from her and leaning forward he kissed her deeply in the mouth. He didn't let her speak and he was very gentle.

'Come to bed with me, Terese.' She put her arms round his neck and shut her eyes.

'Take me there.'

It was like flying when it began, like the sensation in dreams of having wings and soaring high above the earth. They moved together, ascending together towards the summit and its unbearable goal of physical and emotional explosion, and in the same seconds they reached the point of momentary disintegration, with its total loss of identity and sense of separate being. He heard her cry out through the sound of his own triumph. So far had he lost himself in what they were experiencing that the words he had spoken to her in the final throes of making love were said in German. But her sound went on, and now the pitch of it was changing from the indescribably joyous cry of satisfied female love to a fierce and penetrating scream. It was a scream of conscious terror, and emerging from it came the single word repeated over and over as she began to fight and beat her fists against him. 'You! You!'

6

'Ah, good evening, David. Good to see you. Come and sit down. My wife has left coffee for us and some of her excellent chocolate cake.'

Jacob Hoffmeyer was in his sixties; he ran a flourishing export business in the centre of Buenos Aires and he and his family had settled in the Argentine in the late 1930s, during the Nazi persecution. He had arrived with nothing, but the fanatical capacity for work which made his race so many enemies had resulted in a thriving business and a large house in the prosperous suburban area of the city. Jacob and his wife and their five year old daughter had left Germany in time. Every relative on both sides of their family who stayed behind in the hope that things would settle down, went to the gas chambers at Auschwitz. Jacob had established this personally when he returned to Germany after the war. He had searched for them all; his parents who were old when he left, his wife's relations, three brothers with their wives and children, and some cousins, his wife's widowed mother and sister – they had all been taken and they were all dead. He had come back to Buenos Aires, to his business and his nice house, and the rabbi had held the service for the dead for him and his wife in the city's principal synagogue. Two years later they made a trip to Israel, and since then Jacob had been a active agent for Israeli Intelligence.

David Klein was in his thirties; he had been working for Hoffmeyer for the past three years and he was an expert at the kind of tiring leg work which was beyond the older man's capacity. He had tramped the city, making enquiries about Karl Amstat, and he had come to Hoffmeyer's house to report.

He helped himself to coffee, ate a piece of the rich Viennese cake, and then produced his notes.

'A Karl Amstat was enrolled at the University here in 1955; he was a student of Diego Bolsa. His academic record was good, he got his degree in architecture and passed out at the end of his four-year course. He was registered as a Swiss national, born in Berne in 1921.'

'That would make him – forty, forty-one now,' Hoffmeyer said. 'That checks with the New York query.'

'He had no family here,' David Klein said. 'He lived in a boarding house in the Aruña district for two of the four years, I checked there and they didn't remember him very well. Said he kept to himself. Then he moved to another place nearer the University, slightly more expensive, a pensione with full terms. Same story again; a nice, quiet man, spent his time studying, and never brought any friends back.'

'Hmm, yes. He had no friends at the University? No women?'

'I had to go carefully,' Klein explained. 'I went to see Bolsa himself, but he wouldn't see me. I got in to talk to one of his assistants.'

'What did you tell him?'

'I said I was doing a series of newspaper articles on foreign graduates of Bolsa's and following up their careers. I said Amstat was well known in America now and he was one of my subjects.'

'Very good,' Hoffmeyer said. 'What did you get out of him.'

'Not much,' Klein answered. 'He remembered Amstat because he worked very hard and he was much older than the other students. I asked if he had any friends, so I could get the personal angle on him, but he said he couldn't remember anyone. He said the same thing as the landlady and the people at the pensione. He was a quiet man and he kept to himself.'

'There were no graduate groups – no photographs?'

'Not with Amstat in them. The assistant couldn't say why he wasn't in the photograph, but he was noted as absent.'

'You know,' Hoffmeyer said, 'this is beginning to look interesting. Have some more coffee, David my boy. There's something of a pattern here. He comes in 1955 to the University – he may have been here long before that. He has no family and he's over thirty-five – he stays in a boarding house in the poorer part of town. He's quiet and he keeps to himself. Same thing when he's a later student; he moves, all right, but this could be because he's beginning to feel a little safe. He's still quiet, he has no women, no friends among the other students. Any suggestion he was homosexual?'

'None at all. The woman at the pensione said he was good-looking, but not in a way to make out he was queer. Just a good-looking man, very serious. That's what she said. You really think we're on to someone, Mr Hoffmeyer?'

'I don't know,' the old man said. 'This is just the beginning. But, as I said, it shows a certain pattern. Most of them have done, you know, when we pick up the early scent of them. They're all quiet, and they choose unobtrusive cheap places to live. They damned well have to, don't they, when they get here first? Eh? Well, we've got something to check against. I've got the list here. This is not the complete one, my boy, only the suspects we think may have crept in to this part of the world. Now.'

He began reading down the list of names; they began alphabetically, with the rank, army, S.S., or medical in brackets beside them and a very brief note on the crimes they had committed.

'He's too old – over sixty now. This one was a doctor; he wouldn't try to be an architect – I don't think – wait a minute, no, Fritche – it's unlikely to be him, though the age group is nearer. He could be a young fifty. Fritche wears spectacles. Medical officer with the 3rd Panzer Division, seconded to Waffen

S.S., armoured unit where he chose Jews for extermination in Warsaw after the uprising. Note down, Fritche, David. Let's see. No, not him or him.' His pencil went down the pages slowly; he mouthed the words as he read; two more names were written on David Klein's pad and ringed round twice.

'That looks like it, but one minute, and I'll just make sure.' He turned the papers back and started again.

'There's one here. Brunnerman, Gestapo, S.D. Section IV, counter-espionage. Wanted for extermination of Jewish population of Lodz 1944. Thought to have escaped to South America, last-known clue in Spain in '49. Nothing since. His age fits, so does the description, as far as it goes. No spectacles, no distinguishing marks. Father a professor at Stuttgart University. That means an educated professional background.'

'But there's nothing more to go on.'

'No, nothing; Fritche and the last two, Kronberg and Elsner, were tracked to Brazil and Chile and then lost because they moved on. There's nothing to say Brunnerman ever got here. But put the name down just the same. You never know.'

'It's a short list,' David Klein said. 'That ought to simplify it. Is there anything else you want me to do?'

'No, I don't think so. We know where our

man is, if he is one of our men, and he'll be watched in New York. I'll send these names through to Tel Aviv where they've got the complete dossiers and let them get on with it. When they've got something for us they'll let us know.'

It was a complicated process, but made much simpler by the fact that dossiers relevant to war criminals wanted for crimes against the Jewish people had been handed over to the Israelis by American and French Jews working on the War Crimes Commissions and in the Deuxième Bureau in Paris, when their own governments had given up the chase.

It was all unofficial; the photostat copies and often the originals had found their way to the chief officers of Israeli Intelligence, together with anything that might be relevant, family snaps, old identification passes, handwriting samples, everything that could identify a man after he had been hidden for twenty years under a dozen different names, in any of a dozen countries. The two men talked for a while about ordinary things; David Klein was married and expecting his second child. Hoffmeyer asked after his wife, and talked about his own son and daughter. There would probably be a wedding there too, with his boy getting so serious about the daughter of a friend of theirs. It would be nice, to have more grandchildren. It kept the family going. It had so nearly been wiped out completely. Hoffmeyer liked David; not just because he worked with him and was a clever boy, but because he typified the young generation of Jews, like the children he had seen making the Israeli state. He had been shocked by the women at first, by their mannish attitudes and their military service. But he had come to understand what all this meant. They were the children of parents who had not known how to fight. The generation before them had gone unresisting to deportation and death, and this was the young people's reaction to that sheep to the slaughter mentality of their race. David Klein was one of the new Jews; once his race got up off their knees, and faced the Gentile world on equal terms, there would never be another list like the one he had put away in his desk. Six million had gone down without a struggle. The men and women who did Intelligence work were not only dispensing private justice. They were proving that it was no longer safe to kill Jews, because now the Jew had learnt to use a gun. The next morning Jacob cabled his subsidiary office in Tel Aviv. 'Please check following personnel against export list for employment in our area. FRITCHE. ELSNER. KRONBERG. BRUNNERMAN. Regards. Hoffmeyer.'

Fritche had spent time in Holland. Their agent there would be contacted and the information cross-checked with what was known about him from his activities in Warsaw. They had got one S.S. major in Portugal because it was discovered that he had had a hernia operation; the scar on the man living in Lisbon under the name of Franken proved to be the same operation scar as the one recorded on the S.S. officer's dusty personal file in his divisional personnel records. He had personally shot twenty-five Jews at Mauthausen and sent their heads to the Professor of Anthropology at Stuttgart University because he wanted specimens of prime non-Aryan skulls for his collection. Three Israelis had stood over the major until he shot himself in his own bathroom.

Elsner, Kronberg and Brunnermann had all spent part of their S.S. career in France, the last two had been stationed in Paris. Paris would look into what was available on them; the French were most co-operative in these matters so long as it was done discreetly. After all, there was a thriving German tourist trade in France. Check and cross-check. It was the Israeli boast that they had never got the wrong man.

There was no swinging light-bulb signifying consciousness this time; she was naked and unable to move, but the hands holding her were not thrusting her under the water in an icy bath, or bringing the glowing eye of a cigar butt to rest on her skin. His hands were firm because she had struggled so violently, but she wasn't tied down on the table in Freischer's interrogation room, it was the weight of her lover's body that kept her still.

'Don't cry, don't cry,' he kept saying. 'Nobody's hurting you, darling heart, it's all right, it's all right.'

She had gone through it all again in those few seconds; the mental block had disintegrated under the release of that tremendous climax: memory came rushing back like water through a burst dam. Now she had committed the crime she had tried to confess to Kaplan when he was treating her with drugs; she had gone to bed with her German interrogator and collaborated. Now, with her memory returned and the confusion about time and place receding, she made the final betrayal.

'His name was Raoul,' she said. 'Raoul Duclos, and he lived in a house in St Germain des Pres. That's what you wanted to know, wasn't it? That's what I wouldn't tell them afterwards.'

'I'm going to put the light on,' he said. 'Be calm now, you know where you are, Terese. You're in Chicago, in my apartment.' He moved cautiously away from her; when the bedside light came on she cringed, and he took her in his arms and let her hide herself. The impossible had happened; he had taken the gamble and lost. There was nothing he could do about it that didn't involve harming the woman beside him, trembling with shock in his arms. And he could never hurt her; he could only wait and see if she intended to hurt him. That would emerge later, when she was over the nervous crisis, when she had stopped weeping and regained her self-control.

'I have some brandy here,' he said. 'Will you be all right if I leave you for a minute, just to get it from the living room?'

'I'm all right,' she whispered. She pulled up the sheets and covered herself. Kaplan had made her forget; Kaplan had pulled down a blind over that window into hell, from the Avenue Foch to Buchenwald, and the act of love had released the catch and sent it shooting up, showing her everything. He brought the brandy and helped her sit up; he held the glass to her lips while she drank, very slowly.

'You're my interrogator,' she said. 'The first one, the one I nearly told about Raoul.'

'Yes,' he said. 'I am.'

'I wanted to tell you,' Terese said; she took the glass from him, holding it very tightly to stop herself from shaking. 'I wanted to go home with you, didn't I?'

He looked into her eyes and the pain in them was unbearable. He turned away from her and for the first time in his adult life he shed tears. 'Oh God, if only you had – if only I'd got you out of it.'

'They broke my fingers with a hammer,' she said. 'One by one, each time I didn't answer the question. I'm married, aren't I? and my husband's name is Robert Bradford. I live in Boston.' She paused for a moment, marshalling her life, and then went on. 'We're very rich and he loves me. I know I've been happy. I can feel it. I know everything about myself. It's just that it doesn't seem quite real.'

He heard the undertone of hysteria in the last words, and caught hold of her, ready to fight it. 'Drink the brandy down; come on, drink it.' He put his hand against her face, shielding her, and bending he kissed her hair.

'Go slowly, Terese, go slowly and it'll be easier for you.'

'Why am I in bed with you now?' she whispered to him. 'We made love to each other, didn't we – that's what did it. That's when I knew who you really were.'

'Yes,' he said. 'You got your memory back. Everything came back to you after that.'

'We're lovers,' she said. 'That's all that's really happened. It didn't happen then, but it has now. I don't even know your real name. It isn't Amstat, is it?'

'No,' he said. 'It's Brunnerman, and my Christian name is Alfred.' She moved away from him a little, looking at him, into his face.

'We're twenty years older. How strange, you've hardly changed at all.'

'You haven't either. I thought you were so pretty then; I can remember looking at you, sitting in that office of mine, and thinking, What a pretty girl, what the hell is she doing here? How do you feel now? My poor darling one, you're trembling so much. Try to be calm, trust me and relax.'

'It's mad,' she said. 'The whole thing is a nightmare and we can't wake up. Hold me, for God's sake!'

'We've woken up,' he said. 'Accept that. It's all in the past, you can look back later – later you can think about it, but not now. Now you must be good and quiet, and let me comfort you.'

'I want to sleep,' she said. 'It's too much, too many things coming at me from every-where at once. I'm so cold, Karl.'

'Let me warm you; come close to me.'

'I can remember Joe Kaplan too,' she said; the brandy was seeping into her system, dulling the after-effects of shock. 'He was my doctor after Robert found me. Do you know about that?'

'No,' he said. 'And you're not going to tell me, not yet. You're going to get warm and close your eyes and sleep for a while.'

The light went out and they lay together in the dark; she still trembled, but it was spasmodic and before long her breathing became regular and she slept. 'My name is Brunnerman.' He hadn't even tried to protect himself against her. All his mental reservations, the years of denying his own existence and living a lie in the effort to make it the truth, had been sacrificed when he told her his real name. The solution came to him, and because there was no possibility of it, he was able to think about it and reject it calmly. He ought to kill her. It was the only way to make sure he would never be discovered. He ought to kill her as she lay asleep beside him. He put his hands up to her throat, gently, and kissed her; she stirred and he stroked the narrow proportions of her neck and the hollow of her collar bone. When he brought his hand down over her breast she woke and turned to him immediately. 'I love you,' he said in German.

'Oh, Karl, Karl, hold me to you. I'm still afraid. Comfort me...'

There was a moment in that second love-making when she resisted; he overcame her quite deliberately, as he would have had to do if she were a virgin of eighteen and he had just seduced her. They went back together to the first relationship between them and it was properly resolved with skill and tenderness on his part, and complete acceptance on hers. He didn't let her talk again that night; he slept very briefly and woke if she moved. By the time the morning light showed through the slits in the curtains, they had been lovers many times.

It was mid-afternoon before they woke properly; he found her sitting up, watching him quietly. For some moments neither of them spoke. Then she put out her hand and laid it on his shoulder.

'Have you any food here? I'm hungry.'

'I'll ring for it; they'll send it up. Terese...?'

'I'm all right, Karl. I know that's what you're going to ask, and I'm all right.' She smiled at him, and it made her look a very beautiful woman. The odd immaturity which had kept the years from showing in her face had gone in the course of the night. She was thirty-seven years old, she was in control of herself now. 'I'm going to take a bath. Order something for me, please, darling. I'm too tired to think what I want for myself.'

They dressed and ate eggs and steak on rye in the living room; the service restaurant sent the order up, and she poured coffee for him, while they sat opposite to each other. If they had been married and were in his fantasy honeymoon suite with the Rhine castles and the view out of the window, they would have taken breakfast together like this.

He gave her a cigarette, and then when the meal was over and cleared away, he didn't know what to do. Or what to say. She had called him darling. 'Please, darling.' When she looked at him he could see nothing but peace and fulfilment in her face. But it couldn't last; it was just a temporary euphoria because she was herself again and able to turn her mind back as well as forward. He understood this feeling because he had it himself. She had given him back his identity; now she had her own through his intervention in her life. She was still warm from the discovery of her capacity for love, and this warmth included him at the moment. But it wouldn't last; he was convinced of that. She came close to him and touched him.

'Who are you wanted by?'

This was what he had anticipated, only it came far sooner than he thought it would. There was no point in lying; he had lied enough.

'The Jews. I'm on their list. Like Eichmann.' He got up and moved away from her; he didn't want her to touch him, to be near him. He waited, and the question came.

'What did you do, Karl? What do they want you for?'

He turned and said dully, 'Do you really want to hear it? Do you want to know what I really am, after what we've been to each other?'

'I want to know,' she said. 'I've got to know. What happened?'

'It was during the retreat from the East,' he began. The words should have been difficult to say, but they came fast as he started to describe it. 'I was dismissed from the Gestapo after I sent you to hospital. I didn't care, I wanted to transfer anyway. You were the finish, as far as that kind of work was concerned. I wanted active service, and they gave it to me. I was sent to a Waffen S.S. division to fight in Russia. Terese, you will never be able to imagine what that war was like and I only came in at the end. The cold, the hunger, and always the dirty, filthy fighting. No prisoners, no quarter – atrocity for atrocity. My commanding officer – God, I can see him so clearly even now! – I never saw him without a greatcoat; he was just a face with ear-muffs to keep his ears from being frostbitten and a helmet pulled down on top of it. He scratched himself through his clothes, and the only thing that interested him was finding cognac from somewhere and shooting Russians when we caught any. He wasn't a man, a human being. And he was my commander. If you'd asked him what I was like he'd have probably described me the same way. My men weren't men at all; they were machines, they fought like machines too, and they killed in the same way. We did a lot of killing, Terese. We were being beaten and we knew it, and this made us mad, mad like machines, so that we felt nothing, not even hate, not even excitement. We just exterminated, because those were our orders, and we had never disobeyed. Then we got to Lodz and there was another order.' He stopped suddenly.

She was sitting very still, a cigarette in her fingers, with a long drooping ash on the end of it, watching him and listening. He could feel the sweat coming out on his face and through the pores of his body as he stood there, trying to tell her how he had given the command for four thousand people to be killed in cold blood. He took a cigarette and lit it, his hands shaking, and then he sat down away from her.

'Do you still want to know?' He asked the question and she nodded. She couldn't speak; she could only sit and listen and feel a sense of cold growing inside her and spreading over her. He was hunched up in the chair, turning the cigarette over and over in his hands, taking deep breaths of smoke in between words.

'We were told to round up all the Jews and take them out and shoot them. Outside the town, and bury them so they wouldn't be found.'

'Oh God,' she said. 'Oh my God!'

'It was bitterly cold; our orders were to do this, and then drive the Polish population out while we set fire to the town. This was the usual pattern; everywhere our division came across a Jewish pocket we wiped them out. But it was the first time for me. I'd come in at the end. I remember my commander coming in with the order and throwing it to me; we were in a house in the city, but all the windows were gone and it was so cold that we ate and slept in our clothes all the time. He'd got some cognac and he was happy for the day. "See to this, Brunnerman, and make it quick. We're leaving tomorrow after we've fired this place. Get them all rounded up and we'll do it in the wood we passed on the way. We start in three hours." That was all he said, and I did it, Terese. I sent my troops out and they herded all these people together and then we started off in a scout car, following the line of march. It was only a few miles, not more than four or five, and I remember the wood. There'd been an engagement with some of our tanks and the Russians and there were burnt-out wrecks on the way. I kept thinking how slow the line was and wishing they'd get on, get on. Can you believe it if I tell you something?'

'I can try.' She said it in a whisper. 'I can try and believe it.'

'They weren't people to me at all,' he said. He got up suddenly and began to walk up and down the short space from one wall to another. Up and down, up and down, while he spoke. 'Himmler once watched an execution like this one, and he fainted outright. The women and children upset him. So he issued an order that only the men were to be shot en masse. The women and children were taken away in special vans and gassed. We didn't have any vans. I went into the wood, Terese, while that bastard sat in the car keeping himself warm and getting drunk, and I watched them dig their own graves.'

'I don't think I can bear any more,' she said suddenly. 'I don't think I can listen to it.'

He didn't seem to hear her; he just looked up, confused because he had been interrupted, and went on.

'I couldn't see them as human beings who were going to die. They were bundles, bundles of rags that moved about, making noises in a language I couldn't understand. If they cried for mercy, I didn't understand a word. They were filthy inhuman creatures; they didn't have faces, they weren't people at all. You couldn't tell the differences between the men and women; they all looked the same, like beasts. They weren't Jews to me, Terese, because that would have made them people again. They were just animals. It doesn't make sense now,' he said. 'It didn't make sense as soon as I'd done it. I knew then. It's not even an excuse to say I would have been shot if I'd disobeyed that order. I should have disobeyed. But I didn't. I did as I was told and they were shot, and buried. Four thousand of them. There were so many; you lose the sense of reality when it comes to numbers like that. It's easier to kill hundreds by remote control than to put a bullet into one individual human being. I don't think I would have done that, Terese. I don't think anything would have made me go up to one of those people and see they had eyes, and then shoot. So I just gave the order and let my men do it. But I murdered them, just the same.'

There wasn't a sound after he had finished. He went back to the chair and sat forward, his head between his hands. She didn't move or speak.

'That's what the Israelis want me for,' he said at last. 'I used to wish to God they'd find me sometimes. I've run and run for twenty years. It would have been better if I'd given myself up after the war and let them hang me at home. I haven't tried to excuse myself to you, because there's no possible excuse for what I did.'

He made it a statement and she didn't contradict him. He heard her get up and he didn't move. He went on sitting in the chair. The front door of the apartment opened and then shut, and he knew she had gone. He leaned back and closed his eyes; he was very tired and his capacity for feeling anything was gone. He sat for a long time, and then got up and went into the bedroom to pack. He wasn't going to run away again, he was going back to New York to wait for the police or the Israeli executioners, or whoever came for him. He didn't care and it didn't matter. He had put himself into her hands and it was up to her what she did with him. He folded her clothes and put them away in her valise; he was methodical and slow because there was no hurry now.

'You needn't pack for me,' she said behind him. 'We've still got one more day together.' He turned and she was in the doorway; she had been crying.

'I thought you'd gone,' he said.

'I thought I had too.' She walked towards him, and he caught her in his arms.

199

'Oh God, Terese, my love, my darling, I thought you'd left me.'

'I tried to,' she said. 'I tried to walk out and go home and I couldn't. I can't leave you, Karl, because I'm part of you now. There's nowhere else for me to go any more.'

'Even though you know what I did,' he said, 'you can still say you're part of me?'

'I was walking,' she said, 'round the streets, going over and over what you told me. You asked me if I'd believe something – when you said that they weren't people to you when it happened. Well, I do believe you. I've seen it happen myself. I saw it with the prisoners at Buchenwald.' She felt him stiffen. 'Yes, I was there too. That's where they sent me from the hospital. What I saw in those compounds when I first got there weren't people to me, either, and I was half crazy then. But not completely. I was still clean; they were filthy. I hadn't had time to change from a woman into a *thing* because of what starvation and dirt and indignity had done to me. I couldn't pity them; they made me sick with the way they smelt, the way they crawled round or sat in their own dirt. I couldn't see them as men and women because they had become animals. When I did stop feeling this way it was because I'd sunk to the same level. I know what you saw in that wood at Lodz. I know how they

looked to you. Nobody else might understand this, but I do. And I still love you. Do
you believe that?'

'I don't dare,' he said. Now she was
holding him; the roles were reversed for the
first time. 'I wasn't going to try and run. I
didn't care whether I was caught or not,
because I thought I'd lost you.'

'You'll never lose me,' she said. 'If you
hadn't tried to help me, you would never
have gone to Russia. I realised that, too,
during my walk. If things had been different
with us – if I hadn't been obstinate and held
out just too long, I'd have betrayed my
friend. We'd have been lovers then, and you
wouldn't have been sent away. Instead I'm a
Resistance heroine. It makes me ashamed,
knowing the truth. I'm a fake, Karl. Terese
Bradford is a fake and so is Amstat. Only you
and I are real, together.'

'It was the telephone that did it,' he said. 'If
Knochen hadn't rung down, you would have
given way, and our whole lives would have
been different. But I want you to know this,'
he raised her head, and kissed her, 'you
would never have collaborated. I know that
now, though I didn't then, not at the time
when I was working on you, trying to make
you break. I was an expert at it; it was my
speciality, making friends with prisoners,
undermining them. That's what I did with

you, deliberately. But I fell into my own trap, that was the irony. I wanted you myself. I took advantage of you, my darling, because you were a girl and alone and very frightened. I made you tired and hungry and confused, and then I woke your senses, just to destroy your will to fight me. You hadn't a chance against me, so don't blame yourself. But you were special to me and I failed you as much as myself when I let them take you. Do you have any idea what I feel every time I see those scars on your right hand? Do you know what it means to me to imagine how they hurt you?'

'It doesn't matter.' She was guiding him to the next room; they sat together, still embraced. He was near breaking down and she knew it.

'Nothing matters to me now but having you,' Terese said. 'I don't care who you are, my love, or what you've done. I don't care about the past any more. All I want is the future.'

'With me? Going on with me – do you really want that?'

'I told you,' she said simply. 'I walked out of here to go home. And that's when I realised I had no home to go to; I don't belong to Robert Bradford, or to his family and his friends. I'm not part of them. I'm as much an outcast here as you are. We don't belong

202

in this comfortable country among all these nice conventional people. They wouldn't like us if they knew what we were; you'd be a murderer and I'd be a kind of freak – something that ought to be in an old movie about the war. I'm sure none of Robert's family know what really happened to me, and they wouldn't like it if they did. Concentration camps put people off. I turned back and came here because this is where I *do* belong. With you.'

'And do you still love me?' he asked. 'Knowing everything, will you still let me touch you, make love to you?'

'I've nothing to live for if you don't,' she said. 'And we have the rest of the day together. Tomorrow we can think about the outside world.'

7

They had been back in New York for two weeks; he had finished his final designs for the department store and decided that it was one of the best pieces of work he had ever done. Being in love was a new stimulant; it made everything important because he felt so vitally alive himself. He had a contract with a florist to send flowers to his apartment and have them arranged three times a week, so that when Terese came to him she found roses in the bedroom. He had got rid of the bed, and given away the calf-skin cover; he intended to have the whole apartment re-decorated and to let her tell him how she wanted it. It had become a home because she went there, and the bedroom was beginning to look the kind of room he would have had at home in Frankfurt, except for the white leather walls. They would be changed too, but Terese enjoyed choosing with him and discussing, so there wasn't any hurry. He had never been so happy in his life as in those two weeks after they got back. And Terese was happy too; it showed in subtle ways, which he could see, like a new confidence in herself. He wondered how the husband could be so blind that he didn't notice how his wife had changed. Amstat could meet him now quite openly, just as he had met Julia at a cocktail party given by a mutual friend. He still hated them as a form of social entertainment, but he went because he knew the Bradfords would be there, and he couldn't lose the chance of seeing her. Julia had gone up to him and held out her hand. She did it with a style which he couldn't help admiring.

'Hello there. How are you?'

'Very well. And you? You look wonderful.'

'Thanks. Let's move over here for a minute. Thanks for the flowers, Karl, and the note. It was nice of you to send them.' They had made her cry when they arrived; he had done something sentimental and she could not be angry with him any more. It really was ridiculous how much she missed him, he had no idea as they stood talking, how much she wanted to beg him to come back. He was at the party to see Terese; she had come there to see him.

'I just wanted to say I was sorry,' he explained. 'I behaved very badly that night. I was rude and I said things I didn't mean at all. I hoped you would forgive me. I hope you have forgiven me.' He saw the colour coming into her face; it was the first time he had ever seen her blush. 'And forgotten me,' he added. 'Except as a good friend.'

She managed to smile and she shrugged. 'I've done both, my dear,' she said. 'Forgiven and forgotten. We had a lot of fun together and I guess I behaved pretty badly myself. By the way, how is it going?'

'How is what going?' He took a whiskey-and-soda from a passing waiter's tray.

'Your new affair,' she said. 'With Terese Bradford. Oh don't look like that, darling, I know all about it, everyone knows all about

205

it except Bob. That ultra-bitch Vera saw the two of you lunching one day and she's had a ball, spreading the news around. You ought to be more careful, you two.' It was said with a smile and without malice.

'I just want you to know that I'm not jealous any more. And you needn't worry about me saying anything to Bob, because I won't. He's too nice to hurt, and I have a soft corner for you too, in a way, now that we're just friends.'

'You're a nice woman, Julia,' he said suddenly. 'And we will be careful. I'm very grateful to you.'

'They've just come in,' Julia said. 'Go on over, you don't have to waste your time with me. You really are crazy about her, aren't you?'

He had forgotten her when he saw Terese moving through the crowd of people; he turned back to her then. 'Yes,' he said. 'I am.'

'Goodbye, Karl. Nice to have seen you.'

'Goodbye, Julia.' He took her hand and kissed it.

'My,' she said, 'only you could click your heels like that, my sweet, and get away with it. Americans are so uncouth, I've always said so. Good luck.' She turned away from him and the crowd swallowed her up. He had forgotten himself. Christ! He had clicked his heels and kissed her hand as he had been taught to do as a young officer. Careless, careless – stupid. He called himself a variety of names and moved in the direction of the Bradfords. It was because of Terese, because he relaxed all his pretences when they were alone. Old habits were reasserting themselves, unconsciously he was slipping back. He went up to Bob Bradford and held out his hand.

'Hello,' he said. 'Hello, Terese, how are you?' He made a point of shaking hands with them both, very casually, just to make up for the slip he had made with Julia Adams. But nobody had noticed, or would see anything significant in it if they did. He indulged his curiosity now whenever he met Robert Bradford, and studied him intently. He was interested in the man because of what he had done for Terese; he wasn't jealous of him because in spite of it all he had never made her love him. He could afford to be curious without resenting him at all. He had asked her once if she felt differently with her husband now; it was the stirring of an an intolerable jealousy, but she had put it simply and directly to him so that he didn't have to think of it again. Nothing had changed between her and Bob. And nothing would change. He had a right to her gratitude and to whatever affection she could give him, and he was always going to have both, as long as he wanted it. That part of her life was the same, and it had no connection now with the life that she and Amstat shared together. That belonged to them alone, and it was her real life, and she was her real self only when they were together. He must not, she had said gently soon after they returned from Chicago, confuse her loyalty with her love. She could only give one to Robert; he had both and he ought to be content with that. He was, and he had never asked that sort of question since. Under different circumstances he might have liked Robert Bradford, even made an attempt to get to know him on a less superficial level than the dinner parties and casual encounters like their present one. He was good-looking, virile, and everybody liked him. Julia had said that – 'He's too nice to hurt' – Terese, so passionately engrossed with him, still sheltered her husband and refused to leave him or allow him to be hurt. He was the kind of clean-cut American who would have been killed in five minutes by any one of his own troops or by him in his combat days on the Eastern Front. He didn't have the fighting, aggressive spirit in him which still smouldered in the European character, expressing itself in wars. Bradford was the best example of the New World; he and the woman he loved were true products of the old one, and the American generosity of spirit would always be taken advantage of and at the same time resented by the European. It was interesting to think about, though irrelevant, and he addressed himself to Bob, keeping Terese till later, when they might slip away for a few words alone.

'I've been up to my eyes these last few weeks,' Bradford was saying, 'playing my sister's favourite game – trust-busting! Never make a trust for your children, Karl, because whatever you do, it's sure to be wrong at some time or other!'

'I'll remember that,' Amstat said, 'but I've got a long way to go before it's an issue.'

'You need a wife,' Bob said. 'That's my great theory for everyone. Get married; there's nothing like it.' He put his arm round Terese as he said it. 'Is there, sweetheart? How about finding a nice girl for Karl and making him settle down? Too bad you and Julia didn't make it.'

'Yes, it was a pity,' he agreed with a pleasant smile. 'But she's already had two husbands. She mightn't share your enthusiasm for marriage; I'm not sure I do either, on that count.'

'Well, maybe it's because I've been so lucky then,' Bradford said. 'I'm a complaisant bastard, aren't I, darling?'

'Not really,' Terese said. 'I think you're

right. Karl ought to settle with a nice girl.'

'Just make sure she doesn't keep changing her mind, like some women I know,' Bradford said. 'A couple of weeks ago we were all set for Portugal. Now I can't drag her away from New York. You just never know what's coming, do you?'

'With women – no,' Amstat said. 'But being unpredictable is part of their charm.'

Their moment alone came soon after, while Bob went in search of a drink. 'Don't talk to me, darling,' she said. 'I think it's beginning to show on us. I feel so awful when I'm with Bob and I see you. He hasn't any idea, poor darling.'

'Are you going to find me a nice girl, then?' he said quietly. 'A nice American wife to marry me and decorate my apartment for me instead of you? What time will you come tomorrow?'

'About five. I'll let myself in and wait for you.'

'I'll be there,' he said. 'I wish it was now. I wish we could go back together now.'

'So do I,' she said. 'Please, please, Karl, go away before Bob gets back to us. I can't bear having you both together.'

'Can't you come downstairs, can't you slip away for a minute? I want to hold you, I want to kiss you – come down in the elevator with me – you can come back.'

'My God,' she said, 'there's Joe Kaplan just come in. Darling, we'll have to wait. We can be together tomorrow for a long time. We can make love as often as you want tomorrow. I don't want him to see us together. Please go away now.'

'You're right,' he said. 'Until tomorrow, my darling. I'll be there waiting for you.' They shook hands again, and she saw Joe coming towards them as Amstat tried to ease away. He didn't succeed because Kaplan deliberately blocked his path.

'Hi, Karl – you have to rush away so soon?' He stood in front of Amstat, with his wife beside him. They had met often in the last few months. It was normal to stop and talk for a moment.

One thing he and Terese had agreed between them: no one must suspect that she had got her memory back. The most likely to detect a change was the man who had made her lose it originally; that was what made Terese afraid of him now, and that was why he felt so uncomfortable standing talking to the man, against his will.

'Are you very busy right now?' Kaplan asked. 'I often wonder whether architects are nine-to-five men like the rest of the professions. Except medicine, of course.'

'Yes.'

Vera Kaplan was beside them now, smiling

maliciously from one to the other of them, not knowing which one to attack first.

'Always on call, aren't you, Joe? Such a bore, I find it. Nobody asks you to dinner when you're always running off in the middle of the soup, or you're an hour late getting there. Architects aren't like that, are they, Karl? They must get plenty of time off.'

'If we do, it's a very bad sign,' he said coldly. 'Personally I'm glad to say I'm very busy. I even work at home.'

'Something interesting?' Kaplan asked. 'In New York?'

'I'm doing a department store and office block in Chicago,' Amstat explained. 'I make a trip down there once or twice a month if necessary, but most of it is done here.'

'How nice.' Vera smiled up at him.

He had never met a woman he disliked more; it almost made him feel sorry for the Jewish doctor, being married to her.

'You must come round and have dinner one evening. We keep meeting all the time, and we've never gotten down to inviting you. Would you like me to ask Julia? Or is there anyone else you'd like to bring along?'

'I can't think of anyone,' he said. He spoke directly to Kaplan. 'I should be delighted to visit you, at any time. And I would be most happy to have Julia with me. She's still one of the nicest women I've met in New York.

So many of them are such bitches. Forgive me, I have a dinner engagement, and I must go. I'm late already.'

'Nice to have seen you,' Kaplan said. 'We'll do that – we'll fix something, as you're going to be in New York all the time. Within the next month, maybe? I have a medical conference in ten days, so, that ties me up a little. Vera'll call you.'

'I'll look forward to it.' He made no mistakes this time. He gave them a casual American wave and pushed his way through to the hallway.

'Vera'll call you...' she said. 'Like hell I'll call the bastard! Did you hear the crack he made at me!'

'You asked for it, honey,' Joe said. 'You can't cut slices out of people without them cutting back. And I didn't ask him to dinner – you did!'

'I wanted to embarrass him, that's why,' his wife said. 'I wanted to let him know we knew what he and Joan of Arc over there are doing in their spare time. He's just a bloody Kraut, who's ashamed to admit it.'

'That's one thing I wouldn't go round saying,' Kaplan said. 'That could land you in court. You better be careful, Vera, that's something different from telling everyone he's sleeping with Terese – oh, I know you've had a ball with that story. But you say he's

213

pretending to be Swiss and you're impugning him professionally. He could take you to the cleaners for damages; I have a hunch he's just the kind who'd do it, too.'

'Well, you thought he was lying, when I told you,' she said. 'You agreed with me, he was a phoney.'

'I'm not so sure,' Joe said. 'Maybe he was mixing up the hotels; maybe you were – I'm pretty sure he's Swiss. I can smell a German a mile off. He's not one. Come on, let's stop arguing about it and say hello to Bob and Terese; they're right there.'

'I can't wait,' she said.

Joe caught hold of her arm and she stopped. 'Don't start anything there,' he said very quietly. 'Not one crack, Vera, not one word, do you hear?'

She glared up at him. 'Still protecting her? Still in love with her, are you?'

'I'm protecting Bob,' he said. 'What she does is her business – I wash my hands of that side of it. But he's not going to be hurt to please you. Stay out of it, Vera, do you understand? Stay out of this from now on, or I'll walk right out on you. I mean it!'

She pulled her arm away from him. 'I'm not going to be threatened by you,' she said. 'I'm going home. You can go and talk to them on your own. And go to hell, while you're at it. And if it is her that you're protecting – God help you, Joe, if I find out!'

He let her go, and then went to find himself a drink; he didn't show his feelings; he polished his glasses which was a mannerism he couldn't stop, but by the time he came up to the Bradfords he was in control of himself inside as well as out. He was glad Vera had gone home. It was the luck of God that she was obsessed with Amstat's sexual relations with a woman she hated; she was too busy beating Terese with that stick to think about the real issue. He was sure he had frightened her off the scent that he was following. There would be a row when he got back; tears and reproaches and the same, stale accusation of guilty involvement with his best friend's wife. And it was not true and never had been true. What he felt about her now, knowing she was cheating Bob, had nothing to do with personal jealousy. He was disappointed in her, and he was angry too, but it was on Bob's behalf. He wondered whether she had found her sexual freedom through the medium of adultery and lies. He had no wish to know any more.

He had established one point that night, which was important, and started on another. Amstat would be in New York for the next few weeks, and that kept him nailed, except for Chicago, while he waited for news from Buenos Aires. He could fix Chicago when he got home, just to keep a watch there.

'Hello, Terese – how are you, Bob?'

'We're fine,' Bob Bradford said. 'You've got a drink, Joe? I'm fresh out, and so are you, sweetheart. I don't know why they pay a waiter, he's never around when you want him. I'll go and bring back something.'

'No, darling,' Terese cut in. 'Don't go, I don't want any more.'

'I do,' he said. 'Just one for the road, while we talk to Joe.'

Kaplan offered her a cigarette. 'You don't have to avoid me,' he said. 'I only give advice, I don't expect it to be taken.'

'You're angry with me, aren't you?' She fumbled, looking for a lighter. After a moment he took his out and lit her cigarette.

'Not angry. I told you, Terese, it was up to you what to do.'

'Well, as it happened, Joe, it wasn't up to me.' She looked at him for the first time, and there was something in the eyes that he had never seen before. Pleading, and guilt, and something else too, which was difficult to describe. 'It was up to Robert. I did what you told me; I asked him to take me away. I begged him. But he said no; he had to stay here and help Ruth milk out some more money from the Bradford trust.'

'I'm sorry,' Joe said, and he meant it. 'I

216

take it all back. You still feel the same way about the guy?'

Now he could name the difference in her. Reserve; the child-like trust in her relationship to him as patient, doctor and friend, no longer existed. She had shut him out.

'I managed it alone,' she said. 'I kept away and talked some sense into myself. It never came to anything after all. So you don't have to be angry with me for that either, Joe.'

'No,' he said. 'I'm glad, Terese. I have a feeling Mr Amstat wouldn't have been worth it in the end. Here's Bob – I guess we change the subject?' He smiled at her, and it was a friendly, relaxed smile; he had an impassive face, which had showed nothing to Karl Amstat. It showed nothing to Terese either to disclose that he didn't believe a word she had said.

Amstat was working when the doorbell rang. He had had dinner alone in a quiet restaurant downtown, and gone home. He looked at his watch; it was eleven-thirty. He wasn't expecting anyone; he was not a man who encouraged the casual caller. But it might be Terese.

'Mr Karl Amstat?'

It was a middle-aged man standing outside; he was dressed very soberly in a dark blue suit, and button-down-collar shirt, he carried a short-brimmed hat with a blue band. Amstat had never seen him before.

'Yes,' he said curtly. 'Who are you? What do you want; it's very late.'

'My name is Smith, and a friend of yours asked me to drop by and see you. A Mr Brückner. Can I come in?'

Amstat held the door open and let him pass through. Brückner had been his German contact in New York; he had managed the introduction to the architectural firm when Amstat first arrived. He had provided money and paid certain expenses for him until he was established. Then he had simply dropped out of Amstat's life.

'Sit down,' he said, and the man laid his hat on a chair and settled himself on the sofa. He sat forward in a very unrelaxed position and he spoke with a vulgar West Side twang. He was a second-generation German who ran a successful manufacturing business; he had been a Bundt member as a young man and then been drafted into the American Army where he had served in the Far East. He had been very happy to help his fellow Germans after the war, and though he wasn't rich, he contributed regularly to the funds for supporting them. He had never had to deal with anyone so high ranking as a Gestapo Standartenführer before, and it made him uncomfortable. He felt he ought to be standing up.

'Would you like a drink, Mr Smith.'

'Er, no thank you. All right if I smoke?'

'By all means. Help yourself from the box there. Now, why have you come here, Mr Smith? It's nearly six years since I heard from our friend Mr Brückner. Has something gone wrong?'

'No,' Mr Smith said. He decided to speak German. 'Please understand, Herr Amstat, I am only carrying Herr Brückner's message.'

'Then deliver it,' Amstat said. This was an underling, a lower-middle-class little man, unsure of himself before an officer.

'If there's nothing wrong, why are you here? Why do you come and disturb me at nearly twelve o'clock at night!'

'I apologise,' the man said. 'I apologise profoundly; but I acted on instructions. Herr Brückner wanted me to see you and to do it as inconspicuously as possible.' The effort was too much for him and he stood up. The move irritated Amstat; he had fallen into the old arrogant S.S. attitude so quickly that he was shocked at himself. He vented his self-disgust on the embarrassed sheep in front of him.

'For God's sake, man, sit down and stop behaving as if you were on a charge. We're both civilians. And speak English.'

'Brückner's worried,' Smith said. He began

to talk quickly, and he became an American again. 'He's sick, that's why he called me up and said I should come over. He's not happy about what you're doing, Mr Amstat, he's not happy at all. We keep an eye on our people, just to make sure they're not in trouble; it's all part of the service. And it's not a bad service, I guess you'll allow that?'

'It's saved my life,' Amstat said. 'I suppose that gives you and Brückner the right to spy on me for the rest of it. Go on.'

'It's your association with this Mrs Bradford,' Smith took out a handkerchief and wiped his face and neck.

'She's a Frenchwoman and we have information to suggest she was in prison at some time in the war. Brückner thinks this could be dangerous to you.'

'That's very thoughtful of him,' Amstat said. 'Anything else?'

'Look, Mr Amstat, if this woman was in prison, or mixed up in anything, she's not the sort of person you should go around with. She just might pick something up. It draws attention to you, going around with a foreigner. I guess you mix in pretty stuffy circles, all very high class and society page, but Brückner thinks this is going too far. The last thing in the world you ought to do is draw attention to yourself!'

Mr Smith paused; he had begun to gain

confidence while he went on telling this steely bastard what the score was; he had a moment of rebellion against his own sense of inferiority. He might be ex-Gestapo and high ranking and belong to the snob class in the old country, but the emphasis was on the ex. Former, used to be.

He was on the run and he owed people like him, Smith, or Schmidt, as his father still called himself, and Brückner and German Americans all over the country, everything he had at that moment. He needn't be scared by him; it should be the other way round.

'Mrs Bradford was not in prison in the war,' Amstat said. 'She was born in France, that's all. There is no danger to me in our association, as you call it. There is no possible connection with the past. We met in New York for the first time. She's one of a wide circle of my friends.'

'It's not just you,' Smith said. 'If anything came out about you, you could endanger others; you could bring trouble on people like Brückner and me and all of us who've helped you. You're not the only man we have to look out for – there are others. We have to think of them!'

Amstat hesitated; this last point was true and he knew it. There *were* others; murderers, like himself, men like Freischer who had stubbed his cigar out on the breasts of the woman he loved. The marks were still there, very faint and white now, but still visible. Killers who had never pulled the trigger, but drawn up the plans, discussed it round the conference table, and checked the figures at the end of the month.

'You helped me,' he said. 'Thank you, Mr Smith. You and Brückner and the rest. Now I prefer to stand on my own. You needn't watch out for me any more. I'll never come to you for help again, no matter what. Now get out of here.'

'Okay.' Smith got up, reached for his hat and put it on. 'But I should watch it; the Kikes are tricky people. They don't give up easy; we've lost quite a few in the last few years.'

'So I've heard; it's very sad. But they won't catch up with me. Close the door quietly, please; you mustn't forget to be inconspicuous.'

Smith turned with his hand on the latch; he wore a ring with his initials on the middle finger.

'You won't give her up? That's final?'

'I told you.' Amstat made a move forward; he hadn't realised how close he was to taking the man by the collar and throwing him into the passage. 'Get out!'

'Okay,' Smith said again. 'Okay. From now

222

on, you're on your own.' He went out and shut the door; at the very last moment he decided not to slam it, as he would have liked. It wasn't possible, of course; he knew they couldn't carry out that threat and leave someone like Brunnerman to be picked up. The Kikes had a nasty habit of asking questions before they killed their victims. In Smith's eyes they really were victims, honest-to-God Germans who were being victimised for carrying out orders. All this bleating about gas chambers and concentration camps, as if they hadn't done the world a service, getting rid of them. America could do with a few million less. He took the subway home and wondered what the hell Brückner would say when he told him. Ungrateful son of a bitch; he'd have been in some ditch with a dozen bullets in him, years ago, if it hadn't been for the blood-tie policy of the old Bundt members who stepped right in to help when the war ended. Money, time, trouble, an efficient spy system to combat the Kikes; and all the thanks he got was to be kicked out of the apartment. They would keep a watch on Amstat, whether he liked it or not.

'Darling,' Terese said, 'why is it always so wonderful?'

'I don't know,' he said. 'Is it so wonderful

223

for you? Always?'

'Every time,' she kissed him. 'Sometimes I think to myself, today will be different. Our moods won't match – we'll have a quarrel, or Karl will be getting tired of me. And it's never true. I love you more and more, do you know that?'

'You have a great capacity for love.' He said it seriously. 'You're a very female creature, my darling. Very brave and very deep. The best kind there is. I wish to God I could marry you. This isn't enough for me, just having you in an afternoon, stealing a few hours together. I want you with me all the time.'

'This can't happen,' she said. 'You mustn't start saying this. I can't leave Robert.'

He reached up and pulled her down. 'You'll leave him one day,' he said. 'Because I'll make you. You're not the kind to lie for long. He's lost you to me already.'

'I won't hurt him,' she said. 'It's the only thing I can hold on to, not hurting him.'

'Very kind,' he said, and kissed her. 'I like you to be kind, Terese, I like you to be soft and tender-hearted. Open your mouth to me. Now, my love, now.'

At the end, when she was dressing, he said to her, 'I have to go to Chicago again next week – can you come down with me?'

'I'll try,' she said. 'I'll think of something.

But it's so difficult.'

'I know,' he said. 'That's why you'll have to divorce him in the end. And don't say you won't again, or I won't let you go home at all tonight.'

'It wouldn't be too hard to make me stay.' Terese came over to him. 'Do you really love me, Karl? Do you love me in the same way as I love you – not just for making love, but really? For myself?'

'Really,' he said. 'For yourself. You're the only woman I should ever want to marry. I don't want you as a mistress, Terese, I want a wife. I'll take you out somewhere tomorrow. We'll meet in the afternoon and drive out.'

'We could go back to that pretty village, Chappagua, and walk around for a while. Do you remember when we went there, and I said I'd go to Chicago with you? It was the first time you kissed me.'

'I remember,' he said. 'We'll go there tomorrow. Darling – people know about us. Julia told me, everyone knows through Vera Kaplan. We must have been seen dozens of times.'

'I told Joe Kaplan I was in love with you,' she said, 'before anything happened between us. He told me to go away, that's why we were going to Portugal. Only Robert couldn't leave at that time. Do you know, if he had, we wouldn't be together now?'

'I didn't know you had told Kaplan,' he said. 'Does he know about us now?'

'I'm not sure,' Terese said. 'I said I'd got over it, but I'm not sure if he believed me. It doesn't matter anyway. It doesn't matter who knows so long as they don't tell Robert.'

'They will,' he said. 'One day. I'll pick you up at three tomorrow, outside my office, sweetheart. And we'll go back to our Indian village.'

'Joe! There's a personal call for you from Buenos Aires!' He didn't show surprise; they had instructions never to use his private number unless there was an emergency. He turned to his wife as he picked up the telephone. 'This is a patient; close the door, will you, honey?'

'What makes you think I'm interested,' his wife said. She went out and he spoke; the line was very clear.

'Personal call to Dr Kaplan. Is that Dr Kaplan speaking? Go ahead, please, Dr Kaplan is on the line for you.'

'Hoffmeyer here; so sorry to disturb you at home, but we've been trying to contact you at your office this week and they said you were away on a conference. How are you?'

'Fine,' Joe said. 'I was in San Francisco. What's come up?'

'We've had a report about your friend Amstat. It seems a bit confusing, and before I send it on I thought I could cut out some of the irrelevant details for you if we talked on the phone first. Does he have any difficulty with his hearing? Does he wear a deaf aid?'

The old file on Hugo Elsner said that after an illness in childhood he had become partly deaf. This barred him from active service in the German armed forces, so he had enlisted as a concentration-camp guard in Poland and rose to be commandant. He had personally executed two hundred and eighty Jewish male prisoners by shooting them in the back of the head, and more than 150,000 were gassed and incinerated during his two-year term. He had disappeared since the war and was last traced to Chile. The deaf aid was his only distinguishing mark.

'His hearing is perfect,' Kaplan said, and then repeated it. 'He has no trouble with his hearing at all – he doesn't wear any kind of an aid.'

Hoffmeyer drew a line through the name of Elsner. Other details were also at variance with Kaplan's brief description. Elsner had a large nose and dark eyes. This did not connote Kaplan's explicit 'Aryan appearance'.

'Okay, that cuts it down by one,' Hoffmeyer said. 'What's the height and weight factor?'

'Around six one or two, around 180 lb. Very fit physical specimen.'

Kronberg a major in the Reichswehr, wanted for blackmailing French Jews by threatening to denounce them to the Gestapo or the Vichy Militia and then informing on them when they had given all they had in securities, valuables and jewels, was five feet seven inches tall and weighed 135 lb. Aryan appearance – blond hair, regular Germanic features and blue eyes, last heard of living in high style in Rio in 1949 on the proceeds of his wartime extortions. He too had got a warning and vanished in time. A change in weight was possible but no short man could grow six or eight inches. Hoffmeyer crossed his name off too.

'Does any of this help at all?' Kaplan said. 'Wouldn't you just like to send me on the whole report?'

'How much time have we got?' Hoffmeyer asked. 'Is your friend going to stay around for a while?'

'He says he'll be here for the next month; I don't see that he has any reason to move around right now; he did say he had business in Chicago, but that's been covered.'

An agent in Chicago had reported back to Kaplan already. He knew every detail of Terese's second visit to the apartment; he even knew about the flowers Amstat ordered for her, because the apartment janitor remarked on them. She had been lying, as he suspected. They were lovers in New York too; they were being watched everywhere, and everything they did was known.

'Well – things take time, you know how it is.' Hoffmeyer hesitated for a moment. Then he decided to trust his own judgment.

'I'll send you on the one report that's left, Dr Kaplan. The trouble is, it isn't much. But it's all we've got that might help this particular diagnosis.'

'You don't hold out much hope then?' Kaplan asked. 'You don't think you can be of any help?'

'I wouldn't like to commit myself. There's very little, as I said. But there's no harm in sending you this one report and you can form your own opinion. If by any chance it was the right one, we'd need a first-class specialist team to handle it. But – I don't think they'll be needed. You'll have it by airmail, Doctor. My kind regards to you and Mrs Kaplan. Sorry to have disturbed you at home, but we like to get these things cleared up. I have my own report to make out, too. Goodbye.'

'Goodbye,' Joe Kaplan said. 'And thanks for calling.'

Hoffmeyer had been crossing off possible

suspects; one wore a hearing aid, one was obviously the wrong height and weight. Both must have surfaced in South America or even America at some time and then been lost. It didn't sound as if Amstat was what Kaplan thought he was. The masquerade wasn't important. Unless he fitted in somewhere with this one report, this one man that Hoffmeyer hadn't cleared from their conversation, he was not an escaped war criminal on the Israeli list. And the old man hadn't sounded very hopeful. Well, he shrugged and went back into the living room. Even if Vera had picked up the extension or the operators listened in, they wouldn't have made anything out of what they heard. Airmail from Buenos Aires. Five days, a week. He didn't say anything to his wife and she went on reading the latest edition of *Vogue* as if he hadn't come into the room.

Ruth Bradford Hilton had been trying to make up her mind to talk to her brother for some time. There had been many opportunities; they spent some part of every day together, usually in conferences with lawyers while her husband sat in without attempting to take part. Bob had been wonderful over the whole business; she needed a cool head and a guiding hand in these situations. She was a woman who reacted very strongly to being thwarted; she had an equally powerful dislike of interference from outside. Her husband would never have been allowed to pull her up as her brother did, or to sometimes insist that the trust lawyers and executors were right on some points, and their side in the wrong.

She really loved Bob, and closeness in families as rich as theirs was very rare; especially among the old families. They had lost the close, clan attitudes which the Latin and Irish still fostered as a legacy from their immigrant beginnings. Ruth loved Bob, and she was finding it hard to stand by and see him being made to look a fool.

She said this to her husband, after they had left the Bradford's apartment.

'Give me a cigarette, darling, I'm worn out!' He did as she asked him and he sat beside her and patted her knee. He admired her and he was very fond of her indeed. He hadn't the slightest objection to being run by her or to keeping in the background in affairs that concerned her money. He was quite rich himself, though a beggar by his wife's standards, and he had not married her for her money.

'You look damned tired,' he said. 'I'll be glad when it's over. We might go away somewhere. Ruth. Why don't we join Bob and Terese in Portugal? Lovely place, Estoril;

had some of my gayest times there before the war.' He never attempted to pronounce his sister-in-law's French name properly; it made it sound long and English with a final flat A.

'They're not going to Portugal,' Ruth answered. 'She's changed her mind; she's fallen in love with New York, it seems. After fifteen years of paying as short visits as possible, they look like taking root here.'

'But I thought she went to Boston quite often still,' her husband said; he knew from his wife's expression that she was upset about something. He knew from experience that it would very soon come out.

'Yes, she goes to the house. At least that's what she tells my bloody fool of a brother. It just so happens that the last three visits to Boston didn't take place at all. I wasn't checking up on her, I just called the housekeeper about those tapestries – you know, I told you about them, darling, we lent them to the Metropolitan Museum two years ago for an exhibition. They needed some slight work done on one of them, and I'd heard of a French firm that specialised – oh, the details don't matter, and I forgot to mention it to Terese, so I called up the housekeeper. It was pretty obvious that Terese hadn't been near the place. She'd made a couple of calls, but she'd never stayed a night there when she was out of New York.'

'Oh.' He made a face. 'What do you think it means, then?'

'Oh, darling, for God's sake, don't be so naïve. She's got a boy friend, that's all. And she's spending the time with him when she tells Bob she's at the house. Or visiting friends, or whatever the hell the last excuse was. I don't think I can sit around and let her get away with it!'

'Any idea who the man is?'

'No. But that doesn't matter. What does matter is that she doesn't make a fool of my brother. The more I think of it...' She got up and began moving round the room; she looked like a small, angry lioness. 'The more I think of how good he's been to her – and let's face it, sweetheart, she's a nobody! She's a girl he brought back here, without a memory or a background and some sentimental story about an Allied bombing raid. She could have been anything. And she had that Jew backing her up. I suppose it was all part of the old pal's act; here's my best friend and here's my entrée to a nice fat practice if I take care of his little French wife for him. It's all very well, I can tell you think I'm being nasty, but my brother could have married any girl in the States; damn it, he could have had the world's pick, with his looks and background and his money! So this little tramp is not going to turn around and cheat him now. Not with me standing by, anyway.'

'I should sit down, Ruth, and calm down,' her husband said. 'Come on, my dear girl, don't go off the handle like that, it won't do any good. What Terese's background is, is neither here nor there. She's been married fifteen years and you've all been quite happy about her.'

'Mother wasn't exactly an enthusiast,' Ruth interrupted. 'But Bob was impossible; he wouldn't let anyone even talk to her at first, without he sat there, watching over her.'

'But you did, didn't you? You liked her, and were quite happy about it?'

'Yes,' she admitted. 'Yes I was. But because it seemed to be working out well; Bob was happy with her; she never put a foot wrong, it looked like an ideal marriage. Except they had no children. But he was like a bear with a sore head if you tried to mention that! I know what you're getting at, darling – how do I know that it's changed – just because she spends a night or two away and doesn't tell the truth about it – but it's more than that.'

'What else is it?' he asked.

'People are talking,' she said. 'I can feel it; every time their name comes up I can see in people's faces that they know something and

I don't. And she's different too. She's dropped the little-girl-lost act; she's – oh, I don't know how to put it – she's changed completely. It's ridiculous to say someone in their thirties suddenly grows up, but this is it. This is what I feel about her. I used to feel sorry for her in a way; she seemed so withdrawn, so dependent upon Bob. So long as he didn't find it a burden. I felt it was all right. I pitied her for it. But not now. She's a different person; even when she walks into a room, I notice it.'

'Does Bob realise anything?'

'If he does, he's too proud to say so,' his sister said. 'I don't know what to do. I feel like asking her round here and telling her exactly what she can expect from all of us if she does anything to let Bob down! Or I can go to him. I can warn him. I think that's what I'll do!'

'Oh well, I suppose you won't take any notice of me, sweetheart, but if you took my advice you wouldn't interfere at all. I certainly wouldn't tackle Terese; she'll only tell Bob and that could cause a major row between you. He's very fond of that girl, you know. I'd leave it alone, if I were you. It'll probably work out in the end.'

'It'll work out in a divorce with Bob settling a million dollars on her – that's what usually happens. And then she marries some creep that she's been sleeping with and they get fat on it. You would say I shouldn't interfere!'

'All right, darling, go ahead. If you must do something, you might try Bob direct. Personally I think he'll bite your head clean off!'

'Oh so do I,' Ruth answered. 'But all the same, I think I'll risk it.'

8

'Darling,' Terese said, 'I can't go to Chicago with you this week. I'm running out of excuses, and I just can't think of anything.'

'You can say you're going to Boston – what's wrong with that?' They were walking together in Central Park; they had lunched together in Chinatown, and taken a cab to the Park. It was a beautiful spring day, and they walked like lovers, hand in hand through the trees.

'I'll get caught; I can feel it. Everyone in our circle is gossiping about us, Karl. I can't make another trip out of New York so soon again. Even Bob is beginning to ask questions.'

'What sort of questions?'

He had her hand in his arm and he squeezed it. Once already he had stopped and turned her round to kiss her. They were going back to his apartment afterwards; it had become part of their pattern to delay being alone, to eat and talk and go out, with the desire growing in them until by mutual need they hurried back to the apartment block and shut themselves in. Love; he often said the word to her, and it was an endearment and a question. This was something he had never believed possible for a man to feel for a woman. In his mind, a woman had always fitted into a certain category with the label 'inferior' clearly marked. A woman was something that gave a man pleasure and children and was responsible for the wise administration of his home where his personal comforts had priority. His own mother, a dignified and austere woman, had filled this niche to perfection for his father. It was the ideal of German womanhood, and it had nothing to do with the way he felt about Terese Bradford. She had never been his type. He could remember liking tall, big-breasted women when he was young; he had never been attracted by the slim, delicate type, large-eyed and easily breakable. Not until she came into his office in the Avenue Foch. He could never have enough time with her; not just to make love to her, but to talk, to laugh, to share living. And to express the tenderness that overflowed from him towards her.

'What sort of questions?' he said again.

'Oh, why must I go so soon again? Couldn't I just telephone? He misses me.'

She said it sadly, because it was true. Robert missed her, and he was showing it. The real reason he felt her absence for a night or two once every ten days, or even once in three whole weeks, was because she was really far away from him when they were in the same room and the same bed. She had gone from him; she was sorry for him now to such an extent that it hurt her to look at him, but nothing could alter the truth. She belonged with the man who was walking beside her; and he belonged to her. He treated her as if he would never have enough time to make up to her for what had happened twenty years ago. He wouldn't even let her walk in a cold wind.

'It can't go on,' he said.

He said it every time they met and she had stopped arguing with him.

'He'll find out, and then you'll have to choose between us. Him or me, my darling. I lie awake wondering what you'll do when that time comes. And then I say to myself, "She'll come to me. She'll leave him and come to me. And we'll be married.'"

He had refused to marry Julia; now that he wanted to secure Terese for himself, he had begun to push the obstacles aside. No marriage in New York, because of papers and questions – all the difficulties he had envisaged when Julia used to try and win him round to the idea. He couldn't marry, he couldn't ever trust a woman to get that close to him. Now no woman would ever be closer to a man than she was to him. They could fly down to Mexico, and marry there.

'I want to make a proper life for us,' he said. So much had changed; all he had wanted was to stay alive, then to make money, be safe, be comfortable and do his work. Now he wanted to make plans, to live completely like other men.

'I want you to be my wife, and find you at home when I come back and beside me when I wake up in the morning. I want to plan holidays with you, and talk to you about my work. I want you to get ill, so I can care for you. You'll have to leave him, Terese, and come to me. I'll never let you go, you know that.'

'I can't have children,' she said. 'I never gave any to Robert, and I couldn't give any to you. Why do you love me so much, Karl? Why do we love each other more and more?'

'Because we are alone here,' he said.

'That's part of it. We can't escape the past; it's all we really know, my love. I'm still Brunnerman and you're still Terese Masson. We haven't changed except on the outside. Let's take a cab and go home now.'

In the taxi she put her arms round him. 'How long will you be in Chicago?'

'Three days, perhaps four. I'm nearly finished.'

'It's so long to be without you,' she whispered. 'I don't think I can do without you.'

'Then come with me.'

'No, I daren't. I'm not ready to hurt Bob yet; I can lie to him because I love you, but I'm not able to see any pain in his face, and know I caused it. I'll go to Boston, and I'll stay at our house. You fly up there from Chicago and we'll find somewhere to be together. I'll book a hotel room. We can have an afternoon, an evening.'

The cab pulled in and he paid it hurriedly, while she slipped into the entrance of the apartment block. They went up in the elevator together, and let themselves in.

'I'll come to you in Boston,' he said.

It was a thick envelope, sealed with blue wax and decorated with a long line of stamps, marking it 'Air Mail, Express'. It measured ten inches by six, and it had taken eight days to reach Joe Kaplan's office from Buenos

Aires. His secretary had not opened it; he had given her instructions to leave his mail to him for the next fortnight; he was expecting something highly confidential. She had been working for the doctor for five years, she liked him. He was considerate, and gave her chocolates on her birthday. She brought him the package, and smiled.

'Here's your mail, Doctor. Is this package what you've been expecting? It's from Buenos Aires.'

'That's it, Dora.' He smiled up at her. 'Open the other stuff, and deal with it, will you? Thanks.' He began sawing it open with a paper knife. There was a photostat of a file, several copies of typed foolscap, and, at the back, four photographic prints. They accounted for the size and shape of the envelope. He didn't do more than look quickly at the pictures; he had seen many like them and a good few that were worse. Then he opened the photostat copy and began to read. It was taken from the original in the Gestapo files at 8 Prinz Albrecht Strasse in Berlin, photostated and documented for reference after the war when the War Crimes Commission was being set up.

Alfred Brunnerman. Born February 1919, Frankfurt, parents Professor Freidrich Alfred Brunnerman and Frau Brunnerman, born Minna Elsa Neustadt. Educated privately, student at Frankfurt University from 1934 to '37, member Hitler Jugend, recruited S.S. '38. The details of his service in the S.S. followed; like all photostats, it was difficult to read and, as an old copy, it was beginning to fade. Kaplan read on slowly; he understood German very well. There was an identification photograph, but taken when the subject was still in his early teens and newly recruited into the Führer's personal army. It showed a round, rather unformed face with close-cut hair and a fixed stare. It didn't look like anybody in particular and a hundred eighteen-year-old boys in general. In 1941 Brunnerman had transferred to the S.D. Section IV of the Gestapo itself. His record began to soar from there. He was quite a Nazi, Kaplan thought; quite a super specimen.

'Intelligent, diligent, displays outstanding qualities of initiative and leadership.' Promotion was rapid, like bullets being fired. Transferred to Paris under Obergruppenführer Knochen and promoted to Standartenführer for outstanding intelligence work. That was where the file stopped. He read it through quickly again. He didn't allow himself to get despondent because he hadn't found anything at the first glance. He began reading the foolscap sheets. They were mostly scraps. A piece of information here and there.

Brunnerman had taken up his post in Paris; his file at the Avenue Foch had been lost after the war. Its last appearance had been in 1946, when the French were conducting an investigation and had undoubtedly 'lost' it, so that they could conduct the search in their own way. It had not reappeared since, and presumably any photograph attached to it was also mislaid. There weren't any others discovered so far.

This particular report had been compiled by the Israeli contact in Paris; he was a respectable jeweller in his seventies, and his entire family had been deported to Germany in 1942 and exterminated. He had good friends in the Deuxième Bureau, and they, in turn, made discreet enquiries which disclosed that the Paris file on Alfred Brunnerman had not been handed over to the Israelis, and all they could find through their Resistance records, many of which were missing or suspect because of Communist affiliations, were a few names of French prisoners and collaborators, who had had a connection with the man, and the inconclusive report on these and the missing file itself by a Colonel Baldraux of the French Military Intelligence after the war. Colonel Baldraux, it noted, had died in 1957. Joe Kaplan lit a cigarette; Hoffmeyer had not exaggerated when he said that there was almost nothing known about the man. His height and description fitted Amstat on the German dossier, but this meant nothing. It was the only detail that did fit him, as far as he had read. He picked up Baldraux's report. This was a copy, too. 'This former Gestapo officer was last heard of during the final stage of the Russian invasion of Germany, and posted missing, believed killed. However, we have received a report from the Russian military authorities that an S.S. lieutenant, who belonged to his company in the Waffen S.S., said Brunnerman was alive and had deserted in Germany in 1944. On the basis that he may be alive, we are making enquiries for the S.S. officer Brunnerman, for his criminal activities against members of the French civil population while in the Paris section of the S.D. Counter-Intelligence Group IV. I am aware that he is on the official list of war criminals responsible for the massacre of Jews at Lodz, but our investigation is not connected with atrocities committed anywhere but in France, and against French nationals. In the course of my enquiries, I have interviewed three surviving members of the Resistance with whom he was concerned: Jean Paul Belmont, François Laffont, and Eduard de Bré. These described him as an expert in psychological interrogation, but did not suffer direct brutality under his direction. The first and last named were subsequently tortured by his subordinates, and Laffont was being held by us on charges of giving information to the Gestapo when I made my enquiries. I was unable to question a woman member of the Paris Resistance, who had been interrogated by Brunnerman, a Terese Masson, because she was married to an American officer and he refused to allow me...' Kaplan stopped. The name enlarged into huge black capitals in his mind. He actually put his finger on the place where it was written.

Terese Masson, TERESE MASSON. He moved his finger slowly on to the point where he had stopped reading the dead man's report.

'Refused to allow me to question her. As a result of torture and imprisonment, she had lost her memory. Gestapo records on Terese Masson record a preliminary examination by Brunnermann, which was unsuccessful. By comparing her dossier and his personal file at the Avenue Foch, it appears that he was relieved of his duties and sent to the Eastern Front on suspicion of going "soft" on Masson. She was given medical treatment at his order, and this was noted against him. I protested strongly to the American Major Bradford, as I felt that there must have been a closer relationship between Brunnerman and Madame Bradford than was normal in these circumstances. I am sure she had valuable information to contribute, if I had been allowed to ask her a few questions.' Kaplan stopped there. Terese Bradford, the former Gestapo victim, was having an affair with a German pretending to be Swiss. Terese Masson and an association with the Gestapo interrogator, Brunnerman. A closer relationship than was normal. That was Baldraux's impression.

'She's had some kind of sexual trauma with one of the bastards.'

He had said that himself, to Bob, when she was at the base hospital in Germany. Whatever had happened, had happened with this man, with Alfred Brunnerman. And whatever he had done to break her had broken him too. He had gone soft on this particular victim, and lost his rating as reliable. Terese Masson. He looked at the name again. From the other side of the world, the past was linking up with the present, a man without a face, who had been hunted unsuccessfully for twenty years, was linked to Terese Bradford. He had remembered his own words, and they were spoken long ago. Now he remembered hers, when she had come to him in that same office asking for help because she was in love with another man, with Karl Amstat. He was familiar, she had said, 'It's as if I've always known him.' It was a common cliché people used, but now it had another meaning.

'I'm in love with him, really in love.'

She had been frigid for twenty years; Bob, with all his love and care, had never broken through to her. She had never felt anything for him or for anyone until she met Karl Amstat. And she had reached out blindly for something that she recognised subconsciously. That was the real meaning of why Amstat was familiar. They had met before.

Vera's gibe came back to him too, the first piece in the puzzle that had led to other pieces, and perhaps the most important because it was the one that matched with Baldraux's fragments. 'If she suffered so much under the Gestapo, how can she go to bed with a German...?' Vera had been so nearly right. But not *a* German. *The* German. The one she had wanted to tell, to go home with. That had come out too, when he was probing the wound of her experience, and it had been so deep he sewed it up again. Brunnerman hadn't tortured her; Brunnerman had tried to help her. An expert at psychological interrogation. He must have fallen face down in his own dirty trap. Kaplan lit a cigarette; he wasn't shaking, he was icy calm. The pieces were fitting one by one, and now he had a picture. The same height, the same build, the same age, the same Aryan type, and the same woman who had been involved with Alfred Brunnerman. And the same mistake that got him sent to Russia. He had taken up where he left off, twenty years earlier. He knew now who Karl Amstat really was.

In all probability, so did Terese by now, but she hadn't given him away. That figured too. Kaplan unclipped the photographs and looked at them. It might be twenty years, but he was going to die for what they showed. He didn't waste time with cables or codes now. This was a big one, and he had very nearly got away for ever. He switched on his intercom and said, 'Dora? Get me a Mr Karl Amstat on the line, will you? It's an architect's office right in the centre of town; it'll be under his name. Thanks.'

The pictures were spread out in front of him. They had been taken by the Russians six months after it happened, and most of the bodies in the opened trenches were quite well preserved because of the extreme cold. The four prints were slightly different, but what they showed was the same. Corpses, semi-decomposed, heaped one on top of the other; here and there an arm or a skeletal piece of leg stuck out.

'Is that you, Karl? Hello, it's Joe Kaplan here. How are you? Fine, we're just fine. We were wondering if you were free for dinner any night next week?' He listened for a moment; he had taken his glasses off and they lay on the pictures of his people in their shallow graves.

'Well, that's a pity. How long will you be in Chicago? Maybe we could arrange something for the week after? Okay, we'll call you then. Have a good trip.'

He put the receiver back and wiped his mouth with a handkerchief. He felt unclean after speaking into the phone. His secretary buzzed and he switched on. 'Your first appointment's here, Doctor.' He had forgotten completely; he couldn't even remember who it was, and he had looked at his appointment book when he got into the office. 'Who is it, Dora?'

'Mrs Harper.'

Mrs Harper: forty-eight, married to an executive with an engineering firm; three teenage children, and an anxiety condition which took the form of a neurotic fear of going mad. She was an unhappy, uncertain creature, the victim of an approaching menopause and a husband too busy to give her the constant reassurance that her illness needed. Her dependence upon Joe Kaplan was pathetic, and she was a constant and often time-wasting patient. But time and patience were what she needed to rebuild the crumbling confidence which was the root of this delusion. 'Tell Mrs Harper I'm tied up right now. I'll have to keep her waiting. Otherwise she can make an appointment for tomorrow.' A minute later, his secretary buzzed back.

'Mrs Harper says she doesn't mind, Doctor. She says she'll wait.'

They always waited, sometimes for an hour or more if he were held up; it was the first sign that they were getting well when they felt confident enough to give up an appointment.

'Okay,' he said. 'I'll buzz you when I'm ready for her.' He put through the call himself. It was a number in Detroit, a private number, and it was the last link in a long and complicated chain.

'Kaplan speaking,' he said. 'You know about Hoffmeyer's report?'

'We've been informed,' the voice on the other end said.

'I'm sure it's Brunnerman. No doubt about it. Yes, a real lucky strike, this one. You can send the team up.'

'It may take some days. Where is he?'

'He'll be in Chicago from the eighteenth to the twenty-third next week. I've just spoken to him and confirmed this.'

'Very good work. We'll take him there.'

Kaplan put his glasses back on, rearranged the papers and the photographs, put an extra clip on them, and shut them in his office safe. His part was over. Now it was the execution squad from Israel which would be flying in. He had a drink of water, took out Mrs Harper's file, and made himself go through it to get his concentration back. At the end of twenty minutes, he felt ready.

'Okay, Dora. Send in Mrs Harper now.'

Amstat was asleep when the phone rang; for some minutes, it went on ringing and he thought it was part of a dream; when he finally woke and switched on the light he saw it was four o'clock in the morning.

'Mr Amstat?'

'Yes – who is that?'

'Brückner. Five of them left Tel Aviv the day before yesterday. They're after you. You haven't any time to waste; pack a bag and get on the first plane to Washington. There'll be a ticket and the necessary papers and money in the luggage office under the name of Dressler. Follow instructions exactly and you may have a chance. Are you listening? Are you there?'

After a moment, he answered. 'Yes,' he said. 'I'm here.'

'You don't deserve help,' said the voice at the other end. 'But, as Smith said, we've got other people to consider. We can't afford to let them catch you. You had no right to

251

disregard our warning.'

'I told Smith I wouldn't take your help again,' he said. 'If I have to run, I'll run in my own way.' He hung up. Five men had left Tel Aviv. Brückner knew what he was talking about, and he had been a fool to turn him down. The first plane to Washington and ask for a package for Dressler at the other end. He was due to meet Terese in Boston that weekend. Now he had to throw his clothes into a bag and run, begin the endless paper-chase across the world, leaving it all behind, not even saying goodbye. That was the obstacle; it was such a small thing, such a piece of sentimental nonsense, that need to see her once again and tell her why he had to go. A telephone could do it. Now, he could pick it up, and put through the call, and say it to her quickly, Goodbye, Terese. I've been discovered, and they're after me. He wasn't going to do it. Not like that. If he had enough time to take a plane, then he could choose his own direction. He got up and began packing. He opened the door of his apartment, locked it, and went out leaving the hall light burning. He went down the back stairs and out through the service entrance at the back. The street outside was empty. He was being watched, that was obvious, but not at that hour of night. They must think he was safe where he was at that hour. He walked for nearly five blocks before he saw a single cab, crawling slowly along in search of a drunk or a whore with a client. He told the driver to take him to the airport. At 7 a.m. he boarded a plane which caught a connection to Boston.

They stood facing each other in the enormous drawing room; the Aubusson carpet had been woven for Louis Philippe and his monogram was the centrepiece; there were wall panels painted by Fragonard, and the pretty women with their unrealistic lovers flirted in the trees and pavilions under skies that were always blue in a landscape full of flowers. It was a treasure house of the past of other countries, other cultures, and at nine in the morning it made the two people feel a sense of emptiness, as if they were meeting in the Frick Museum. The housekeeper had answered the door when Amstat rang; he had phoned Terese from the airport, explaining nothing except that he was coming straight to see her. The housekeeper had shown him into the drawing room because the small study wasn't quite ready. She disapproved of Mrs Robert always using it, and leaving the famous drawing room with its furniture collection and its tribute to the taste of the old Mrs Bradford shut up and unused.

'Karl, what is it? What's happened?'

He didn't come towards her, or touch her. He had rehearsed what to say and if he took her in his arms, he wouldn't be able to say it as it should be said.

'I've come to say goodbye, Terese. I can't stay long or keep our date for this weekend; I've just come to say goodbye, my darling.'

'No! No, you can't, Karl!' As he didn't come to her, she ran to him, and the chance to get it done was lost. 'What's happened, darling? Darling, what's the matter?...'

'I had a call yesterday,' he said. 'They're on to me; I've got to run for it again.'

'No, no, darling! No!' she kept repeating it. 'How could they find you?...'

'It doesn't matter how,' he said. He made her look at him and kissed her. 'Don't cry, Terese. I don't want to see you cry. I was a fool...' He broke away from her, but she caught at his hand. 'I shouldn't have come here; I've only upset you, hurt you! It was selfishness. I wanted to see you just once more.'

'Where are you going?' she said. 'Oh, Karl, darling! Don't hold me off; come and sit down somewhere – how I hate this room! There's nowhere comfortable to sit, no proper chairs or sofas. Come into the study.' She had always disliked this room; she had felt a stranger in it, and now she hated it, and the house and everything in her life it represented. 'Come with me! Down the passage here; this is my room.'

She drew the curtains back, and opened the windows; it was a comfortable room, but still dominated by her dead mother-in-law's desk, which had come from the Trianon and was too valuable to be moved.

'At least you can sit down here without feeling it's a sacrilege! Now, sweetheart. Let's be calm, let's talk this out together. Tell me exactly what happened.' She had stopped crying; she wiped her eyes and waited.

'I got a call in the middle of the night; the people who helped me before – I told you about it. The Israelis left some days ago; I don't know how my people knew, but they have a good intelligence system. They set up an escape route for me – papers, money, the usual thing.' He sat there, holding tightly to her hand, knowing he should have been in Washington, D.C., and on his way under another name.

'I didn't take it. I'm going alone from now on. If they catch up with me, they catch up with me. I'm tired of running, anyway.'

'They'll kill you, won't they?' she said. 'This is the murder squad, isn't it?'

'Yes. They won't take me back with them. I'm not important enough.'

'You're important to me,' she said. 'You're the most important thing in the world. How much money have you got?'

'A few hundred dollars. Don't worry about that, darling. I've managed on less.'

She looked into his face and smiled; she had always been beautiful within the limit of her type of delicacy and colouring; now love irradiated that beauty. It warmed him, as if he were suddenly in sunshine.

'I'm going with you, Karl,' she said. 'Don't argue with me, I've made up my mind.'

He shook his head, fighting the resolution, the passion which she was conveying, silently, as they looked at each other.

'You are not coming with me. You don't understand what may happen.'

'I called them the murder squad,' she said. 'I understand exactly. And I'm going with you. What happens to you happens to both of us from now on. I belong to you, Karl. You can't leave me behind, and I won't let you. We go together.'

'It's impossible.' He said it very gently. 'You have no idea what life will be like. You've been comfortable, safe – look at all this! If I escape them, and I think I will, it'll mean odd jobs, dirty boarding houses, back-street living. Years of it, maybe. I asked you to leave your husband, but that was different. I could offer you something then. I had a future. Now I've nothing. I'm going, Terese. And I'm going alone.'

She got up and lit a cigarette. She seemed quite calm and confident too.

'I would rather live in one room with you for the rest of my life than spend one more day here. I'm not going back to Robert – ever. You said the moment would come when I left him, and it has. I'm finished now. I love you, and you're all I've got to live for. It's as simple as that. If you've got to run, I must run with you. If you die, I die too. I told you once, when I knew who I was, and you told me what you'd done, that I ran out thinking to go home and realised I'd no home to go to. It's still true; I don't belong anywhere here. I only belong to you. And I'm not soft, just because of all this – as you call it.'

She held out her right hand to him.

'Finger by finger, with a hammer. I can take anything you can, my darling, and you can't deny that. We go together.' She came up to him and held out her hand. He took it and kissed it.

'All right,' he said. 'All right, God forgive me, all right, we go together. But if there's any danger, you've got to promise to do what I say!'

'I promise,' she said. 'If there's danger, I'll do what you say. How much time have we got? And where are we going?'

'We must get out of here,' he said. 'They'll be watching the airports by tomorrow, when

257

they find I'm not in Chicago. New York, Washington, everywhere – and the seaports, of course. They'll expect me to run south, try to get across the Mexican border and then down. I've been trying to work something out. I think we should try and do the unexpected. We can drive right across the States and then turn up north somewhere in Montana or Washington and over the Canadian border.'

'If they watch the airports, we're limited to the railroads or the highways,' Terese said.

'I've no car, and we need something fast and reliable.'

'We have two cars laid up here,' she said. 'Just waiting in case Robert or I want to go down the street. So we have a car. And we have money too. I can draw ten thousand dollars from the bank here – more if you like, but it might cause comment. And there's this...' She touched the inch-square diamond on her finger. 'And the few things I brought with me to look pretty for you, darling; they'll come in very useful later on. I'm going to tell the housekeeper to make a packed lunch for us, while I get some things together.' She went to the desk and pressed a foot bell under the carpet. 'I spent the first year of my marriage here; my mother-in-law used to sit in this room in the mornings writing letters and going through the menu.

After she died I remember sitting at this desk trying to find the courage to ring for Mrs James, who let you in. I couldn't do it. I couldn't do it for three months; I used to go and get things for myself or wait till I ran into her to ask about something, rather than put my foot on that bell. Thank God I'll never have to worry about ringing it again.'

'What are your cars?' he said.

'A Bentley convertible and a Ford; the Ford's last year's model, the Bentley's new.'

'The Ford sounds the best,' he said. 'Fast and not so conspicuous. We don't want to be noticed. That's very important.'

'We won't be,' she said. 'Because they'll be looking for one man, and we'll be two. From now on, we've got to behave normally – till we're away from here. Oh, Mrs James, we're going on a picnic lunch and then I'll be driving back to New York afterwards. Will you have something ready for us in an hour, and you can shut my room up. I shan't be here for the weekend, after all.'

'Very good, madam. Is there anything the gentleman prefers in a packed lunch?'

'What would you like, Karl? Mrs James is a magician at these things – she can produce anything you fancy.'

'I've no preference,' he said. 'I leave it to you.'

'We leave it to you,' she said to the house-

259

keeper. She had been in awe of her for years; now she wasn't afraid of anyone. 'Thank you, that's all, Mrs James. We'll be using the Ford, so you can put everything in the boot.' When the door closed, he got up and took her in his arms.

'Loving, and brave too. I have everything in you; I don't deserve it.'

'Kiss me,' she said simply. 'And then I'm going to pack.'

'What the hell is going on?' Vera Kaplan said. 'That's the second call you've had from Buenos Aires in two days.'

'Professional calls,' Kaplan said. He was trying to read the *New York Times*; it was a day old, but he had picked it up because it was the first thing he could get hold of; he had to read or do something to cover himself.

'Like the one from Detroit yesterday, I suppose?' she said. 'I listened in on the other line, darling. It didn't sound like medical talk to me.'

He looked at her with real contempt. 'I didn't think you'd sink so low, Vera. You've no reason to check up on me.'

'Thanks, I believe you,' she said. 'Let's just say I'm curious, and you don't talk to me much these days. I've been in the dog house so long I feel like barking when you come in the door! What are these calls anyway? Don't try and tell me that man from Detroit was talking about a *patient*. Who's got away from whom?'

They'd lost him. That was the final report from Detroit yesterday, and he had just confirmed it with Hoffmeyer. When the commando squad got to Chicago, they were too late. Amstat's apartment was empty and no one knew when he left. He hadn't gone back to New York either. He had just vanished forty-eight hours ahead of them.

He and Vera had been married for eighteen years; she'd fallen out of love with him, refused to have children because he was a Jew and she hadn't been able to rise above the prejudice against his race. It had ruined their marriage and soured both of them in different ways. Perhaps the time had come for her to face just how very much a Jew he was.

'A German war criminal,' he said. He put the paper down and sat back with his hands folded. 'A man who had four thousand of my people murdered during the war. We've been hunting him for twenty years, and we thought we'd got him. But he was tipped off somehow. He's got away.' She was staring at him, trying to make sense of what he was saying.

'War criminal – what war criminal? You're

not making sense. What do you mean *we've* been hunting him...? Who's we, for God's sake?'

'The Jewish people,' her husband said. 'You heard about Adolf Eichmann, didn't you? I guess you did because you kept saying it was all so illegal to kidnap him like that...'

'I said it was bringing up old sores,' she interrupted fiercely. 'I said it was making a race issue when it was all over! And it was.'

'Killing six million people is making a race issue too,' Joe Kaplan said. 'We feel we have a right to do something about it. The Jews in Israel took up where all you Gentiles left off. We got Eichmann, and by God you'd be surprised how many more of those bastards have been picked off here and there. We're sick of just standing there until somebody decides to start something; building up out of the ashes, running from one country to the next with all we can carry on our backs. We've got a country now, and we're a people. And I'm a part of that people, Vera.'

'You're an American Jew,' she said. 'You've got about as much connection with those gangsters in Israel as I have. You're not making sense with this royal "we".'

'I work with the Israelis,' Joe Kaplan said. 'I've worked with them for years, looking for guys like Eichmann. And I've found one, thanks to you, and now it looks as if we may have lost him. So you'll understand why I'm a little out of sorts?'

'What do you mean?' She said it very slowly. 'What do you mean thanks to me?'

'You put me on to him. Karl Amstat. If it hadn't been for you, we'd never have suspected anything. But you were right, honey, right all the way. He was a German. He was a guy who murdered Jewish men, women and children, after they'd dug their own graves. And he's not going to get away with it. We'll find him. I promise you, we'll find him.'

She had moved backwards, still staring at him; she looked sick and white. 'You,' she said. 'You're mixed up in this? You're mixed up in kidnapping and killing people in cold blood – oh, Jesus God, what did I marry?' Her voice rose and then began to crack into tears. 'What in God's name did I marry!'

The phone began to ring, and she stopped; she didn't move to answer, nor did he, and it went on ringing. When he left his chair and went over to pick it off the cradle, she made a noise like an animal at his approach and ran out of the room.

'It's Bob,' the caller said. 'Joe, you've got to come right over. Terese is missing.'

Bob Bradford knew his sister very well; when she invited herself back with him after they left the lawyer's office he didn't think it was because she wanted company or a drink. She had something on her mind, and he wondered with some impatience if it was another divorce. They sat opposite each other and talked trivialities, and after about ten minutes, he said, 'Ruth! Come out with it, whatever it is!'

'I was about to,' she said. 'I gather Terese is away again?'

'She's up at the house for the weekend. Why?'

He knew that grim jaw-line and the go-to-hell look in Ruth's blue eyes.

'I've been trying not to interfere,' she said. 'But the time has come, Bob dear, when you've got to face facts. She is not at the house; she's cheating on you.'

She put down her glass, and waited for the storm to break on her.

He waited too, deliberately. 'Say that again, will you? I want to be sure before I throw you out of here. For good!'

'You can lose your temper, if you like,' Ruth said. 'You can say anything you like to me, but it's the truth. Terese is not at Boston. I've known this for some weeks, and I hoped you'd do something about it, but apparently you're just as blind as ever. Mrs James hasn't seen her in three months. And there's talk going around; they haven't named a name to me yet, but any minute now.'

'You're a liar, Ruth,' he said. 'My wife has never done a dirty thing in her life. And I spoke to her the day before yesterday. At the house.'

'Then it's the first time she's gone up,' his sister said. 'She wasn't there the other times. Look, Bob, we're family. We love each other, and we've always stuck together. I wouldn't say something to hurt you unless I felt I absolutely had to! But you're a laughing stock, a fool, and, Christ, I just won't sit back and let it happen. I'm not making it up – she wasn't in Boston all the other times. Okay, she was a couple of days ago, but now where is she?'

'In Boston,' he said. 'Until tomorrow morning, as it happens. And just before I do tell you to get out, I'll prove it to you. I'll call her there.'

It was after speaking to the housekeeper that he put the call through to Joe Kaplan.

'Why him?' Ruth asked. She had a very stiff drink in her hand and she was standing over him trying to make him take it. 'Why Joe Kaplan?'

'He's her doctor,' Bob said. 'If something's gone wrong, he'll know what to do.'

'He's a psychiatrist,' Ruth said. 'What's he got to do with Terese? Are you telling me she's had some kind of a crack-up? What's been going on, Bob, for God's sake?'

'There's an awful lot about Terese you don't know,' he said. He shook his head and pushed the drink away. 'He said he'd be right round. Where the hell is he?'

'I'm out of my depths, Robert,' she said. 'What don't I know about her?'

'That she worked for the Resistance in the war. She was captured and tortured by the Gestapo. I found her at Buchenwald, when we liberated the place. If you want details of what they did to her, I can give you those too! Joe pulled her out of it; she didn't lose her memory – it was blotted out on purpose to make her forget the way they held her under water in a bath-tub till she nearly drowned, and burned her and broke her fingers!' He looked up at her, his eyes sunken in his face, and they were the same fiery blue as her own. 'My wife's not a spoilt little tramp like the rest of you. About the time you were on your first matrimonial junket with that creep Charleton, she was in Buchenwald! I hope,' he said angrily, 'that you feel as small as you ought to, trying to blacken her to me!'

'Why didn't you tell us?' Ruth went away from him; she began sipping the drink herself. The whole thing sounded unbelievably distasteful and horrifying. One read about these things. One didn't actually meet the people ... they were all in D.P. camps or hospitals or something. Her mind whirled round and round trying to adjust to what she knew of the war and equate it with her brother's wife, with Mrs Robert Bradford the Third. 'Why didn't you tell us?' she repeated. She had a clear memory of her mother in the Boston drawing room, dressed for a reception at the Cabot Lodges', and the question answered itself.

'Because I didn't want to see the look on your face I see now,' he said. 'Because it was none of your bloody business. Joe! Thank God you've come! You know Ruth, my sister? What took you so long?'

'I had a call to make on the way,' Joe Kaplan said. 'Now tell me exactly what happened.'

'I called home to speak to Terese, and the housekeeper said she'd left on Thursday morning. She was coming back here.' He hesitated, and then he said, 'There was a man with her, Joe. They went off together. I think she's been kidnapped!'

'Anyone the housekeeper knew?'

'No. I asked that immediately, but she said he was a stranger. A foreigner; she said Terese called him Karl.'

Joe Kaplan looked from his friend to his sister, whom he knew only slightly. She looked as if she had smelled something bad under her chair. He took Hoffmeyer's envelope out of his pocket and threw it on the coffee table.

'Before we go any further, Bob, I'm going to say I wish I didn't have to tell you this. But there's no way round it. Terese hasn't been kidnapped, and there's only one Karl she'd go off with. Karl Amstat.'

'I said she was cheating!'

Ruth burst out with it; her face had begun to redden at the vulgarity of the whole business, the housekeeper's astonishment when her brother called, the whole shoddy mismanagement of the affair. 'I said she was a cheat and I was right.'

'Perhaps.' She didn't like the Jewish doctor's tone. 'But this is rather different to the usual all-American roll in the hay. Bob, before you read this stuff, I'll make it easy for you. Karl Amstat's real name is Alfred Brunnerman. That's who Terese has gone away with – and they're just two jumps ahead of the Israelis. While you read through this, I'd like to call Julia Adams and ask her to come over. She lived with that bastard for two years – she may know something about him that might give us a clue where they've headed.'

Julia was in watching television when the call came; she spent most evenings at home since Karl left her, not because she was allowing herself to mope or recriminate, but because she hadn't any enthusiasm for going out and starting with someone else. Not for a while, she decided. Amstat had meant more to her than she had known, much more than a man she liked going to bed with and would gladly have married, because this had been true of her two husbands and numerous boy friends in between. It was more than that with this one; she was intelligent enough to suspect that it had its root in his command of the situation; this was what had made the novelty for her. The partnership had never been equal, either in bed or out of it, and this was something she felt she wouldn't easily find again within their circle. Joe didn't say what he wanted; he just said it was urgent, and he couldn't talk on the phone, so would she please come over to Bob Bradford's apartment as soon as possible. There was silence when she walked into the room; Bob was sitting hunched in a chair; he looked up when she came in and it seemed to be an effort for him to get up. Ruth was standing, and there were two patches of high colour on her cheeks, like misplaced rouge on a grotesquely pale face. Only Joe Kaplan seemed normal, but more serious than usual.

'Well, hello, everyone,' she said. 'Who's died? Oh God!' her tone dropped suddenly.

'Bob, darling, what have I said?'

'Nobody's died, Julia,' Ruth answered her. 'We're just a little shocked, that's all. I think you will be too.'

'Sit down,' Joe said. 'I'm sorry we had to drag you out like this, but something's come up. I'll explain it to you.' She looked at the three of them, and sat down. It was Joe who offered her a cigarette. He turned to Bradford.

'Do you mind if I tell her, Bob?'

'No, no,' Bob said. 'You go right ahead, Joe. If there's anything Julia can tell us, it might help. I've got to find her.'

'Terese has run off with Karl,' Joe said. 'I know you're not surprised, Julia, but it's more complicated than it seems. We have to go back a way, quite a long way, to the war. Terese worked for the French Resistance; in the course of that work she was caught by the Gestapo and questioned by one of their officers. A – relationship developed between them – it's too long to go into the hows and whys right now, but it did, and it was highly emotional. I think I could say this particular guy went too easy on her for personal reasons...'

'Why not say they fell in love?' Julia said. 'It could happen, even to a German, I guess?'

'Possibly,' Joe said. 'It didn't save Terese from being ill-treated by other Gestapo, and

270

when Bob found her she was in a concentration camp and a pretty sick girl. I treated her there, and I made her an amnesiac because I felt it was her only chance to start again. Bob married her, and we made up the story about the air raid, and all the rest of it.'

'But why?' Julia looked from one face to the other. 'Why the lies? For Pete's sake, she was a heroine. What were you both hiding up?'

'You see, Ruth,' Bob spoke for the first time, 'everyone doesn't think of it like you. Thank you, Julia, for what you've said. Unfortunately, my family doesn't equate the kind of experience my wife went through with taking one's proper place in good American society – whatever the hell that's supposed to mean!'

'There was another reason,' Joe interrupted. 'The real reason, Bob. Be fair to Ruth and your family. We didn't want anyone asking questions which might have jolted Terese's memory. We didn't want it to come back.'

'I can see that,' Julia said. 'But I don't see where you're leading. She's run off with Karl, and because of her mental state you're anxious about her, is that it?'

'She's run off with the German who interrogated her! That's who your boy friend is – a war criminal called Brunnerman, wanted by the Jews for murder!'

Ruth couldn't keep it in any longer. Then, having done it, she saw the expression in her brother's face and went to him, trying to put her arm round him.

'Bob, darling, don't get so upset. I know it's awful...' He took her arm and disengaged it.

'Go away from me,' he said. 'Go to hell and go away from me.'

'Amstat is a German war criminal,' Joe Kaplan explained to Julia. 'A lot of them escaped after the war and settled in places like Argentina or Chile or Brazil. Amstat hid out for twenty years, until he met Terese here and was fool enough to try and take up with her where he left off. My people, the Israelis, are looking for him, but we've lost him. We didn't know until now that he and Terese were together. We wondered if you might know where they'd go – have any memory of something said to you. But, first, because you were in love with him yourself, I'd like you to look at these. That's what was done in Poland at his order. That's why we want him.'

He laid the four photographs down on the table beside her. Nobody spoke; she picked them up and looked at them, quickly and then slowly, examining each one. She got up so suddenly that they slid to the carpet at her feet.

'I'm going to throw up,' she said. 'I know where the bathroom is...'

'And that,' Ruth said bitterly as she ran out, 'would be most people's reaction to this. I'd better go to her.'

'I'd leave her alone,' Joe said. 'It's just shock. It's the best thing. They're not very pretty pictures anyway.' He bent down and put them back in the envelope. He had gone to his office and brought them for this purpose. Julia was out of the room for some minutes. When she came back, she was very white, but she had put on lipstick and smoothed her hair; she looked herself again.

'I'm sorry about that,' she said. 'But I'd never seen anything like that before. It was one of the children's bodies that did it.' She took a cigarette and lit it. 'I'll tell you anything you want to know, Joe, but I want to ask Bob something first. Does she know who he is – does she recognise him?'

Joe answered her: 'Obviously, if they've run off together. She's got her memory back – through him. He's probably the only person in the world who could have brought it back.'

'Okay,' Julia said. 'Now, tell me, what kind of a woman is your wife that she'd go off with that? With a man who did what I saw in those pictures?' She didn't wait for an answer. 'I lived with that man for two years. I wanted to marry him. Do you know why I vomited just now? Why I really vomited? Because he'd touched me! Because I'd been to bed with a man who'd done that to human beings! I'm sick, Bob, sick to my stomach at the very idea of it. I don't think I'll ever feel clean again. What kind of a woman is your wife? You haven't told me! She knows what he is, doesn't she? She knows what he did, and she's with him now, helping him? Sleeping with him? Thank Christ I'm just a plain American woman. Joe, ask me anything you want – anything I can do to help you get him, just ask me! Could I have a drink, please? Some brandy?'

'Did he ever go on holidays with you?'

'No, not with me. I liked the sun; he never wanted to travel. I remember him saying he hated the sun. I thought he meant Argentina.'

'He probably did,' Joe said. 'He didn't go shooting, climbing, have any cabin he rented for trips – anything like that?'

'No,' she shook her head. 'Not that I ever heard of; he wasn't a very communicative type. I can understand why. Where do you think they've gone?'

'He left Chicago and disappeared, that was nearly four days ago now. Until Bob called to say Terese was missing, we didn't know which direction he had headed. But he went to Boston, picked her up, and they left together on Thursday. They've probably gone south again, trying to get into the South Americas eventually. That's where most of them get swallowed up. They have money and a car, and two, maybe three, full days' start. Our people were watching the airports, naturally, but for one man, not a couple. Bob! Where's Terese's passport?'

He raised his head; Julia looked at him, and he seemed to have become a weary, middle-aged man in the course of the last hour.

'It's right here, with mine. I always keep the travelling papers. We've never been abroad apart.'

'Then they haven't left the country,' Joe said. 'My God, that's something to go on!'

'America's a big place,' Ruth said. 'They could hide out for ever here.'

He turned and looked at her; he was a slight man, bookish and short-sighted, the Jewish professor or doctor, the conventional Semitic intellectual type, but he had a dignity and a sense of purpose which was old in his race when the North American continent was uninhabited jungle and desert. He dominated them all for those few seconds.

'We'll find him,' he said. 'There won't be any place on earth big enough for him and people like him to hide in. I'm only sorry, Bob, Terese is with him.'

'She doesn't know what she's doing,' her husband said. They had abused her, both the women; Joe hadn't commented, but he too condemned. Terese was his wife and he loved her; he tried to say it, but it wouldn't come out properly; it came out as an excuse.

'She's ill – she's not responsible! None of you have even tried to be fair! Joe, for God's sake, we've got to find them! – I've got to get her back. She could get hurt in this. Nobody's thought of that! You talk about the Israelis catching up with Amstat – what about Terese?'

'I told you,' Joe said. 'I'm sorry. I don't think she's sick, Bob, or doesn't know what she's doing. I think she's crazy about him. If it's possible that a man like that could feel anything so human as love, he must be crazy about her. They won't leave each other now. As far as her safety is concerned...' He shook his head. 'I can't give any guarantee at all. I'll drive you home, Julia – that was a large brandy on an empty stomach. If you think of anything, call me – day or night, it doesn't matter. Good night, Bob. If I hear anything I'll let you know at once.'

In the car neither he nor Julia spoke until they were almost at her apartment. 'He'll be killed, won't he?' she said.

'Yes,' Kaplan answered. 'And if she gets in the way, she'll die with him. There's nothing I can do to stop it.'

9

They stayed two nights at a small hotel on Lake Itasca; it was a clean, unobtrusive place, and they registered as Mr and Mrs Hudson with an address in Newark. They had been travelling at a fugitive speed for the first two days; the Thursday they left Boston, Amstat drove all night while Terese dozed beside him, and she drove most of the following day; they covered nearly a thousand miles in twenty-four hours, and then he insisted that they spend a night so she could rest. They toured the cheap rooming-house area of Chicago and found a place to spend the night. But the choice was a mistake, a return to his old habits when he was on the run and alone; the scruffy boarding houses were all he could afford in those days; now there was something suspicious about a man and a woman, especially a woman dressed like Terese, with that indefinable air of money about her, driving a good car, staying in a place where travelling salesmen of the bottom grade and an occasional out-of-town visitor were the regular customers. He and she stuck out like sore thumbs, and, feeling this, they paid up and left very early the next morning.

The next night they chose a hotel in Minneapolis where they fitted into the general scene much less conspicuously. They shared the long hours of driving, Amstat insisting that she changed over after two hours because the high speeds and long monotonous highways were especially tiring. After Minneapolis they turned off the highway and made their way up to Lake Itasca where they felt able to relax a little; he took a double room with a private bath, and watching them together the hotel manager decided that they hadn't been married very long. They sat out on the terrace and held hands like honeymooners. He was a sentimental man with an over-worked, short-tempered wife, and when he pointed out Mr and Mrs Hudson to her, she took a long, calculating look at them as they came in and went over to the elevator to go up to their room.

'Nice-looking couple,' her husband said. 'Nice to see folks like that. He's so crazy about her it's like a neon sign.'

'Yeah,' his wife said. 'That's because they

are not married; that's for sure!'

'Not married?' He was genuinely pained at the suggestion. They were high-class people, the Hudsons; he was a foreigner of some kind, probably Norwegian – the manager had worked it all out in his mind, and placing his residents was a favourite game he played while his wife did the accounts. They were class, these two, especially the woman. He thought she was pretty enough to eat in a pie, as he put it to himself, and the last thing he wanted his wife to say was something that tarnished the image he had created for them.

'What you mean, not married? We don't have that kind of thing in this hotel.'

'George,' she said, and she shook her head at him from side to side, very slowly as if he were an exasperating child. 'We do have that kind of thing in this hotel, and we'd be well down on the year's take if we didn't. We get married people and unmarried people, only you like it all nice and tied up with ribbons so you keep your eyes shut. I've been running this hotel for fifteen years, and five years in St Paul before we married, and I can smell 'em! Those two aren't married to each other. That's for sure. Anyway, it's just none of our business.'

'You've got a nasty mind, Hilda,' he said. He was really disappointed and he knew that his wife was certain to be right. She had a nose for people; she could smell the ones who were going to give a rubber cheque for the bill, and she could smell the ones who were on a weekend when they shouldn't have been. There was no escaping Hilda's instinct, but there were times when he resented it, and this was one of them. Then she said something unexpected for her. He often wondered why she took such a jaundiced view of people.

'He's sure a good-looking man, though. Takes real care of her, too.'

'I told you,' he said. 'They're a nice couple.'

'Yeah,' his wife said again. 'Maybe it's because they're *not* married. The guy up in fifteen says he's checking out tonight – wants his bill before seven.'

'They're leaving tomorrow,' the manager said. 'I mean the Hudsons; early in the morning. I'll get number fifteen's account made up.'

'Okay,' his wife said. 'Then let me have it and I'll check it over.'

The previous night. Terese had slept beside him so deeply that he couldn't bear to touch her; he let her rest, and they had breakfast together in their room and then went for a walk before lunch. She looked less strained and pale, and the crisp spring air had given her colour. Again and again he had blamed himself for giving way and taking her; the courage was there, and the will to stay with him, but she was taxed to the limit by the anxiety, and she was not physically strong. She came up to him in the bedroom that afternoon and put her arms round him. He held her against him and stroked the back of her hair.

'It's been a lovely day today,' she said. 'Do you know something ridiculous, Karl?'

'No, what? What's ridiculous?'

'I'm so happy,' she said. 'I've had the happiest day of my life today being with you. Why haven't you made love to me?'

'Because you're tired,' he said. 'Because this is exhausting you, my darling. I wanted to last night; I've wanted to so much today.'

'Well, so have I. I want to now.' His desire overcame him so quickly that he took her to bed without saying anything more; they didn't talk because there was no need that wasn't filled by the simple act of union. Afterwards, she kissed him.

'Will you get tired of me one day?'

'Never. Have you really been happy today?'

'I told you – happier than ever before. I feel free for the first time. I'm with you now, and that's all I can see ahead of me. Just the two of us together.'

'I shouldn't have taken you with me,' he

said. 'I tell myself this a dozen times a day. I shouldn't have done it. Every time I see you beside me in that car, when I think of what's involved, if I get caught—'

'You won't,' she said. She sat up and made him look at her. 'You're not going to get caught. Do you have a gun?'

'No. I haven't carried one for years.'

'Well, then we'd better get one, hadn't we?' she said. 'Two. I can remember how to shoot.'

'No,' he said fiercely. 'No, there's not going to be anything like that! You're not going to be involved in anything – listen to me. No, don't argue, listen to me! You promised if there was any danger, you'd do what I said. You promised that in Boston.'

'That was Boston,' Terese said gently. 'That was to make you take me. I'm sorry, darling. I never meant to keep that promise. I'm with you right through in this. It's the only way.'

'Oh God,' he said. 'What a fool I was – what a damned fool, to listen to you!'

'Don't say that,' she pleaded. 'Please, darling, don't say you wish you hadn't taken me. I love you. We love each other. It was right we went together, and you know it!'

'I don't know any more,' he said. He came back and sat on the edge of the bed. He took her hand and held it. 'We've been travelling for nearly a week now; I've seen you so tired you could hardly get out of the car; I see the strain of it in your face and it's hardly begun. That's why I decided to stay here for two nights.'

'Because of me? When we should have gone on and not wasted time? Oh, Karl, Karl, you fool – why can't you trust me? Why take a stupid risk? I can sleep in the car! Listen, sweetheart, we can go tonight. We can start off as soon as it's dark.'

'Tomorrow morning,' he said. 'I've told the manager. And whether it's a risk or not, you needed the break, and we'll travel differently from now on.'

'How? How differently?'

'We'll take it more easily, get along as far as we feel like during the day, and rest up each night. I've worked out a route that will get us to the Canadian border within the next week. Here, I'll show you.' He spread the map out on the bed; he had marked their way with a pencil.

'We go back on to Interstate Highway 94, just here, about seventy miles from where we are. We get on that and we stay on it as far as Forsyth; then we branch off on to U.S. 12 and go right through to Spokane; then due north and over the Canadian border at Cascade or Grand Forks. There are motels all along the highway; we can spend the nights there until we get to Spokane. We should do the journey from Spokane up to Kokanee Glacier Park in one day. After that, my love, we can breathe a little.'

'How about money? Will we have enough?'

'More than enough,' he said. 'But I think we should do one thing; I think we should trade in your car now, and get another.'

'Yes,' she said. 'Robert must know I've gone by now. It's safer to change cars. When we get to Canada what will we do?'

'I'm not sure. Stay around the tourist centre at the Glacier. We can find somewhere to stay for a few weeks. I can get work. And you, my darling, will have to get a passport. That may take a few days, but it should be simple enough, you're an American citizen.'

'And then where? Where do we go after that?'

'I've been thinking,' he said. 'I think we should go somewhere completely different. Not the South Americas; I don't want to go back to that part of the world again; and anyway, it's not safe any more. This is going to be my last run, Terese. Our last run. I think we'll go to Portugal. I know there are one or two people – Germans like myself – who have settled there, and nobody's come after them. I think we'll go to Portugal. Would you like that?'

'I'd love it,' she said, and she smiled. 'I was planning to go there anyway, don't you remember? We can sell my jewellery there too.'

'Yes,' he said. 'If we have to...'

'The ring would fetch – oh, probably forty, fifty thousand dollars. Robert bought it from Tiffany's for me. I believe it's very good. And I have my emerald clips and a pearl necklace and another brooch with diamonds. We won't be poor, my love. We can buy a house, you can open an office and start again. It will be a new life.'

She reached over and kissed him. 'Don't say you're sorry you took me with you. It hurts me when you say that.'

'It's because I love you,' he said. 'Don't you understand that? Don't you understand that I can't bear for you to be in discomfort or think of you in danger. I lose my own courage when I think like that. I've taken you away from your husband, away from security and wealth, and given you – what? The chance to run like a hunted dog, to have no security, no settled future, just a map route with a question mark at the end instead of a destination.'

'It's what I want,' she said. 'You won't understand because you're a man, my love, and you don't like me in a situation which you can't control. You see it in terms of a night's sleep for me. I see it as my whole life.

In your way, you see it too, or you wouldn't have let me come with you. It wasn't weakness, Karl, because you're not weak. It was what you knew was right for us too.'

He smiled at her and held her gently in his arms. 'I am very lucky, as I've said. So often I've said this to you. I'm so lucky to have you. I'll make you another confession and you can laugh at me if you want. I don't like selling your jewellery and living off the money.'

'I know,' she said. 'I could see it in your face when I mentioned it. When we're in Portugal you can buy me another ring.'

'For fifty thousand dollars? It may take a long time.'

'I'll wait,' she said. 'Don't you think we ought to go down to dinner, Mr Hudson?'

'I think we might. We have an early start tomorrow.'

'The season's picking up,' the hotel manager said. He was sitting opposite his wife and his sister and brother-in-law, and they had just eaten dinner. 'That was good, Hilda,' he said to his wife; he wiped his mouth with a checked table napkin and gave everyone round the table a big smile. She was a very good cook; she was a good woman in so many ways, and whatever people said about them, Jews were hard workers. It was just a pity that she

286

wasn't a little more – soft – sentimental. He chased the criticism away because it came too soon after his appreciation of her cooking. Her sister and her brother-in-law owned a garage outside of town and ran a second-hand-car business. They saw quite a lot of each other, and Hilda and her sister were very close. The brother-in-law, Leo, was too much of a hardhead, but he didn't mind him really; it was important to keep the women happy. In fact, he often tried to put business in Leo's way if he could. If anyone at the hotel wanted a car checked, or repairs, he always called Leo's garage. That reminded him of something.

'Leo, did you get a couple come to you to trade in a Ford convertible a couple of days ago?'

'No,' Leo Hyman shook his head. 'Nobody's traded anything in a week. I was going to say the season ain't picked up as far as I'm concerned! How come – you recommend them to come to me?'

'Yeah,' Hilda said. 'He did, Leo, I heard him. They were paying the bill and the fella asked where he could buy a car around here. George told him, go to Hyman's garage out on the fourth boulevard; they have a good stock and he'll give you good terms. Ask for Mr Hyman himself and say I sent you. That's what George told him. I was there, right behind the desk, I heard him.'

Leo Hyman finished a glass of beer, and his wife answered. 'They didn't come to us then,' she said. 'Like Leo says, we haven't sold a car in a week and nobody's come in with any Ford convertibles. Was it a nice car, Hilda?'

'Very nice; big and no marks I could see. Looked almost new, too. What a shame, Leo. But then George couldn't do more than give your name and tell them to go there, could he?' She spoke defensively and her brother-in-law said quickly, 'Sure, sure, George, it was real good of you to try.'

'Funny,' the manager said. 'I even wrote the address for them. They were foreigners, anyhow he was, and I thought maybe they wouldn't find it, so I wrote it on a piece of paper and gave it to him. I couldn't figure why they'd want to trade in a beautiful car like that, anyhow.'

'There was something funny about them,' his wife said. 'I knew it the first time I saw them, but old hearts and flowers over there wouldn't listen to me!'

'I only said they were crazy about each other,' her husband said. 'And you said, Ah, they're not married. Right away, Hilda says they can't be married or they wouldn't be so happy. I ask you, why not?'

'They weren't married,' Hilda said flatly.

'You just don't see further than the nose on your face, George, but I do. I saw her luggage and the initials weren't right. She was no Mrs Hudson, that's for sure.'

'What were the initials,' Leo Hyman said.

'T.B. Large and clear on her suitcase. I saw the boy bringing it downstairs, and I thought to myself, married my fanny! And they were rich too. I know clothes when I see them, and what she was wearing didn't come from any chain store. You know money when you see it, honey...' She spoke to her sister. 'Like alligator shoes and matching purse, and everything personal in gold. Little things, like a cigarette lighter and a lipstick case – that sort of detail. They were loaded. And they were having it on the side, that's all. George believes it all, of course; Mr and Mrs Hudson. Funny name for a Norwegian, Hudson.'

'How do you knew he was Norwegian?' Leo asked her. He had been picking his teeth with a split match during most of the conversation. Now he stopped and put the match in his vest pocket.

'I don't,' George answered. 'But he was no American; he had some kind of an accent, like Norwegian or German or something, and he looked kind of blond and a big guy. I guess he was Norwegian. Maybe they just decided not to trade the car in after all.

Maybe that's why they didn't go to you, Leo.'

'Sure, most likely. What was the dame like – what were her initials again, Hilda?'

'T.B. Pretty, blonde. Around thirty something, but you can't tell the age on those women; they spend all the time in the beauty parlour. How's your mother, Leo? Is her leg all right now?'

'She's fine,' he said. 'They're made of tough material, the old people. Ruby and I went up the weekend and she was great. She sent her best to you and George.'

The conversation drifted between the four of them, eddying between business and family topics in two streams that sometimes met and interflowed before they separated again. Not long after, the Hymans left. It was well past midnight, when the call came through to the number Joe Kaplan had spoken to in Detroit. Hyman's wife was in bed and fast asleep in the next room.

'I might have a lead for you,' Leo Hyman said. 'It's one in a million but I guess it's worth passing on. A guy stayed at my brother-in-law's place two days ago. Big, blond, foreign guy; had a dame with him, small and blonde. Called themselves Hudson, but the dame's suitcase had the initials T.B. on it. They weren't married, my sister-in-law said. They wanted to trade in a new car, or near new, and they didn't come to me with it. Ford convertible. Could be, yeah. Jewish name put them off, maybe. Okay, glad I called you. Yeah, sounds as if it could be the bastard. The descriptions check. Okay. Any time. Bye.'

Joe Kaplan let himself into the apartment; it was past seven-thirty again and he was tired. His days at the hospital always left him feeling drained and often depressed; so many people were beyond help, and he suffered with them and blamed himself for not being able to do more, help more. His temperament inclined towards the failures in his estimate of himself; the cures gave him a sense of personal fulfilment which had taken the place of the religion he hadn't practised since he was a boy. It had been a long day and not rewarding; he had given everything of himself in the medium of attention and involvement, and he felt empty. The apartment he came back to was empty too, because Vera had packed up and left him. It was odd how little he missed her as a person. There were traces of her in drawers and the medicine chest; she had left a pair of gloves behind and some personal laundry, which the maid had asked him what do to with – she had left debris, rather than traces of the years they had been together, eight of them in that apartment. Joe hadn't argued; she hadn't given him the opportunity. She had just packed and left, and sent him a letter saying she would like a divorce. He had known it was going to happen because she had moved out of the bedroom after he had told her about his connection with the Israelis. She couldn't bear him to sleep near her or touch her. She had gone over to the other side with a completeness that only proved how hard she had found it staying on his for so long. He didn't blame her; he just waited for her to make up her mind when to go.

He came in and went to the dressing room she had introduced into his life, and changed his shoes and took off his coat. It was all over; the rows and the reconciliations and the patching of the threadbare marriage with sex and gestures of affection, which weren't strong enough to overcome the resentments and the secret hates. He remembered the night they had driven to the Bradfords for dinner – how many months ago now? – it seemed a lifespan. They had quarrelled before they left because she was jealous of Terese, and then they had made a joke in the car and stitched up another tear in their relationship. But the tears were too many and the thread of love was rotten; it snapped at the first strain. She had been jealous of his work, and jealous of Terese Bradford because she symbolised the war which had been waged against his race, and Terese was all the more important because she didn't belong to that race.

That was the real reason behind Vera's suspicion; everything she objected to had the Semitic slant hidden beneath it, and hidden so well that she couldn't see it herself. It had been easier for her to say, 'You're in love with her...' and turn it into a sexual misdemeanour on his part, when what she really meant was, 'She fought the Germans and you feel so strongly about her because the Germans killed the Jews and you're a Jew, and I can't take it. And I can't forgive you for making me such a miserable social coward that I'm ashamed of my own husband.'

He had accepted the failure and told her she could have a divorce, if she went to Reno and got the thing through. He felt nothing but emptiness; he was more unhappy about Robert Bradford than he was about himself and Vera. Their friendship was finished now; they kept in touch but there was a hostility which Bradford didn't bother to conceal. Kaplan had failed his wife; he didn't care about Alfred Brunnerman or what he had done; all he cared for was his wife's safety and this was in jeopardy because of Kaplan. And he clung to the illusion that she was ill and not responsible, like a climber stuck on the cliff face with only one good rock to hold on to; if he let go, he fell and Joe had given up trying to make him face the truth. He hadn't seen it himself, and he was trained in the study of the human mind and emotions. He had guided Terese out of the morass of horror and pain which had engulfed so many people in that old, boring war of twenty years ago. He had re-made her and allowed himself a lot of pride when he saw her and his great friend, Bob, together. He had played God, and sat back to contemplate his own wisdom and success in solving one complicated human problem. He had been closer to her than anyone, even the man she married, and it turned out he hadn't known her at all. She had defeated him and all he stood for; she had gone with Brunnerman because she loved him. There was no medical cure for that complaint. He was having a drink and reading the paper when the phone rang. It was Julia.

'Sorry to disturb you, Joe. Any news?'

'Yes, we've got a new lead. At least we think so, and we're checking on it fast; we've had quite a number of false trails, you know; this could be another one. How are you?'

'I'm fine. I'm at home tonight, so I thought I'd call. I tried to talk to Bob, but he won't speak to me. He isn't talking to Ruth either.'

'I know,' Joe said. 'I'm sorry for the poor guy. He's got to defend her, and he's not had much help from any of us.'

'Maybe that's because there's not much of a defence; I keep seeing those pictures, Joe, and I'm on sleeping pills right now. How's Vera?'

'I don't know,' he said. 'She's left me, but I guess she's all right. I'm sorry about those photographs; you'll forget them after a while.'

'Maybe. I'm sorry about Vera. I didn't know. What happened?'

'Too many things,' he said. 'She couldn't take them all at once. I don't blame her. What are you doing now, Julia?' He hadn't realised how lonely he was until she called and he began to talk to someone. It was still early and he hadn't eaten. 'Why don't you let me take you out for dinner?'

'Why not?' she said. 'I'm not doing anything, you're not doing anything either. Come on over, Joe, and we'll have a drink first. I'd like to hear about this lead you think you've got.'

'I'll be round in fifteen minutes. Where would you like to eat?'

'Somewhere quiet,' Julia said. 'I don't think either of us feel like El Morocco at the moment.'

They sat on in her living room, drinking

until they discovered it was too late to go to a restaurant, so she made an omelette and they ate together in the kitchen.

'You really think they've gone North?'

'I just don't know. But it could be right. The descriptions fitted, the initials on the suitcase, even the car make. Bob keeps a Ford in Boston and that's what they drove off in. I think we're on to them, Julia. I think the bastard's making for Canada, because we expect him to go south again. And they can get across. We'll probably lose them if they do. It's a big country and it's sparse; there are thousands of miles and Christ knows how many routes to be covered. We're just not that organised.'

'You seem pretty well organised to me,' Julia said. 'Joe, how does this thing work? How did you get the tip that they might be on Lake Itasca?'

'It's not too difficult,' he said. 'I'm a little high, Julia, and I'm talking too much. But I'll tell you this. We have a system, and it works through ordinary people – people like this guy with the garage. They don't go round with guns or codes or anything like that; they just get a word now and then to keep their eyes open and call a certain number. Maybe nobody contacts them in years. But if the need comes up, like now, we have people all over the States and they have friends. It's one of the great complaints about us. We're everywhere, like bad weather.'

'The woman noticed her suitcase,' Julia said. 'What a bloody stupid thing to overlook.'

'About as bloody stupid as taking her with him,' Joe said. 'But he did. Do you still feel bad about him – about yourself and him, I mean?'

'I don't think about it,' she said. 'Funny thing Joe, I don't want to go out with men, or anything. I think of that bastard and everything in me goes cold. I feel thoroughly dirty. I won't feel clean until he's dead. I'm high too, or I wouldn't have said that.' She lit a cigarette and drew on it. 'I wanted to marry him. Did you know that? I really wanted to marry him, and I kept asking him and he wouldn't. Jesus, when I think of it. What was wrong with me, Joe? Are women really that blind, that they could go to bed with a man and not sense *anything* about him? I don't count her – she knows, she knows he's a killer and she doesn't mind, but I didn't. I slept in that bed through there with him for two years – I even cooked breakfast for him right here and ate it, sitting like we are now, and I never noticed anything about him. And there must have been something. Nobody can do that and stay the same as other people. I just don't believe it!'

'If you're looking for an answer from me, I haven't got one,' he said. 'I spend my life looking into people's motives, digging into the dark places. I'm not prepared to dig for Brunnerman; I don't know whether he's like other people or why he murdered a lot of men, women and children, and I tell you, Julia, I don't care. I just want to see him get it, that's all.'

'You used to be fond of her,' Julia said. 'Like a kind of Dutch uncle. Do you care about her now?'

'No,' he shook his head. 'I don't give a damn about her either. I better be getting back, it's late. Thanks for dinner, Julia. It was nice.'

'It was nice for me, too,' she said. 'Don't sit alone, Joe, just call up and come round any evening.'

'I will,' he said. 'Good night.'

'That's a nice car,' Leo Hyman said. He was standing in the foreground of a garage ten miles away from the Lake. He had phoned every garage in the area asking if they had a Ford convertible in good condition as he might have a customer. The fourth call brought him out to the small place on the road to Park Rapids. The Ford stood out in the front; it had been polished and it shone in the bright sunshine; it was getting really warm and the trees were coming into flower.

It was one year old, and the number plates were the same as the ones on the car he had been told to look for; the numbers were on a piece of paper in his pocket. 'The condition's perfect,' the garage owner said. 'Hood, inside fittings, engine, automatic windows, every god-damned thing. It's like a new auto – I guess it's hardly been on the road at all.'

'What's the mileage?' Leo asked.

'Twenty thousand – Boston registration, here, I'll show you the papers.'

They went into the little office at the back beside the petrol pumps and Leo looked through the insurance certificate for the car. It was insured under the name of Robert Garfield Bradford of Boston, Mass.

'How much?' Leo asked. He gave the papers back.

'Fifteen-fifty to you. Trade price,' the man said.

'Okay, I think we'll make a sale,' Leo nodded. 'I'll have to bring my customer out to see it first. He's a fussy bastard, but if he likes he'll pay. Say two thousand to him, uh? You give me four-fifty bucks and we're all square. Say, what did you trade the owner in exchange for this?'

The man laughed. 'A Chev,' he said. 'A nice black Chev; they must have been crazy.

I offered them the Chev for a thousand two fifty bucks and the Ford, and they didn't even give me an argument!'

'How do I know you did a straight trade?' Leo said. He had a square stony face and he watched the man out of eyes like pebbles. 'I want to see the bill book, bud. If it's okay, maybe we can raise your piece to two thousand. Otherwise, no deal.'

The bill counterfoil was genuine; it gave the same description of the car the man and woman would be travelling in as the man said. A black Chev. But he couldn't remember the number plates and Leo decided not to press it.

'I'll bring the guy out this afternoon,' he said. 'I think we'll make the sale.'

When he got back to his garage, he put the call through to the Detroit number again. 'It's the Bradford car, no doubt about it. Yeah, I saw the papers. It's them, for sure. A Chev, black, a newish model, saloon. No number plate, couldn't get it. He thinks they were headed west. Okay. They should be about five hundred miles on by now. Sure. Macht gut.' He hung up, and went back to his business; there was a car in front waiting for petrol.

The highway stretched in front of them like a broad concrete river, which never seemed to turn. Cars and lorries flashed past them, horns whining and dying away as they disappeared in front. Amstat drove at a steady seventy, which was the minimum speed allowed on the highways; the one thing they couldn't afford was an accident. It was monotonous and nerve-racking; there was a radio which they switched off, because the combination of pop music and the endless traffic noises made it impossible to talk. In the evenings, they stopped at one of the big, brassy motels along the way, booked a room for the night and slept, exhausted.

The relationship was changing between them, subtly, so that they were unaware of the alteration; it had seemed impossible to him that he could feel any deeper for her, both mentally and physically, but this was happening. It gave him a sense of peace which was extraordinary. Love didn't consist of the high peaks of pleasure; it was more potent in him when she was fast asleep beside him, one arm curled over his body, and he tried to shake off her mood of optimism and see the truth of what their life must be. It was his last run. He had said that and he meant it. He could never do this again, whatever the consequences; he had lost the impetus. It was Terese who kept him driving on, studying the maps, encouraging and making light of the situation. It was easy to talk about Portugal and a new life. She, in her sweet ignorance, had no idea of what life meant without the cushioning of a million dollars.

She and he both talked as if Portugal meant safety. He had said that to himself about New York, and seen that it was no safer than Buenos Aires. Nowhere was safe for him. He could make one new life after another, think up a new name and start again, but at any time the façade could collapse, with Brunnerman standing naked in the public view.

And she would share this with him, this anxiety, this uncertainty which he felt would never end except in death. And that was when he discovered the extent to which he really loved her. He had lost hope for himself; he didn't want to die, but she was the one thing that made living worth the trouble. And the same dark red Pontiac had been following them for two days. He had noticed it soon after they left the Stay Way Motel outside Bismarck; he remembered seeing it in the morning, and after they pulled off the highway and ate the packed lunch supplied by the motel, he noticed it again in the afternoon. It was still with them when they stopped for the night; the place was smaller and less brightly decorated; it had a seedy look about it and the cabin wasn't very clean. He suggested they eat in the diner, because the room was so depressing, and there were two men sitting there, already eating. They looked up and stared at him for a moment; then one said something to the other. He hadn't felt fear like that since the retreat from the Eastern Front. She sat opposite him, touching his hand and talking, and he said yes and no, while he watched the two men at the other table. Neither looked up again. When they went back to the cabin, he saw the Pontiac was in the parking lot.

They left at dawn the next day; he paid the bill to the clerk who was half asleep, threw the cabin key down, and got the Chev out and on to the road before it was completely light. All night lorries went down the route like clumsy rockets; there was hardly a private car in sight. He turned to Terese, sitting dozing beside him, and pulled her closer into his side to keep her warm. He kept his foot hard down on the accelerator and by ten o'clock they had covered over two hundred and eighty miles. Traffic was normal now and he had to slow down; he had been driving at a lunatic pace for almost five hours. By noon, he saw the red Pontiac in his rear mirror.

'Darling,' Terese said. 'What's the matter?'
'Nothing, sweetheart.'

'You keep looking in the rear mirror – what is it?'

'There's a car behind; I think the driver's been drinking. I'm going to pull into the next lay-by and let them pass us. We don't want any accidents if they try and overtake. Light me a cigarette.'

She did as he had done that day at Chapaggua, when it was just beginning between them; she put the cigarettes into her mouth and lit both. For some reason, she remembered it though she had lit his cigarette in that way since they left Boston. It made her feel the physical pain of her love for him, that memory and all the memories that came after it. When they pulled into the lay-by, he took her in his arms, and kissed her; holding her close to him he watched the Pontiac with the two men in it flash by them. In those few seconds, he made up his mind what to do, and in the hours before they reached another overnight stop, he thought out how it must be done.

'Is that Dr Kaplan?'

'Speaking,' the voice said on the line.

'This is Karl Amstat here.' There was a pause and he thought they had been cut off. 'Hello? Dr Kaplan – are you there?'

'Yes. Who is calling again?'

'Amstat, Karl Amstat. You remember me,

we've met often in New York.'

'Sure, of course I remember you. You were coming to dinner one night, and the next thing we heard you'd left.' Even over the telephone line, Amstat could hear the excited undertone running through the banal half-phrases, so typical of telephone conversations. His instinct had been right; he had picked the only Jew he knew, and it was going to be easier than he had imagined. Kaplan was one of them. He couldn't quite hide the emotion in his voice.

'I need your help,' he said.

'Sure, anything I can do at any time. What's your problem?'

'My real name is Alfred Brunnerman, and your people, the Israelis, are going to kill me. Does this make sense to you?'

'Yes.' There was no insincerity in the voice now. It answered shortly and it was as curt as his own. 'It makes plenty of sense. Why are you calling me? What are you asking – mercy?'

'No,' he said. 'I've many things to be ashamed of, Kaplan, but being a coward isn't one of them. I have Terese with me, and I want to make a deal. Can I make it with you, or can you make it for me? You're the only Jew I know.'

'You couldn't know a better, as it happens,' Kaplan said. 'I can make the deal so long as it doesn't include you.'

'Your people are after me,' Amstat said. 'They've been following me for two days. If they come in after me, Terese will get hurt. I don't want that, you understand? I don't want anything to happen to her. You haven't any quarrel with her – I want her safety guaranteed.'

'And in exchange for that?' Kaplan asked.

'I'll meet your people at a definite place; I'll come out, and they can do what they like after that.'

'Where are you now?'

'At Helena, Montana. We should be at Spokane tomorrow night and there's a motel on U.S. 10 where we'll stop tomorrow – place called Rock-a-bye Motel. They can find me there.'

'All right,' Kaplan said. 'I have to contact them. And you'll stay there?'

'We'll be there from tomorrow evening. At eleven o'clock, I'll come out of the cabin – alone. I won't be armed. You have my word on that.'

'I'll take it,' Kaplan said.

'And no one will go near Terese? She won't be harmed? You promise that?'

'I promise,' Kaplan said. 'Just so long as you stick by the deal. You come out alone, at eleven o'clock. No gun. Just walk outside.'

'I'll be there,' Amstat said.

'We will be waiting for you.'

He hung up, and instead of leaving the booth, he waited inside it for a minute, and lit a cigarette. It hadn't been so difficult; it was much less difficult than pulling the trigger on oneself, and he hadn't been able to do that, years ago, when the weight of his guilt seemed too heavy to bear. He had lost the sense of it now; Lodz didn't matter any more. The dead were dead; the blood was lost in the soil, the bones had rotted into fragments. He felt nothing any longer, not even brave because he had sentenced himself to death to save Terese. His only sensation was one of relief that the major terror of the last few hours was lifted from him. It was so acute that it was almost an hallucination, where the cabin door burst open and before he died, he saw their bullets hitting Terese and her body dropping like a broken doll. That wouldn't happen now. When he came out of the booth and walked back to the diner where she was waiting for him, he was whistling; he felt happy. It was almost over, and they had forty-eight hours together without fear.

After Joe Kaplan called Detroit, he tried to ring Julia; he had to talk to someone, but there wasn't any answer. She was out. It still seemed impossible; he couldn't quite believe that the conversation with Brunnerman had ever taken place. It was a fantasy, a wish fulfilment, dreamed up because he had been so sick with worry and frustration the last few days. The special squad from Israel had completely lost the trail. The report from Lake Itasca was the last they had on Brunnerman, and the only Jewish-owned hotel near the highway they were supposed to be on had turned out to be a joker instead of an ace. The husband and wife were middle-aged, American-born Jews; he had had a report direct of the reaction to questions and then a straight appeal for help.

'We're Americans; we don't want any part of this killing business. Look at all that nasty talk about that Eichmann guy, and everyone saying us Jews did something illegal. And kidnapping ain't right. Look, it's twenty years ago – you can't hate for ever. We're not getting mixed up in any trouble. We don't go for murder – you got something on this guy, why don't you call the cops?'

A blank; an obstinate, disapproving blank. That had been the first of many. In the process, they had lost Brunnerman and the woman, and the search was at a standstill; Detroit was beginning to think they had branched off and gone south, just to confuse the issue. The Israeli team were standing by, waiting. Then the call came through, the call he had just taken less than half an hour ago. That was the crazy part, the fantasy. They'd got away; three more days and they were over the Canadian border, and they were safe. Whoever Brunnerman thought was following him, it surely wasn't the Israelis. That was the incredible link in the whole improbable chain. 'Your people are after me, they've been following me for two days.' It was probably a couple of commercial travellers on the road. Kaplan could have laughed out loud at the irony of it. He had given himself up to them because of a mistake. And because he had a woman with him that he loved; he wouldn't risk her life any longer.

Joe sat on by the telephone; he had forgotten to call Julia again. He was a psychiatrist, a mind-doctor, head-shrinker, witch-doctor – any variety of names, contemptuous and otherwise, would fit what he was supposed to be. He was supposed to know about people, know enough to attack the problems they couldn't overcome themselves, supply the missing personality parts and send out a whole product, or nearly whole, into the pressures of ordinary living.

Here is a problem for you, Doctor. Solve this one for me, will you? Take a man, an intelligent, well-educated man from an upper-middle-class background, father a professor, and tell me why he joins one of the most vicious organisations in the world. How come that kind of man works in the Gestapo? He's a psychopath, a paranoiac, a sadist – out come all the easy answers. He ends up by ordering a mass murder. Men, women, little children, weeping in the snow, standing on the edge of their graves, while his men set up the machine-guns and he stands there, watching, listening, waiting till it's all properly organised, like a well-trained German officer should, and then he gives the order. Fire!

Four thousand people die; a speck in the dust heap of six million dead, but they were his personal contribution to that dust. A psychopath, a paranoiac, a sadist – the pattern is perfect except for the one glaring flaw in it. He is capable of human love. Madmen only love themselves. The truly evil are supreme narcissists, ruthlessly self-obsessed, without pity or imagination. Brunnerman killed thousands, but he can't let one woman die to try to save his own life. He shouldn't be capable of this; he shouldn't be capable of loving anyone, but he is. As capable as she is of dying with him if the moment came. Understand all this, Dr Kaplan, and you have solved the real riddle of the universe. The incomprehensible working of the human heart. He left it until the afternoon of the second day before he went over to see

Bob Bradford and tell him he could charter a plane and fly down to get his wife.

They hadn't spoken for some days; when Joe came in, Bradford asked him to sit down as if he were a stranger. He didn't offer him a drink or a cigarette. He looked quite grey round the temples and forehead, and the boyish, enthusiastic look, which gave him such attraction, had gone for ever.

'Would you mind telling me why you've come here?' he said. 'I thought I'd made it clear I didn't want to see you, not till I have Terese safe and home with me.'

'That's why I came to see you,' Joe said. 'Look, Bob, be reasonable; I want to help Terese as much as you do.'

'Then call off your bloody murderers!' Bradford shouted at him. 'Call them off till we find her! By Christ, Kaplan, if anything happens to her, I'll tear the roof off! I'll have you and every bastard tied up in this indicted for murder! And if you don't think I can do it, just try me.'

'You can do anything you want,' Joe said quietly. 'You're a very rich man, and you have friends in high places. I know. It just happens that she's safe and I know where she is; I came to tell you, that's all.'

Bradford swung on him; he was a big man and he gripped Kaplan's coat front and shook it. 'Where is she? For Christ's sake,

Joe, where is she?'

'She's at Spokane, Washington State. At a motel on the U.S. 10 called Rock-a-Bye.'

'And that bastard – that German? Joe, if he's hurt her...'

'He won't have, don't worry,' Kaplan said. 'That's the last thing he'll do. He's giving himself up. Her safety was the deal. She'll be okay.'

'You've got him, then?' Bradford had let go of the smaller man; he felt embarrassed by his loss of control. He had been tempted to shake him like a dog at one point. Kaplan looked at his watch. It was a quarter to five. 'In another six hours, we will have,' he said. 'It's timed for eleven.'

'The murder,' Bradford said slowly.

'The execution,' Joe answered him. 'I thought you'd want to take a plane and fly down and be with your wife. That's what I came to tell you.'

'Joe,' Bradford stepped in front of him. He looked lost, and miserable, ashamed. 'Joe, she's going to need you too. I'm sorry for the way I've acted – for what I said just now. I'm going to bring her home, take care of her. I want her to forget all this – this bloody nightmare. Will you help me?'

Kaplan made a gesture; it brought his shoulders up and his arms out from his sides, the palms upwards. 'Bob, Bob, let's sit down a minute, shall we? You go and charter your plane while I mix us both a drink.'

'I have a plane standing by,' Bradford said. 'Ever since she disappeared. I can be aboard in an hour.'

'It'll take you seven or eight hours to fly out there,' Joe said. 'If you get there before the time, things could go wrong. Our boys won't let anything stop them now. Sit down and have a drink and listen to me. Bob. For our old friendship's sake!'

'What do you want to say,' Bradford said. 'That I'm fooling myself? She wasn't kidnapped, she went with that sod of her own free will? Okay, I've had time to think, and I'll admit you're probably right. But she's sick, Joe; she's had some kind of breakdown.'

'I don't think so,' Kaplan said. 'I think it's much simpler than that, and much more complicated. I think she's just crazy in love, Bob. That's what you'll find when you get there. You won't find Terese as you imagine her. You'll find a woman who's just lost the man she loves. I'm trying to prepare you for something.'

'What?'

'I don't think she'll come back with you,' Kaplan said it as gently as he could. 'I don't think the old life will mean anything to her now. Not even gratitude to you. I don't think she'll come home now.'

'I don't believe you,' Bradford said. He stood up. 'I'm not listening to you any more. Joe. You've lost your sense of proportion over this. You get on and kill the guy, and leave Terese to me. We won't need your help after all. I'm going now. You can see yourself out.'

The Rock-a-Bye Motel was visible three miles down the highway; it flashed a neon sign in letters six feet high from the front, beckoning the night driver to a meal and a bed, the Washington State's best value for twelve-fifty. The black Chev drew in and turned down to the parking lot. Amstat helped Terese out and carried their suitcases. He did the checking in as usual and paid in advance for the night's lodging. A boy took them to cabin number eight, and opened the door for them.

'You folks want something to eat? I take the orders now; diner shuts in twenty minutes.'

'I'm hungry,' Terese said. 'It's nine o'clock, darling. Let's order something. I'd like some sandwiches, ham on rye.'

'Two ham on rye for the lady,' Amstat said. 'And I'll have the same. And a bottle of whiskey.'

'Fifteen minutes,' the boy said; he was a surly sixteen year old, with an acne pitted face and greasy fair hair. 'You'll have to get

314

it, mister; we're pretty packed out tonight.'

'All right,' Amstat wasn't looking at him; he helped Terese out of her coat. 'Fifteen minutes.'

It was a clean room with a pair of single beds covered in a garish red and green linen; it was much like all the other impersonal, slightly sleazy rooms they'd slept in since they left Boston; except for the two nights on the Lake. When they had eaten the sandwiches, which were slightly dry, and helped them down with whiskey and tap water, Terese reminded him of those two days.

'You know, darling, I've been thinking. Ever since we talked about it. Are you sure Portugal is the right place for us to go?'

'I don't know. Why not? Don't you want to go there?'

'It's too near Europe,' she said; she had a habit of frowning and rubbing the frown with a forefinger when she was thinking. 'I think we should stay in Canada; somewhere quiet. I've even looked up some place on the map; here, I'll show you.'

She got out the big travelling road map, and pointed out two small towns a hundred miles or so beyond the border. She put her arm round his neck and their faces touched as they locked together.

'You mustn't practise architecture again,' she said. 'They know about that. We'll have to live very quietly, in the sort of place where there's no Jewish community – a small country town. We could start a business, a store or something like that, with our money. I don't want to risk applying for a passport and trying to travel again. I don't believe Portugal is any safer than Argentina now.'

'Nowhere is safe,' he said. He went on holding her; while she was talking and showing him the map, he kept his eyes closed. Canada, Portugal, Argentina. Nowhere was safe; it was after ten o'clock, they were probably outside the motel already, just to be sure he didn't try to change his mind. 'If you want to stay in Canada, we'll stay in Canada,' he said. 'Rapid Creek – that sounds a pleasant sort of place. We'll go there, my darling.'

'You look tired,' she said; her voice was tender, and she touched his face, turning it to look at her. 'Very tired. It's nearly over, Karl, don't you realise that? They haven't found us; they're not going to find us. One more day and we're into Canada and safe. We can begin our new life together. No more running away.' She kissed him.

'No,' he said; he smiled at her; the human weakness passed and he no longer hesitated. 'No more running for either of us. We'll have all our lives together. At Rapid Creek.'

'Why don't we go to bed?' she said. 'You've

been driving for all these hours, and you look exhausted. Come, my darling. We've got tomorrow ahead of us.' She undressed first and climbed into the narrow bed; she watched him with her arms above her head; it made her look very young, and she was already so sleepy that her eyes were closing.

'Why don't you get undressed? It's late.'

'I know.' He came and stood beside the bed and looked at his watch. 'It's eleven o'clock, Terese. I want a little air before I go to bed. You must be asleep when I get back. Promise me?'

'I promise. Kiss me good night. And don't be long.'

He sat on the edge of the bed and took her in his arms and kissed her on the mouth. He felt a pain in his body, and it was the pain of leaving her. It wasn't fear at all.

'I love you, Terese. I have always loved you. Never forget that.'

'I won't,' she whispered. 'I love you too.'

He got up and went to the door; before he opened it, he turned and looked at her once more.

'Sleep now,' he said. 'Don't wait for me.'

He opened the door and stepped outside; it was a bright moonlit night and he started to walk slowly ahead into the open space. Shadows among the surrounding trees detached themselves and began to move towards him There was a short burst of shots, and then silence. The boy in the office didn't bother to come out and look; he thought it was a car backfiring and went on reading his paperback.